QUINN

An Urban Fantasy

ANN GIMPEL

CONTENTS

Quinn — v

Book Description, Quinn — vii

Books in the Circle of Assassins Series — ix

Author's Note — xi

Chapter 1 — 1

Chapter 2 — 13

Chapter 3 — 25

Chapter 4 — 37

Chapter 5 — 49

Chapter 6 — 61

Chapter 7 — 73

Chapter 8 — 85

Chapter 9 — 97

Chapter 10 — 109

Chapter 11 — 121

Chapter 12 — 135

Chapter 13 — 147

Chapter 14 — 161

Chapter 15 — 175

Chapter 16 — 187

Chapter 17 — 201

Chapter 18 — 213

Chapter 19 — 223

Chapter 20 — 237

Book Description, Rhiana — 251

Rhiana, Chapter One — 253

About the Author — 265

Also by Ann Gimpel — 267

QUINN

CIRCLE OF ASSASSINS, BOOK TWO

An Urban Fantasy

By
Ann Gimpel

Tumble off reality's edge into a twisted world fueled by lore and magic

Copyright Page

The only constant in my long life is murder. Assassin for hire, to put a finer point on it. I'm an earth wizard. Usually, we're on the peaceful side. Not sure what happened to me, but I never fit in with my kinsmen. They'd have chased me out of the fold —for obvious reasons—but I saved them the trouble. I left on my own. The same way I left the Circle of Assassins because it was too tame for my taste. Or maybe too structured.

Along with my bondmate, an oversized eagle, I've been playing fast and loose with the rules forever. Of course, the rules have changed, but I've rolled with the punches. Never found a policy I couldn't manipulate to my advantage.

There's an old saying about life coming full circle. It's about to snatch me up and spit me out. I can run, but there's nowhere far enough to hide from what I am or the Circle of Assassins.

My first home.

My first nemesis.

Grigori said I'd be back. How in the hell could he have known?

BOOKS IN THE CIRCLE OF ASSASSINS SERIES

Shira, Book One
Quinn, Book Two
Rhiana, Book Three
Kylian, Book Four

AUTHOR'S NOTE

Between Covid-19 and the California fires, I've had a lot of time to dream up ideas for books. Watching too much *Blacklist* and *Warehouse 13 and Stranger Things* probably didn't help. And the last season of *Supernatural*. I will miss Sam and Dean...

Meanwhile, a concept shaped up for me. Assassins have always held a fascination factor. Death is a job for them, but what kind of people are they beneath their knives and guns and poison? Toss a few bond animals into the mix, and the bones for a darkish urban fantasy series took shape.

Within its pages, you'll meet men and women who found their way to an age-old profession. Every king worth his salt had a court assassin, and so has every ruler from olden times to modern. If you're shaking your head saying such things can't happen today, consider "suicides" that are swept under a whole bunch of rugs. Oddly enough, the victims of those suspicious deaths had stories to tell, stories someone wanted silenced —forever.

Quinn would understand completely. And he wouldn't give two hoots about any of it.

CHAPTER 1

Automatic weapons make a hell of a racket. My ears ached. Worse, they'd be ringing for days. Depressing the trigger of my Kalashnikov, I fired another burst in the general direction of the Taliban commando unit. It had been mighty quiet these past few minutes, but I didn't trust those bastards as far as I could see them. It's not accidental the Brits have never won a war against them. For that fact, neither has the US. Mountains are high and wild and inhospitable in this remote locale with a million places to hide and stage counterattacks. No matter how rough things got, local militia had an ace in the hole: they wore their enemy out until they gave up and went home.

I'm not in the habit of giving up. Period. My ace in the hole is I have magic. I'm an earth wizard. Or earth mage. Means the same thing. There aren't too many of us left, not because we died out but because we got tired of dealing with mortals and made a run for other worlds.

They're not perfect, either, those other places. I know. I've shopped them, and I always end up right back here slopping around in mud and blood and guts. Most earth mages are pacificists at heart. No idea what happened to produce an outlier like me.

Afghanistan could be the poster child for human quirks. Over the past few decades, it's transitioned from being run by Russians to the US training the Taliban to overthrow the USSR to the Taliban spiraling out of control and giving the US hell's own time.

I never take sides. I'm for sale to the highest bidder so long as what they're asking me to do doesn't run aground on the few scruples I have left.

More firepower rained from the two men with me on this mission. Spaced fifty feet to either side, they were solid fighters. The mercenary world is small. We all more or less know one other, but not too well. It's not that kind of club.

"Quinn." My earphone hissed static along with my name.

"Yup. What?"

"Think they're dead?" Rafael asked.

Breath hissed from between my teeth. It was the question of the hour. "No. But any survivors are long gone."

"How? I'd have killed anything that dislodged so much as a pebble," he growled.

"Another of their infernal underground tunnel systems. How else?"

"What do you want to do?" a different voice joined the discussion. Leon had clearly been listening in.

More hissing breath as I considered his question. "Move in. Sweep for survivors. Search for anything that looks like a tunnel entrance and drop grenades."

"Works for me," Leon agreed cheerfully. Being on the move was always preferable to staying in one spot.

Rustling from both sides alerted me my companions were on the move. I paced myself to their stride until we arrived at a five-hundred-foot granite wall. Its broken rockwork offered virtually unlimited paths upward to still more crags above. Bodies littered the ground. I never bother to count, and I didn't now. Dead was dead, and these poor fuckers weren't dressed for the minus twenty temps. Maybe we'd done them a favor. Dragging out my phone, I snapped pictures to provide proof we weren't out here with our dicks in our hands jacking off.

A spate of curses from Rafael brought me at a run. He stood over exactly what I'd been certain we'd find. A hole in the ground leading god only knew where. "Got it," Rafe mumbled as he pulled pins and dropped grenades. By the time they detonated, we were a hundred yards away, running over talus blocks and sucking dry cold air. Our work was done, no reason to tarry.

"Fuck me. Bird's still there," Leon shouted and fist pumped empty space in front of him.

"Sure is a pretty sight," Rafael chimed in.

I'd given it fifty-fifty our ride wouldn't be disturbed. Not great odds, but better than the usual in my business. Of course, I didn't actually need the chopper. I can teleport. Saved a lot of explanations, though, since I'd be the logical one to come back with another bird.

It's where not being BFFs came in handy. None of the dudes I worked with asked very many questions. Or any at all about the times I'd bailed them out. Rafael and Leon hadn't worried about the chopper being stripped for parts—or blown up— because they had faith I'd produce another exit strategy on short notice.

Leon headed for the bird at an easy lope.

"Hold up," I yelled. "We don't want any ugly surprises."

"Like it exploding when you hit the ignition?" Rafael arched dark brows. Not that everyone I work with is a clone, but men in this trade all have the same look. Roughhewn with lots of muscles, they've lived through nightmares and keep coming back for more. Truth was they didn't do well in polite society, and they knew it. Kind of like snarling watchdogs; necessary, but no one wanted to get too close to them.

The occasional woman is drawn to this life, but not many. Too bad because there's nothing quite as fierce as a cornered bitch.

I understood all of it too well. Assassins are born, not made. We only feel alive when adrenaline is pumping, and Death's dank breath stinks up the joint. I bit back a snort as I went through the chopper from stem to stern with Rafael and Leon helping. Death was actually a woman, and she wouldn't have appreciated my reference to stinky breath.

"Clear," Leon yelled. Rafael echoed the word.

I'd just yanked the door open when the rat-a-tat-tat of an automatic rifle jerked my attention away from the chopper. More rifles joined the choir. Damn it. I could deal with one, or even two, from the air, but not the dozen or better filling the night with their death chant.

"Fuck. Not home free yet," I shouted. Feeling naïve and gullible—and pissed—I dove for a boulder pile This attack made perfect sense; I should have expected it. The Taliban hadn't bothered to boobytrap the chopper. Why go to the trouble when they could kick back and wait for us to return to it.

Leon zigged and zagged before jumping next to me. I scanned for Rafael, but didn't see him. Rather than wasting magic, I relied on our communicators. "Dude. Make a run for it."

Bullets peppered the rocky ground. Bits of broken granite blew everywhere, deadly as shrapnel.

"Nah," Rafael's crusty voice crackled against my earpiece. "I'm good where I am."

"Hold your fire," I cautioned. "Let's let them burn up more ammo."

"Copy that," Rafe muttered.

For the next quarter hour, we hunkered as bullets splatted around us. I sent a thread of power outward, intent on eavesdropping. Maybe I'd hear something helpful, like if they had enough ammunition to last all night. It had been dark for a couple of hours, and the temperature was dropping—if that were even possible.

The Taliban has always drawn its ranks from small remote villages. Driven by faith, they were fearless fighters and as tough an adversary as I'd come across. I'd fought them before—many times. Often enough, I'd even been approached about switching sides, but some of their activities rub me the wrong way. Human trafficking, for one.

"Christ. Colder than a well digger's ass," Leon mumbled and dragged a hood over his helmet.

Cold weather gear was cush-city these days, compared with the ratty woolen coats we used to have that always smelled like rancid sheep fat. I'd have called him a pussy if I weren't so intent on deciphering a conversation in Dari and Pashto.

I held up a hand. "Ssht."

"No one can hear us," he protested. "Not with all this racket."

It wasn't why I'd silenced him. A trio of the rebels were arguing—in two languages. They hadn't counted on us going to ground. They'd assumed they'd smoke us out and make short work of us. Ha. I'm not in the habit of being easy pickings for anyone, and certainly not this bunch of dicks.

"You need to get out of there," a familiar voice buzzed through my head.

"What do you see?" I asked my sidekick. Some would call him a familiar, but he's been my partner in the assassin trade for

hundreds of years. He's an eagle, but only in a very distantly related sense. In the days he was hatched, they were far larger, true birds of prey. His given name is Roland, but I saddled him with Gwaihir after *Lord of the Rings* became popular. It amused him—after I told him about Tolkien's tale—and he hasn't said not to call him that. Not yet anyway.

"Men are moving toward you," the eagle squawked.

"How many?" I screwed my mouth into a scowl. Counting wasn't the sort of thing he excelled at.

"Too many."

Not the answer I'd hoped for, but I trusted my bondmate.

"We've got problems," I told Leon, assuming Rafael would hear too.

"How do you know?" Leon shot back. "Nothing's changed."

I keep Gwaihir a secret. It's why he was in the air and not down here with us. After a small shrug, I said, "Instincts."

"You've got to do better than that, dude," Rafe protested.

No. I didn't. Since no answer would satisfy him I didn't offer one. He didn't push it, either.

Thoughts collided as options bounced around. We couldn't take the chopper. She'd be shot down before we got off the ground. It only left one option, and it wasn't something I could talk about. I located Rafe easily and crafted the underpinnings of a spell to move us all out of here.

"What you thinking, boss?" Leon nudged me.

"Going to have to trust me," I mumbled and sent a wing of my casting to scoop Rafe into it. Was it worth wasting ammunition? So far, we hadn't fired a shot. The same phalanx of boulders protecting us meant we'd have to move beyond their shadows to use our weapons. I was still listening to the three men haranguing each other. Since I'd established a link, I rode in on it and opened the dirt beneath their feet.

At first, they probably figured it was another quake. The

ground was riddled with fissures from volcanic disturbances. By the time they realized this was something different, that they'd be sucked through layers and layers with rocks sealing their egress, it would be too late.

So much for those three. Were the others worth killing? If I told my comrades-in-arms we were going to open fire, they'd be all over it. Murder has a seductive aspect, particularly when the target is fighting back. Makes it easier to justify atrocities. Not that I've ever required an excuse to snuff out a life.

Leon elbowed me again and angled a come-on-already look out of clear blue eyes. He was right. We'd overstayed our welcome. One of the sheltering boulders exploded, peppering me with rock fragments.

Clock just ran out.

I tightened the wing of my spell draped over Rafael and ignited it. The shithole countryside dropped away, and we catapulted through blackness. No worries about Rafe and Leon. Something about the vibrational force of teleporting rendered mortals unconscious.

We were headed back to Camp Leatherneck Marine base in Helmand province. The CO would be irate about his chopper. Or not. Far from the first aircraft lost in combat, it wouldn't be the last, either. Besides, I hadn't completely given up on it. Our mission had originated at Leatherneck, but I wouldn't bring us down inside the base. I could do a little bit of memory alteration with my buddies, but not with everyone on the base who saw us wink into existence out of thin air.

Too many balls in the air when I wasn't certain who'd seen what. People would compare notes, though, and it made modifying memories a total crapshoot. Gossip ran rampant in spots like Camp Leatherneck. It was the kind of place that turned humans into alcoholics—or addicts. Drugs were cheap and plentiful in the Middle East. The Marines had a sporadically enforced policy about illicit drugs tucked away somewhere. I had vague memories of signing it along with a spate of other hush-hush agreements.

It's a dirty little secret the military hires mercenaries to do certain aspects of their wet work. Places where it would be inconvenient to admit US involvement have made me a wealthy man. Except I was set for life long before the war in the Middle East.

Once I made the mistake of asking a high-ranking Army officer if he had second thoughts about training the Taliban. He'd turned on his heel and left the supply tent. Eh, when you're as old as I am diplomacy isn't a driving force.

My spell, which had been chugging along on autopilot, was running down. Not dissimilar to the barren region we'd left, I dropped us a few miles outside the Marine installation on a high, windswept mesa. A squawk from above told me the eagle had anticipated my moves and beaten me here. Shit. He was worse than a wife, not that I've ever had one. Women are a complication I don't need. I settled Rafael and Leon with their backs leaned against substantial rocks. They had GPS equipment and could figure out where they were once they came around. I expected to be back before then, but plans have a way of derailing. While they were still out cold, I mucked around and planted a memory of us making a run for it.

And then, I deepened their trances to make it believable we'd covered the miles between where we left the chopper and here. Because they were sitting ducks, I swathed them in invisibility and ripped a page out of the small notebook I never gave up carting around.

I've kind of made a transition to the digital age. Sort of. But this was simpler than relying on electronics.

Gone back for chopper was all I wrote before crumpling the paper into Leon's hand. He'd find it and not worry about where I was.

Gwaihir squawked again. I loped toward him, and he flew to meet me, landing heavily on my shoulders. It's always a shock something made mostly of feathers could weigh a good forty pounds. Images flooded my mind of the incoming troops he'd warned me about.

"We're going back," I said.

The eagle pecked the side of my head. His version of a love bite, it always drew blood. "Hurry," he urged.

"Why you bloodthirsty bitch."

"Not your bitch," he retorted in a stock answer to my comment.

The exchange made me laugh. We were friends, companions, buddies, mates. All of the above and more. He'd become my bondmate centuries ago when I was part of the Circle of Assassins. Long story short, Grigori and I butted heads once too often. I could have given him a run for his money, challenged him for control of the Circle, except I had less than zero interest in piloting a rowdy crew of supernatural assassins.

And so, the eagle and I had left sometime during the 1700s. We'd been on our own ever since despite Grigori's parting shot that I'd be back. Not only was it never a consideration, but I wasn't even tempted. I knew what I had there. Likeminded companionship, but at what cost?

Grigori ran the Circle with an iron hand and single-minded purpose. He picked the jobs and parceled them out. He wasn't unreasonable. If I wasn't up for a mission, he offered it elsewhere, but the lack of autonomy grated. The first time I left was for a month, the second for a year, and the third far longer. I hung around for another hundred plus years after returning, but the writing was on the wall. I knew I'd leave, and so did Grigori.

He tried to talk me out of it over flagons of well-aged brandy one winter evening. Ironically, that conversation made up my mind. My leave-taking was amicable, as those things go, and I occasionally run into him or his operatives. I'm not a bridge burner. That door is still open, but it would take a whole lot to entice me to sign back up.

Different terms, for one thing. A world where I picked my assignments, sought them out on my own. I wasn't a neophyte, and I didn't require protection from the baser aspects of my nature. I could burn down the world leveraging earth magic—if I wanted. I don't. Everyone has a niche. I'd found something that was as good a fit as I was likely to come by, and—

Another peck reminded me it was time to get moving.

Returning to the battlefield on my own had advantages. The primary one was I could chuck as much magic around as I wanted. I might come up short if I faced a hundred ragtag Afghanis—those dudes were tough as knotty oak—but my bet was the vast majority had decamped.

Didn't matter. I'd kill until the fire raging inside me retreated. It never withdrew for long, but I'd learned to control it, turn it to my advantage so it worked for me not against me.

"Coming with me?" I asked the eagle.

"Still here, aren't I?" Talons dug into my shoulders, treating my layers of cold weather gear as if they weren't there. Blood trickled down my back and chest. I diverted a shot of magic to seal the wounds.

Holding an image of my destination firmly in mind, I wound fire and air into a transport spell. It would take a little longer, but it freed up earth and water to weave into a wave of destruction.

I'd hit the fucking ground on all fours, running for all I was worth. They'd never know what hit them, and maybe I'd get my chopper back. If they hadn't stripped it for parts. Most of the Bell AH1-W's components weren't interchangeable with the Sikorskys—carryovers from the Russian occupation—favored by the Taliban,

Rather than ripping the Bell to shreds, they'd be smarter to fly it back to Taliban central. It pained me to admit it, but my current adversaries weren't short on brainpower. If they'd been inept, their regime would have caved, outsmarted by Western forces.

Training them had been one of the US military's dumber moves.

"I'll take stragglers," Gwaihir announced.

"Eat a few eyeballs for me."

The bird huffed laughter. "I can save you some."

"Nah. They're your favorite. Pay attention, we're almost there."

Power crackled between my raised hands as I prepared to lay a sheet of death a quarter mile wide in my wake. But first, I had to make the transition from teleport channel to terra firma. For a split second I'd be vulnerable, and it would be a pain to have to regroup if someone caught me half in and half out of teleport mode.

The eagle's weight shifted as he spread his huge wings. Seeing him airborne would be enough to send the superstitious jerks ranged against me into a tailspin. Viewing me unshielded, power bubbling around me, ran a close second.

More than ready, I channeled Death's presence. I was her agent, doing her work, even though she'd been horrified the time I'd suggested as much. And I'd been exasperated she refused to dive into the nitty-gritty delight of eliminating marks who were a waste of good air.

We'd agreed to disagree, but one of these days we'd have a

rematch, she and I. The deep gray of my journey channel exploded, leaving me in roughly the spot I'd left. No more phut-phut-phut from rifles, but I didn't let that stop me. Everywhere I sensed life, I sent power chasing after it intent on finishing what I'd begun.

CHAPTER 2

Squeals, screeches, and moans rose all around me in a sweet symphony of lives snuffing out. Gunfire started back up. I ignored it. Bullets are an annoyance. They can't do me much damage. Facing a magical adversary might be fun for a change. Mortals weren't much of a challenge, like mowing through kewpie dolls in a gallery. The eagle's excited cries rose above the barrage of bullets. He was having a good time.

Magic jetted from my hands as I strode forward. It's rare when I drop the glamour that makes me appear more or less human and show my true form. Not that I couldn't pass for mortal, but I was closer to seven feet than six. Dark hair streamed down my shoulders and back, accentuating the Slavic cast to my features. Yeah, I could pass so long as no one noticed my eyes. Like all earth wizard eyes, they're bronze with deep-green centers. I've seen dragons with eyes like mine, but not for a long while.

I didn't need layers of winter gear to stay warm; borrowing heat from the Earth's core was a simple matter, so I settled for unzipping my oversuit. So far, this was too easy. Ceding to power that scrambled their nervous systems until they forgot to breathe, the Taliban force melted to piles of broken flesh and bones all around me. I latched onto the simple joy winning always brought. Sucking air deep into my lungs, I gloried in the copper stench of blood and the nasty reek of spilled entrails. Some things never grow old.

A field littered with the slain was one of them.

The eagle swooped low, casting long shadows in the newly breaking dawn. A few brave rebels fired at him, but he evaded them easily. I've always assumed my sidekick is immortal. If he isn't, he's so long lived it scarcely matters.

Another wave of destruction rolled from me. Damn it. This really was too straightforward. Borrowing liberally from my earth-linked magic, I spawned mini quakes; they rotated beneath my feet, making the ground buck and heave. Maybe that was the coup de grace because the next time I checked for life, the survivors had all left the immediate vicinity. Truly left, not just crouched behind something.

"No more fun," Gwaihir crowed mournfully and circled to land.

"Nope." Riding high on adrenaline and bloodlust, I'd have agreed to damn near anything. I loped to the helicopter and checked to see if anybody had been near it since my walkaround pronounced it airworthy.

"Is anyone else out there?" I asked the bird to take advantage of his aerial perspective.

"Aye. Cowards, one and all, though. They're running the wrong way." He perched on top of the rotor. "Want me to flush them out and head them back toward you?"

It was tempting. If I'd been on a rogue mission, I'd probably not have stopped until everyone who'd so much as twitched in my direction was dead, but I had higher obligations. The military was solid as employers went. They paid well and asked very few questions. The main one was whether I'd fulfilled the terms of my contract; a fancy way of inquiring if the target would bother anyone again.

So long as I said yes and flashed a few pictures around, we were golden, and I'd retreat to one of the spots I hang out in between jobs. Losing this chopper would be a black mark, so I tugged the door open. "Coming?" I asked the eagle.

"In that?" He hooted the avian equivalent of laughter.

"Silly of me to ask," I concurred. "You might want to move off the rotor."

Gwaihir spread his substantial wings. After a couple of flaps, he vanished from sight. Either he'd dialed up his version of supersonic speed, or he'd launched a teleport spell. We'd catch up later at a country house I keep north of Inverness. Not that we'd discussed post-mission plans, but after all the time he and I had put in together, he could second guess my movements.

It cut both ways. I could predict his too.

I shucked my pack and rifle and ferreted out the chopper key from one of many pockets. After fitting it into its slot, I hit the ignition. It took a few tries before the engine sputtered to life, and the propeller spun in lazy circles. I activated the tail rotor next. It might not look important, but it counteracted the force of the main blade and kept the craft flying straight. While everything was warming up, I ran my fingertips over the controls for the craft's weaponry. Bristling like an outraged hog, the Bell had more firepower than she'd probably ever need.

Half expecting a regiment to rise out of nowhere, intent on separating me from the Marine aircraft, I didn't tarry. As soon as my instrument panel said I was safe for flight, I nosed the throttle out. Nimble despite its guns and rocket launchers, the craft leapt skyward.

I can fly anything. Don't spread it around, but I enjoy the

rush of defying gravity. Modern aircraft are primitive by magical standards, but I still get a kick every time a hunk of aluminum parts company with the ground.

Time to think ahead. This job was over. It hadn't been a clean sweep, but a significant chunk of the Taliban force was dead. More would pop up behind them, but they weren't my concern. My assignment had been to locate a particular pod and snuff it out. Normally, I prefer working in tandem with Gwaihir. I'd tapped Leon and Rafael because the assignment had specified a force of three. If one of them hadn't been available, I'd have found a replacement. The well was reasonably deep in our exclusive guild. I've never had to scramble to locate mercenaries who live for the days they don camo and a bulletproof vest and kick some serious ass.

Would the Marines fly us back to London? It was where we'd picked up the specs for this job and met a chopper somewhat bigger than this one that had dropped us at Camp Leatherneck. If they returned us to the UK, Rafael would head for his home in Ukraine. Leon might stick around or fly back to the States. I wasn't exactly sure where his home base was. Like I said, personal info is on a need-to-know basis. If they were smart, even their names were phony.

Mine wasn't, but it was only part of the story. Quinn is my given name, first, last, only. I'd been fielding queries about my last name—or my first—so long, I've developed a few pat answers designed to shut people up. Along with my solo name, I've never signed up for any official documents. Everything from my driver's license to my various pilot licenses and passports were false. Some listed me as Quinn McCullough, others as Richard Quinn. I had go bags stashed in so many locations I sometimes unearthed one I'd forgotten about, one where the phonied-up ID had passed its expiration date.

The high mesa where I'd left my companions spread below

me. Were they still asleep? Or had they begun hoofing it for the Marine camp? I focused jets of seeking magic, intent on figuring it out. They'd hear the Bell overhead; hopefully, they'd figure out it was me. It would be a bitch to be this close to returning the craft only to have it shot down by my associates.

The spot I'd left Rafe and Leon was empty. I didn't see them, but they could have ducked behind something when they heard the whine from my rotors. My earpiece was still in place.

"Rafe. Leon." I augmented their names with magic since the communicators weren't exactly designed for this range.

"Who?" crackled through my earpiece. Rafael probably recognized my voice, but he was playing it safe. In case someone had hijacked my ride—and my communicator.

"Quinn. Went back for the bird like I said."

He and Leon melted from the spot they'd sheltered the moment they heard the squeal of my rotors. I set a flight path and circled to land. Bending low to avoid the rotor wash, they piled in, tucking field packs and rifles behind the seats. Questions hit me from all sides. I answered a few, mostly about how many more I'd killed and whether I'd had to fight my way out of there with the helicopter.

"Can't believe they just gave up," Rafael mumbled.

"I can be damned persuasive. Anyway, we did good. Job accomplished." Turning, I offered high fives. We could celebrate later. I keyed the mic and alerted the camp I was inbound.

The next several hours sped past. We were debriefed, collected the other half of our money, and hopped a ride on a military jet. It stopped a couple of places, so it was late by the time we debarked at an RAF base in North Yorkshire. After a few back slaps and "until next times," Rafael and Leon grabbed rides to Heathrow.

I said I'd find my own way back and walked away from the

base, field pack dangling from my shoulders. We'd left the Russian Kalashnikovs with the Marines. Easier that way since they were illegal most places. No one questioned me about my travel plans or anything else, but I hadn't expected them to. I could have teleported from Afghanistan, but it would have been much harder to explain. Less attention drawn to me by taking the offered transport. The men I worked with accepted I was odd, but they also lapped up perks, like me rescuing the helicopter.

The area around the RAF base was dark and quiet, mostly rural. I walked for an hour, decompressing and wiping out memories of the Afghan countryside. What a grim, depressing place. Some war zones had been beautiful once, but not the Middle East. Unless you counted the mountains. They were high and stark and stunning.

After a quick look around reinforced that I was alone, I whisked myself to the closest of my many homes. I've always loved my manor house in the Scottish Highlands. I picked it up for peanuts in the middle of the 1800s and have putzed around modernizing it ever since. Plastering and replacing fixtures is mindless, restful in between jobs. I'd deliberated between the place I bought and a falling-down castle on one of the Outer Hebrides. The island location would have been more private, but I'm not totally antisocial.

I like the option of dropping by the local pub and hefting a few pints with the guys as we ogle the local lassies. My enclosed courtyard shaped up around me. The fence was built from rocks like most barriers in this part of the world. Trees are scarce because so many had been sacrificed for building materials and fires to warm dwellings.

Gwaihir glided silently to one of many perches near me and fluffed his wings. "Took you a while," he observed.

I shrugged. "Anything new here?" The question was

rhetorical. I wasn't expecting an answer, and I didn't get one. I did pull out my phone, though, and flicked it on. Pings, chirps, and other assorted noises heralded texts, email, voice mail, ad nauseum.

Whoever invented cell phones should be shot. I'd even resented landlines back in the day. But offering any stray person the ability to tag me any time of the day or night was a major invasion of my privacy. I couldn't not have a phone, so my answer to the whole conundrum was to leave the bloody thing off as much as possible. I shredded my latest round of grisly battlefield photos. No need to hang onto them. The Marines had their proof.

The evening was tolerable, by Scottish standards. It wasn't raining or sleeting or snowing. Stars peeked from behind clouds that never departed the northlands, and the start of half a moon was visible. I went through a routine that never varied, checking if my home had been disturbed before I strode inside and dropped my pack in the front hall. Like most buildings of its vintage, the downstairs featured a long hall that ran the length of the structure with rooms opening off both sides. Each room had an individual hearth. The two upper floors held bedrooms, baths, and an armory I'd built myself.

The basement was devoted to an arena where I kept my skills sharp. This was my primary home. Others were more stopping off points, places I stayed if I happened to be close. In truth, I didn't need half-a-dozen homes, but what else did I have to do with my resources?

Yeah. Not very much. How many fancy cars or planes or houses can one man buy?

After reassuring myself no one had been here, I snagged a couple of bottles of Guinness from the double door stainless steel fridge in the remodeled kitchen and returned to the terrace where I'd left the eagle. He was still there, head tucked beneath a wing as he waited to see where we'd go next.

I dropped into a chair, flipped the cap on one of the beers, and tipped it back, enjoying the bitter bite of hops as the ale drained down my throat. I finished it before settling in with all the messages. Most went to trash, but some had potential as new jobs.

"I should take a break," I mumbled. "A vacation."

"You always say that, but you never do," my sidekick observed and repositioned his head so he stared right at me out of shrewd avian eyes. The eagle didn't miss a lick. Ever.

I swiped the empty bottle in his direction; he didn't even flinch. He knew I wouldn't hit him. I was annoyed with myself for a whole lot of things, but the biggest one was lying about how great my mercenary lifestyle was. It met my needs, but it had costs.

I cracked the other beer as a revelation smacked me. Eh, revelation is too big a word since I should have realized this long ago. I'd left the Circle of Assassins because the downsides outweighed the plusses, telling myself I'd finally be free. Except I wasn't any freer than I'd ever been. I was just stuck on a different hamster wheel. No one to blame but myself. I picked my own jobs now, but they weren't any more satisfying than the Circle assignments had been.

Not really.

If I dropped out of sight for a few months, maybe I could figure things out. I'd been on the move since Gwaihir and I left the Circle. My gaze strayed to my phone, and I tapped the display, cycling through the jobs I'd thought might be worth a second look. I had infinite years to indulge in a self-help crusade. Besides, I might not come up with any answers, and then I'd have wasted months of soul searching and browbeating.

Coward, an inner voice mocked.

"Piss on you," I answered. "Practical, that's all."

The eagle squawked and spread his wings. He had zero tolerance for anything that smacked of self-indulgence. When you cut to the chase, overlaying meaning onto the assassin trade was a losing proposition. The bird knew it, and so did I. We killed because it was hardwired into us. Period. End of story.

I brought my phone's display back to life. One potential job was appealing, although I'd be damned if I knew why. Another assassin was trolling for an associate. Usually, I was the one doing the trolling. Not that I don't play well with others, but that's when I'm in control. Like with the last mission where Rafael and Leon answered to me.

I entered my login creds and opened the job scrolling for details. They were distressingly thin. As if to infer signing on required a leap of faith. I shook my head, willing something else to materialize on my screen.

Yeah. Right.

The same set of data points blinked back at me. Nothing had changed. Why should it? It ran counter to my better judgment, but I typed into the response box that I was possibly interested but required more details. Before I thought it to death, I clicked send.

"What are we doing?" Gwaihir asked.

"Damned if I know." I offered a grin and a shrug. While I was waiting, I read through the other possibilities. These were all registry jobs. I could always go out and beat the woods for my own assignments. Or I could return to some shithole like the one I'd just left and spread death in a wide arc. No one would complain, but then no one would pay me, either.

I don't need money.

It's a job. I should get paid for my work, I argued back and put a cork in it. I'd had this argument with myself for too long to contemplate. Killing was like a drug for me, an aphrodisiac. I needed to kill like most people need to breathe. Collecting money was icing on the cake. I'd have killed if no one paid me shit, but that made me a monster.

I set down the second beer, the bottle long since empty, and rubbed the heels of my hands down my face. There it was in a nutshell. So long as I went after jobs and provided a service for payment, I was just like everyone else.

Or so I told myself.

Going rogue meant something entirely different. It laid my sickness—or my hobby or my addiction—bare with nothing to gloss over it. Disgusted with myself, I pushed to my feet. I'd grab a few hours' sleep and see if the mystery job owner had gotten back to me.

I was halfway to the house when Gwaihir made the deep cawing sound that meant danger was near, and he'd ramped into full strike mode.

What the fuck? I twirled to face him, power sheeting from me as I probed the inky night. He'd taken to the air, still shrieking his ire. I felt the same way. Who dared to disturb me?

Power crackled off to one side, lighting the night frosty blue-white. I've never been a wait-and-see kind of guy, so I draped a cage over the power, intent on containing it until I knew what it was. Gwaihir flew closer, tightening up his circles.

The source of the power traded energy for a form. When the sparks cleared, a woman stood in the center of my trap. Hands on her hips, fair hair swirling around her, she rolled deep-blue eyes. "You contacted me," she said in sharp tones. "Release me at once."

"Or?" I challenged, ignoring both her comments. I hadn't contacted a soul, and I wasn't about to let her go until I knew more.

Gwaihir squalled menacingly and flew close enough to the cage to peck at it.

She rolled her shoulders back displaying a choice set of breasts. "Fine. Have it your way. You can't hold me here forever. Once you finally reel in your power, I will make you very sorry."

Something about her tone, or maybe it was her scent, got my blood pumping. If she wanted a fight, I'd give her one. No one dropped in unannounced. Hell, no one dropped in, period. I didn't have friends, or even acquaintances. Nope. I had comrades in arms, none of whom I invited to my homes.

Fascinated by Ms. No Name, who obviously had some command of magic, I withdrew my trap. Spreading my feet shoulder width, I made come hither motions with both hands. "Come on, darling. Love to see what you've got."

"Fucking men," she sputtered and sent a blast of magic dead center at my chest.

CHAPTER 3

Power plowed into me, sharp and stinging with the alluring scent of a tropical sea. Sort of a carrot-and-stick effect. She was lovely, graceful as she ducked and wove, clearly at home in her tall, lithe body. Hunting leathers molded to her curves, and soft deerskin boots laced to below knee level. Clothing like hers had gone out of fashion a couple of hundred years before and would be notable if she'd dropped in anywhere but here. Perhaps she wanted people to remember her, but it defeated the purpose in a trade like mine where being next to invisible was a plus.

Until you weren't. By then it was too late, assuming I'd planned well, which I usually did. Too late for my unsuspecting targets, that is. If I'd been sloppy enough they escaped my net, I had no business proclaiming myself a professional.

I stood my ground, but the force of her blows shocked me. What the fuck kind of mage faced off against me? It didn't take much of an examination to dredge an answer out of the ether.

"You're a sea wizard," I sputtered.

"Give the man a prize," she retorted and loosed another volley.

"But your kind left Earth a thousand years ago. The rest of us pegged you as extinct."

"Do I look extinct?" More of her brand of power blasted into my side. Somehow, she'd made her magic curve around like a wave. It hurt, but it was titillating too, like an exotic breed of foreplay. I needed to get my mind out of the gutter. She was doing her damnedest to hurt me, not fuck me.

I was smarter this time. I warded myself so I'd be less vulnerable. Gwaihir flew between us croaking and hissing. The woman's attention shifted from him to me; her mouth formed an oh, and she cooed at him in Gaelic, telling him he was magnificent. My bondmate has that effect on everyone who sees him, but he's particular who he reveals himself to.

So far, I hadn't fired a shot, but it was about to change. Quick as lightning, I scooted around to one side and rushed her. Magic was too impersonal. I wanted to feel that luscious body smashed against mine. Fighting can be seductive as fuck—if my adversary is a woman. I've tried the dick-on-dick route, but it never did much for me.

I had an arm wound around her neck and another around her torso below her breasts. I'd figured I hang on for the ride, kind of like when you jump on an unbroken horse and it goes through every dance step in the book trying to shuck you off its back. The mounded globes of her ass were jammed against my hips. I've always been a sucker for fine rear ends, and hers was amazing.

The eagle swooped low and dug his talons into her shoulder, beak clacking like it did when something pleased him. Why wasn't she struggling? I had her in a wrestling grip that was difficult to break since I had her arms pinned to her sides. All of a sudden, the eagle made a hooting sound that passed for laughter and launched upward.

Buckets and buckets of cold, salty water whooshed over me as my captive laughed uproariously, right along with Gwaihir. Had he known what she was about to do? From all appearances the answer was yes. More water followed, tidal waves of the stuff. It had to be illusion, but it felt damned real. I sputtered and switched to the way I breathe underwater after almost choking on fluid filling my nose and mouth and lungs.

"Ready to let go yet?" She swished her ass against my growing erection. My unruly appendage always had a mind of its own. This was no exception. I might be drowning, but I may as well die a happy man.

"How can you talk underwater?" Telepathy was the only channel open to me.

"Sea mages developed a few crafty tricks—before we became extinct."

Touché.

Lazy images of underwater sex teased me. I didn't want to let her go, but a lifetime of self-discipline—except when it came to killing—took over. I dropped my arms to my sides. The mini-inland sea vanished as if it had never been there. My clothes weren't even wet.

"How in the hell did you manage it?" I sputtered, expecting to spit out seawater, but there wasn't any.

She turned so she faced me. "Never ask a woman her secrets. Or a mage."

Gwaihir floated down and settled on her shoulders again, making little cooing noises. He could mimic most other birds, and now he sounded like a dove. Suspicion bit deep. "You know her," I said, not making it a question.

Another eagle, slightly smaller than Gwaihir, but still three times the size of the non-magical variety, shot through a hole in the air cawing a greeting. My bird replied in kind and took to the air again without answering my question.

"'Tisn't me he knows," the sea mage said, "but my bonded one."

I wrenched my gaze from the skies where the birds were ducking and weaving, clearly playing with one another, and focused on her. "Why don't you have a whale or a porpoise or some such creature as your bondmate?"

She stood tall and muttered, "If I'd known how dumb you were, I wouldn't have bothered showing up."

It was at least half a lead-in, so I grabbed the opportunity. "Right on. You don't know me. Why are you here?"

Her mouth twisted into a snarky expression. "And I suppose if I knew you, I'd appreciate your brilliance. How in the hell could I operate outside of the sea if I were tethered to a bondmate who required water 24/7?"

"You didn't answer my question."

"Shall we add observant to your other stellar qualities?"

Gwaihir seemed to be having a gay old time with the other eagle, but my patience was within an angstrom of running out. "You have five minutes," I gritted. "Who are you, and why are you here?"

"Or?" She arched a fair brow. "We've already established my magic wins in an out-and-out contest."

"We established no such thing," I countered. Hanging onto my composure had become a nip-and-tuck proposition. "You doused me with invisible water. So what? If you don't tell me what you're doing here, I'll leave. This isn't my only dwelling."

"Take your toys and go home?" she sneered.

Christ. I'm usually fairly even-handed. Not much riles me, but motormouth bitch was getting under my skin.

"I am home," I gritted. "You're the intruder."

"You responded to my posting," she said. "If you weren't interested, why'd you fill out the form?"

Pieces clattered into place, but I didn't care for the pattern they formed. "I requested additional information," I said stiffly, "not an incursion from the aquatic cavalry."

"And I expected..." She frowned before adding, "Not sure what I expected, but you aren't it."

I hate to admit this. Oh fuck, I'm not admitting anything. Her words stung, though. They shouldn't have. I'm comfortable in my skin; my gifts and magic are on a par with the best of them. I can run circles around the Fae or Sidhe. Druids and witches are laughable.

I bit back hot words, settling for, "Leave, then."

"Love to, but I can't."

A distant feral cry told me the eagles were hunting. "What do you mean, you can't?" Breath huffed from between my teeth, making clouds in the chilly night air.

"You're an ideal fit for the job."

"Christ, woman. First you intimated I was a blundering idiot. Now you say I'm perfect for whatever the hell job you put up on the dark web. You don't know me, so your opinions on both counts are badly flawed."

Not sure what I presumed was coming. More disparaging words, or for her to round up her bird and hotfoot it out of my space. Neither happened.

"Is there a place we could sit?" she asked.

I was still clenching my jaw so hard my teeth hurt. "I don't think so. Best thing is for you to go. I've changed my mind. No longer interested in whatever project you put up for hire."

She rocked from foot to foot, standing tall with her shoulders straight. Just like when she'd adopted that posture before, it showcased her Valkyrie build—and her high, rounded breasts.

"We got off on the wrong foot—" she began.

"And whose fault is that?" I shot back.

"Yours. You netted me with magic before my teleport spell had settled. It left me no choice but to fight back."

I opened my mouth to protest she was wrong, but first I replayed how she'd dropped in out of nowhere. "I was defending myself," I snarled. "How in the unholy hell could I have known your unfamiliar magic was related to me indicating I might be interested in a job. Most people message back first." I stopped for a moment, reconstructing the past few years before I said, "No one has ever dropped in. Those like us tend to be careful about revealing ourselves before we have more information."

The twin vertical lines between her eyebrows deepened. "You truly don't recognize the feel of Circle magic anymore?"

"Circle as in?" I prodded, ever cautious where the Circle of Assassins was concerned. Grigori had left me alone for a couple of hundred years, but it was no reason to slip up and cause problems for him and his supernatural hit squad.

While I waited for her to answer, I wove bits of seeking magic around the sea wizard, hunting for telltale markers that would brand her as part of the Circle. She stood quietly under my scrutiny, not shaking it off or warding herself to stymie my efforts.

"Satisfied?" she asked in what for her were neutral tones. Sarcasm rode beneath the single word, but it was muted.

"Circle as in?" I repeated my query.

"Is there a place we could sit?" Maybe borrowing a page from me, she repeated her earlier question as well.

I couldn't hear hunting cries any longer, so the birds were probably feasting on whatever they'd brought down.

Still feeling put out, I stomped across my terrace to the chair I'd occupied before Ms. Mystery Guest blasted holes in my peaceful evening. I wasn't in a gracious host mood, so I dropped into my chair. She could pull one out for herself if she were inclined.

She did and dragged it across from mine before settling into it. "So much for chivalry—" she began.

I chopped a hand downward. "Manners cut both ways. This is my home. Say what you have to and be gone."

After folding her arms across her body, she apparently rethought how defensive it made her appear and splayed her hands atop her thighs. After a terse nod, she said, "My name is Ciara. You already pegged me as a sea mage. My bondmate clearly knows yours, so Grigori was right about that."

She skewered me with her blue eyes, and waited, perhaps expecting me to react at her mention of Grigori. All I said was, "Keep talking."

"I'm a relatively new addition to the Circle of Assassins," she went on. "Up until roughly seventy-five years ago, I mostly worked for Poseidon, but we had a spot of a falling out."

"I'm surprised you get along with anyone," I muttered. Probably should have kept my mouth shut, but I couldn't resist jabbing her back after her comment about me falling short of her expectations.

A corner of her mouth twisted wryly. "Eh. I suppose I deserved that. Not the first time I've been labeled a bitch. Anyway, I had my reservations about the Circle, but it's turned out to be a reasonably good fit, and I love Tory to pieces."

"I remember your bird," I said. "At least, her name is familiar. Back when we were newly bonded, Roland walked me through his family tree, and we've visited his world from time to time. Tell me more about the Circle," I urged. "Things to convince me you're actually part of it and not angling for information to bring it down."

Half an hour later, she'd provided descriptions of all the

guild houses and enough details about mages I'd left behind to convince me she'd been living with them. "If you're a spy for hostile forces," I murmured, "you've infiltrated yourself well."

"Some things require a smattering of faith. Then again, others do not." She tilted her chin at a defiant angle and dug into the sporran-type affair hanging from her waist. After a short search, she extracted an egg-sized chunk of crystal and offered it to me on her open palm.

I leaned forward and probed it with magic. Grigori's distinct magical signature bounced back at me; I took the crystal and held it in my hand. As I expected, the stone grew warm, and Grigori's voice filled my mind.

"If Ciara has gotten this far, she's done well. I told her you'd be a tough nut to crack. Stubborn as a mule. I wouldn't have placed that job post on the dark web keyed to your energy, except a task lies before us. It's huge and daunting, and the Circle needs your help. I'm hoping you'll consider carving out a month for us. We will pay you well. The amount is negotiable, and we can firm it up once you accept."

I waited, but Grigori's message had clearly run through the power inherent in the crystal. The quartz cooled despite the warmth of my hand, and its inner glow faded. I tapped it with a finger. "This is a very old method of communication."

Ciara nodded. "I know. We used a variant of it in the sea with coral as a medium." After a slight pause, she said, "Will you accompany me back to the guild house where Grigori awaits you?"

I leaned back in my chair and crossed one leg over the other. "Not certain. If you let me know which one, I'll give it some serious thought. Why didn't he come? Why send you?"

For the first time since her arrival, something that might have been uncertainty added creases to Ciara's forehead and around the outer edges of her eyes. She studied her hands for a moment, and when she looked up she said, "I shouldn't tell you. He said not to."

"Tell me what?"

"Grigori wanted you to come because you were intrigued, not because you were worried about him."

Her words drove me to my feet. "Why would I be worried about him? He's a werewolf and immortal last I checked."

She pressed her mouth into a thin line before standing so she faced me. "If most of my magical career had been spent in the Circle, I wouldn't answer you. Grigori's hold on his minions is absolute."

"Which is why I left, or one of the reasons. Go on." I did my best to infuse encouragement into "go on." Cheerleading isn't one of my fortes, but I gave it my best shot.

Ciara exhaled long and noisily. "This…problem, the reason Grigori wanted you and every other strong mage who's left the Circle to return, erodes magic. We have no idea where it's coming from, or if its only target is the Circle. But we have to stop it. If we can't, the Circle is finished, and we fear every other mage won't be terribly far behind."

I considered the implications before probing beneath what she'd said to what she'd omitted. "Grigori's power has been impacted. It's why he sent you."

She didn't require words. Her expression, one of mute misery, was all the answer I needed. Grigori might demand absolute fealty, but the assassins he'd handpicked for his Circle returned his loyalty in spades.

"Don't worry," I told her. "I won't out you. No one will know you said more than was authorized."

"I'm a big girl," she retorted. "I make my own decisions. I don't need you or anyone else to cover for me."

"Really?" I leveled my gaze at her. "I thought we'd moved past your prickly phase."

Laughter rolled from her. I'd have thought it out of character as hell, but she had a beautiful laugh. Lyrical, musical, the sound reminded me of hundreds of silvery bells all activated at once. It made me want to amuse her just to hear her laugh, and my dirty mind went from there to all the ways I might amuse her. I cut that line of thought off damned quick before the front of my trousers tented out.

She'd gotten hold of herself enough to manage a few words. "I've always been bitchy. My long tenure in the sea only made it worse. Some of my temper has been modulated by the Circle, but it's part of me."

I've generally believed the oceans were calm, peaceful. Apparently, I'd been way off base. Gwaihir and Tory chose that moment to swoop in for a landing. Bits of bloody meat hung from their beaks, and they had the satisfied look eagles get after a particularly worthy kill.

I turned to my bird. "Well? What was it?"

"Sheep." Gwaihir cocked his head to one side, looking pleased with himself.

I cringed. "Awk. Christ. The shepherds in this area take their flocks seriously."

"No one saw us," Tory squawked. "We were invisible."

"And we carried the sheep away," Gwaihir added.

Ciara folded her arms beneath her breasts. "Was the sheep invisible as well?"

"No," Tory told her bondmate, "but the only one who noticed was the dog guarding the herd. He barked for a long time."

I tried not to laugh, but it was a losing proposition. "You probably gave that poor hound a coronary," I mumbled around gouts of laughter.

"The other sheep didn't even notice," Gwaihir said proudly.

"Like hell, they didn't," Ciara rebuked him. "They were praying to Gaia to spare them from the same fate."

"Since when are sheep a major crime?" Gwaihir asked pointedly and clacked his beak at her. "We used to feast on them regularly."

"Since the advent of modern laws." I flapped a hand his way. "Enough of this. No amount of nattering will bring the sheep back to life." Turning to Ciara, I said, "Meet Roland, my bondmate, but I've been calling him Gwaihir for a few years now."

The same alluring, seductive laugh rolled from her before she said, "I like it. Fits him. May I present Tory."

"Are we going?" Gwaihir broke in. "Tory told me why she and Ciara are here."

I nodded. "Yup. We are. Just let me organize my duffel."

Ciara crossed the space between us and threw her arms around me, hugging me quick and sweet and hard before letting go. "Thank you. I wasn't certain what you'd do."

She'd already stepped away, and I motioned her back. "Do it again. I like that way better than snarky words."

Her full mouth curved in a seductive smile. "If I made a habit of them, you wouldn't appreciate my rare spontaneous displays of gratitude."

"What else spurs you to gratitude?" Damn my cock. It was in full bloom, not bothering with a half-hard stage.

"Maybe you'll find out. Or not. How long for you to repack your kit?"

"Quarter hour. You don't have to wait. If you tell me which guild house, I can meet you there."

She shook her head. "I'll wait."

"Look. I'm not going to change my mind, and I don't require a babysitter."

The bite of her magic washed through me as she tested my

words before rattling off familiar coordinates. Apparently, Grigori was at the off-world guild house, a location I knew well.

Gwaihir and Tory were rubbing beaks and grooming each other's feathers. "I'll go with them," Gwaihir said.

His statement made me chuckle. "So much for loyalty. First pretty face that walks by, and I become an afterthought."

The eagle turned away from Tory. "We often travel separately," he informed me, as if I'd forgotten, "and—"

"Never mind," I cut in. "I was teasing. See you all soon."

Before anything else transpired, like Ciara's gaze straying below my waistline, I turned and loped for the house. I had to admit I was curious about whatever was stealing magic. Beyond that, I was intrigued by Ciara.

Fuck intrigued. She's hotter than a two-dollar bill, and I want to get into her pants.

Speaking of pants, mine were in the way. I'd no sooner cleared the lintel and kicked the door shut than I unzipped. My badly neglected, oversexed appendage leapt into my hand ready for action. My cock wasn't overly picky. Coming was coming. My fingers weren't as cushy as a pussy, but they'd do in a pinch.

CHAPTER 4

I have an embarrassingly diverse collection of sex toys and DVDs, but I didn't need anything to get me in the mood. I was already there. Not bothering with formalities, like finding one of the many beds in the house—or even lying down —I curved my fingers around my cock, teasing the sensitive places as I ran fingertips from base to tip and back again.

In my mind, I peeled the leathers off Ciara, cupping and squeezing her breasts. What color would the nipples be? With her fair coloring, my vote went for more strawberry than copper, but I bet they were generous and they'd form stiff peaks without much provocation.

Reacting to the word "stiff," my cock hardened still more. My balls ached. How long had it been since I'd come? Eh, I didn't want to do mental bookkeeping. I wanted to keep on divesting my imaginary lover of her clothing. But first, I settled my mouth on a breast, sucking and biting until the nipple turned hard as a polished stone.

Meanwhile, I'd traded trailing my fingers up and down my

shaft for grasping it, squeezing, and pumping. Breath quickened, and my heart thudded against my chest as arousal swept through me blocking out all else. Ciara was on her back, sprawled across a soft bed piled with cozy duvets. I cupped a palm over her vulva. The heat of her seared my hand through her clothing.

The trousers had to go, but first, I had to let go of her long enough to unlace her tall boots. The leather was buttery soft, and I worked on the laces and tugged both boots off once they were loose. Her pants had the same type of closure, so I unlaced them and took my time smoothing them over her hips.

A flat stomach and pronounced hipbones came into view as I worked the leather garment down her hips and legs. The pants were warm and smelled like her, musk infused with amber and brine. I've always loved the scents of the sea, but they took on a whole other dimension.

No underwear in the way, so I bent and strung kisses down her belly. Her skin was smooth, silky, enticing. My plan was to settle my mouth over her sex, but hands grasped my shoulders. I knew what she wanted because I wanted it too.

I'd been holding myself on the edge of a mind-bending climax, but no reason to wait any longer. Kneeling between her legs, I pushed into her body fast and hard, matching my hand action to the scene playing out in my mind where she writhed and moaned and told me to fuck her faster, goddammit.

My balls had moved beyond pain. Tight against my body, they were ready. Semen pooled in them and then moved upward before it gushed from me in spasm after spasm of heat and delight. In my fantasy, Ciara came right along with me, her pussy snugging and releasing as it turned liquid with passion. I tightened my grip on myself, and more jism splattered on the floor.

I came for a long while, and it took even longer for my heart to settle back into even double-time rhythm and my gasping breaths to subside. All my homes are self-cleaning. By the time I opened my eyes to survey the mess, the household gremlins had taken care of it.

My next stop was a shower. Between cleaning myself up and sticking a few things in my field pack, my mind cleared enough to think about Ciara's reluctant admission about Grigori. He must be in bad shape to send others to do his bidding. He's always been a hands-on type of leader.

She'd also said he was attempting to recall all the mages who'd left. By that, I assumed she meant those like me who'd left in good standing. The Circle was a forever commitment. Often when mages left, it was because they'd washed out. Those situations never ended well and included Draconian measures like mind-wiping.

I took stock of the contents of my pack. I've never been a mage who relies on potions or powders or crystals or spell books. The Circle maintained comprehensive libraries at all its guild houses, and I'd memorized the bones of the type of magic I preferred so long ago it became part of me.

I did select a few restorative herbs, not that the Circle doesn't have its own healers, but my power is earth linked, so perhaps I could add something to speed Grigori's healing. He's a werewolf, and they're virtually indestructible. But power isn't limitless. While we live forever, we can make judgment errors that cut into the quality of our magical ability.

I shook my head. Grigori was smarter than that. One of his first lectures to new acolytes covered ensuring nothing threatened their magic. Had he grown careless? Or were other balls in play?

I'd find out soon enough.

Ready as I was likely to be, I locked everything, sealed my home with magic, and conjured a teleport casting. My spell ran true, but then they nearly always did. If I was still making rookie mistakes at this point in my profession, I should hang it up.

The guild house courtyard rose around me, unchanged from when I'd left hundreds of years before. Not that stone changes, or wood or glass, but the landscaping was the same. The trees were taller, and the shrubbery more verdant, but they were the same plants.

I recognized them and greeted them through roots tapping deep within the source of my power. Their voices, gritty and harsh and mostly unused, welcomed me in kind. Plants recognize who dropped their seeds in dirt and tended them, and I'd created this garden. And others like it at all the guild houses. Being an earth mage doesn't tie me to Earth. It allows me to tap into latent energy from any world.

Taking the broad stone steps two at a time, I stood before richly carved, twelve-foot doors and invoked the same magic that had always opened them in the past. The building is sentient, and it recognized me. The doors slid open silently, pivoting on unseen hinges.

I raised my mind voice, aiming it at Grigori. *"I am here. May I enter your quarters?"*

No need to announce my name. He'd know my energy. Anticipating an affirmative response, I started for the stairs. The manor house was large and rambling and impeccably furnished with wall hangings, paintings, sculptures, and solidly build furniture. It had always reminded me of a country estate in Cornwall or the Cotswolds. Grigori maintained a manor house in Cornwall, and many of the guild houses resembled it. I'd always assumed he commissioned the Circle's various dwellings, but it wasn't a conversation we'd ever had.

The click of claws on marble drew my attention upward. Grigori was in his wolf form and already halfway down the spiral staircase. Silver with black guard hairs, he was easily double the size of a normal wolf, perhaps triple. Greetings died on my lips. He looked terrible, so thin his pelt hung on him. I started to ask why he didn't stick with his human form since it required far less energy, but it wasn't my place to make friendly suggestions.

He paused when he reached me, said, "Meet me in the grove," and kept going.

Did werewolves grow old? Because he moved as if each step pained him. It felt presumptuous since I was no longer part of the Circle, but if I had I been, I'd have followed him to the grove. Instead, I kindled a quick teleport spell and gathered him into it. When it cleared, a circle of ancient trees rose around us. Linked to Grigori's magic, they shielded events within their boughs and branches from prying ears.

Not bothering to shuck my field pack, I sank into a crouch across from him. "What the fuck?" I blurted, needing to know everything and damned fast before whatever was leaching the power from the werewolf's bones finished the job.

"Never one to pull punches, were you?" Amber wolf eyes bored into me. They were the only part of him that didn't look used up.

"Diplomacy is a waste of time," I said bluntly, followed by, "I almost didn't come. Your, erm, messenger has a few rough edges."

"Maybe so, but she shares a great deal of your type of power. Sending one of the Fae or a Sidhe or a witch would have bought me nothing. And you can see it was impossible for me to make the journey."

Breath rattled from me. I balanced myself by planting a hand on the ground. "Why'd you wait until whatever this is got so bad? Surely, it's been incremental, and you could have intervened before this."

"What makes you think I didn't try?"

Oops. "I might be an insensitive bastard, but you've always been too stubborn for your own good."

"In this instance, I agree with you. I waited too long to bring in our healers. They rebuked me in no uncertain terms, after they failed to identify the mechanism stripping power from me. I'm here because remaining on Earth would have hastened the inevitable."

"Surely not inevitable," I protested, dismayed by his pronouncement. It was so out of character, I couldn't believe he'd actually said it. "Do you know what the problem is?"

His tongue lolled, and he lay down gingerly as if the slightest motion caused him pain. "I have a working theory."

"Let's hear it."

"About two years ago, I ended up in Hell. The why doesn't matter, but for a time I was stuck between forms. After we escaped, and blew enough holes in Hell to slow the demons down for a while, I thought all was well. For a time, my strength returned. Until it didn't. The alterations were subtle at first, so slight I could chalk them up to something else.

"And I did. Finally, I couldn't escape the fact my magic wasn't working the way it should. One job where I provided backup almost went south because I couldn't manage my role. Our healers went over me with a fine-toothed comb but couldn't find anything to fix, although they agree I don't have a whole lot of time left. They've tried energy infusions, energy balancing, counteracting dark power with ours. Nothing has made the slightest difference. I finally told them to stop."

"Is it just you?" I asked, hearkening back to Ciara's implication all magic was on the chopping block.

He shook his shaggy head before laying it atop his paws.

"Wish it were. We've lost half a dozen mages. They simply never returned from assignments. When others searched for them, there wasn't a trace. Not so much as a stray mote of magic suggesting where they'd gone off to."

"Not that I make a habit of hanging out with mages, but I haven't noticed any shifts in my ability," I said. "Maybe my number just hasn't come up, or maybe this isn't as widespread as you assume."

He flapped a paw my way. "I'm not making any assumptions, but the same discrepancy occurred to me. I needed to know if our problem was unique to the Circle or more generic, so I sent people to do some digging."

I rolled back onto my butt and crossed my legs. We were getting to the bones of the problem. "And?"

"Magic wielders who live in groups aren't faring well. Several covens lost enough witches to fold. Some werewolf packs have been decimated."

It didn't make sense. "There used to be safety in numbers," I protested.

Grigori nodded. "Aye, used to being the operative term. What I suspect is demons infiltrated magical circles and planted poison that spread through them. It would be simple enough. Something contracted by touch or via the air."

"Why?" Demons had never been much more than an inconvenience before.

"Back in the day, you listened better. I already told you we planted bombs in several locations. Hell isn't the same place it was."

I sorted through the facts I had, but they weren't adding up. "I can see them being incensed at you and whoever was part of the mission, but why generalize?"

"Do their reasons matter? We need to come up with a way to stop their incursion. As I mentioned, leaving Earth slowed the progression of my illness, but my assassins are still vanishing. So much so, I've quit accepting new jobs until we get a handle on how to quell this problem."

"Did you bring the whole Circle here?"

"Nay. Having us all in one place has never been a good idea. I split us up between guild houses with instructions to keep wards in place. Anyone who shows the slightest symptom is to isolate."

"Does that mean I could get it from you?"

His tail swished. "No. It doesn't jump magical types. Now, if you were a werewolf, then yes you'd be at risk."

I hated to belabor the point, but I did, anyway. "How can you know?"

"We've begun keeping records, looking at who isn't returning. Also, no one who's had contact with me has fallen prey to my wasting sickness, for want of a more descriptive term."

"What precisely are you up against?" I shifted focus from a human world where bacteria and viruses held court to a magical one.

"Not sure how much you know about werewolves," he began, "but the basic mechanism that turns us from human to lycanthropes is a wild type virus, one with two distinct strains of RNA. Whatever happened, and I suspect it was during my tenure between forms while the demons tortured me, is killing the virus. Once it dies, I will too."

"Because it's the key to your immortality." I didn't pose it as a question. Mostly, I was thinking out loud.

He nodded his shaggy head. "It's why I'm aging, why my power is a shadow of what it once was."

"So how come other varieties of mage are susceptible? We don't rely on your lycanthrope genetic alteration."

"I have many unanswered questions. That's one of them. Although, no one else has fallen ill. They've simply vanished."

"Have you considered finding a healthy werewolf and having them bite you?"

"I'd make them sick. Besides, any benefit a new infusion of virus would confer wouldn't last long."

I snapped my fingers. "That's it. Grow the virus in a lab. That way you could get infusions of it until you find a better answer."

He lifted his head from his paws. "The simplest of solutions. Ashamed I didn't think of it, but then I was looking in the wrong place."

"How so?" I asked.

"I sought a magical solution, not one driven by modern science." He paused to take a shaky breath. "That place in the States, the one that has samples of every disease. We'd have to steal it from them."

"Assuming they have it. Might be simpler to find a were and have them drool into a petri dish."

Grigori huffed a series of small growly snorts that reminded me of laughter. "We'd get a better sample from the lab. Not all werewolves are equally strong. Some can't turn humans at all."

"Okay. Lab it is. That would be the CDC, and there has to be a way to check if they stock paranormal material. It's guarded like Fort Knox, but I could pull a team together and see what I can do. Meanwhile, have you considered sending another contingent into Hell and making them sorry enough they leave off?"

"Of course, I've thought about it." For a moment, he sounded like the Grigori I remembered, short-fused and temperamental.

"And?"

"It could still happen." He lurched to his feet. "Take Ciara and the other earth mage. The sooner you return with more virus, the better."

The other earth mage?

"Aw crap, do you mean Loren? I'd prefer not to work with him. In fact, I'd rather select my own team. This mission will be dangerous, and—"

He skinned his lips back from his teeth and growled. "I do not expect you to stay in the Circle, but while you are here and I am still alive, you will take direction from me. If you cannot do that, you may as well leave."

I came dangerously close to telling him to piss off. This was precisely why I'd left. I was sick of taking orders. I'd have remained had he been willing to offer me even a small amount of autonomy. But now I'd laid eyes on him, and seen how depleted he was, I didn't have it in me to turn my back. I can be a total dick, but not to Grigori.

It had cost him to send Ciara after me. Probably more than I'd ever know.

"I will stay and see this problem through to its end," I said, choosing my words with care. "I propose a compromise. How about if Ciara and I take on the CDC?"

The werewolf swayed on his feet. "Can you manage with two of you?"

I ginned up a smile. "Guess we'll find out."

"You've never worked with her."

"Could be a plus. Remember, I have worked with Loren. His crap attitude was one of the reasons I left." I changed topics, not wanting to delve into unpleasant memories. I got along with most everyone, but Loren was an arrogant jerk. He was the only other earth wizard in the Circle, so I'd figured we'd be buds.

Wrong.

Grigori was nodding. "I accept your compromise."

"Can I help you back to your quarters?"

He turned, tail swishing, ears pricked forward. "No. The walk will do me good."

I followed him out of the grove and sent power zinging outward, hunting for Ciara and our birds.

CHAPTER 5

I found them next to a rushing river not too far from the manor house. Many off-world locations don't resemble Earth at all, but this one did. Most of the trees were species I didn't recognize, but at least they looked like trees with trunks and branches and needles or leaves.

Gwaihir and Tory were perched on a big boulder in the middle of the stream. Something dead lay between them, and they pecked lazily at the carcass. Gwaihir squawked in my direction. Tory munched away.

"Well?" Ciara faced me, her beauty even more remarkable than I remembered. Illuminated by daylight, her cheekbones had an Asian slant to them that lent her an exotic look. Her full lips were parted slightly. When she licked them, they glistened, and I had to remind myself why I'd sought her out. Not for a tryst, that's for certain.

"We have an assignment." I borrowed from the Circle's nomenclature. No one was offered choices in the Circle. Once a job was designated—and accepted—you carried it out.

"I'm listening." She spun one hand in a get-on-with-it motion.

"In the spirit of full disclosure, Grigori wanted to include Loren. I put my foot down, and surprisingly he agreed."

"Yeah?" She spun her hand faster. "While I'm glad not to work with him—and frankly I'm relieved you're not as egotistical—I still have no idea what we're doing."

We probably should have retreated to the grove, but this wasn't the type of task one of the other mages would jump on. No one liked breaking into government installations, particularly when we weren't killing anyone. Not unless we had to, that is.

Bending close, I spoke near her ear. "We're going to buy Grigori time to find a solution for his problem."

"Keep going. Damn it, Quinn, don't make me drag this out of you."

"He needs more virus. The one that made him a werewolf. That's what's killing him. The virus is dying off, and consequently he's aging and becoming weak."

Ciara's eyes widened. "Ooooh. I should have thought of that. Hell, he should have. Excellent. Where can we get more?"

"CDC. Maybe. Not sure they stock it." I barely breathed the words into her ear.

"With only two of us? Isn't that place heavily guarded? Particularly the labs where they store lethal pathogens. Maybe we need Loren, after all."

"We do not. Have you ever worked with him?"

She shook her head.

"Well, I have, and he's a nonstarter for me."

I'd had a chance to think about how we'd approach the problem. "Let's keep this simple," I said. "Figure out where they keep the stuff—assuming they have it—teleport in, nab it, and teleport out."

"But they'll have fancy shit like retinal scanners or palm readers," she protested.

"If we hit the correct room, none of that will matter."

Gwaihir had been listening. He flew close and landed on my shoulders. His breath reeked of carrion as he clacked his beak near my ear. "What will Tory and I do?"

It was a good question. "This assignment is...different," I began.

"Not what I asked," my bondmate retorted.

"We're returning to Earth," I told everyone. "We can kick ideas around without the grove's protection, and we require Internet access to see what we can dig up on the dark web."

"Same place I found you?" Ciara arched a fair brow.

I started to say, "Of course," but changed my mind since it sounded patronizing. We'd be equal partners in this endeavor. It meant she had a say in all decisions, even during the planning stages.

"Does that work for you?" I answered her question with one of my own. "I have houses in many other places, and I'm guessing you do as well."

"Been living in guild houses since I signed on with the Circle." She paused for a beat, maybe deciding how much she wanted to tell me. "I used to have a house, actually more like a cabin, near Stephenville in Newfoundland. It's long since been bulldozed under and replaced by urban sprawl. Poseidon wanted me front and center at one of the underwater castles at all times. He resented me clinging to a spot I could retreat to."

"Just another control freak, eh?"

I hadn't planned to make her laugh, but the pleasing trill warmed me. "Didn't mean for it to be funny," I murmured, "but it's kind of the same reason I left the Circle. I needed more autonomy."

Ciara was still snorting laughter. "You have no idea.

Poseidon makes Grigori look like a piker. He killed subordinates who disobeyed. Grigori merely banishes them." Her mirth settled, and she added, "What struck me as humorous was the overlay of modern terms to describe ancient beings."

Computers versus spell books. I got it. I'd been blending the best of disparate realities for so long, I rarely thought about how weird it was.

Gwaihir squawked. Tory had taken to the air and was flying circles around us. The birds were anxious to get moving. I should be too, but I was enjoying Ciara's company, talking with her, getting to know her a little. My priorities were skewed, and I gave myself a brisk mental slap.

Grigori was dying. He needed that virus sooner, not later.

"My place in Scotland, then," I said. "I have solid Internet there, and we'll firm up our strategy. I'd like to have this ball in the air and rolling in a few hours."

I raised my mind voice and keyed it to Grigori. *"We're off,"* I informed him. *"Will check back in once we're done."*

He didn't respond, but I hadn't expected him to. My alert was a formality. He'd feel us depart. "Want to travel with me?" I asked Ciara.

"Nah. Tory and I will get there on our own. I'm going to change into something less noticeable. Be there soon." Turning, she walked briskly toward the manor house.

Did she have someone special here? Someone she meant to say goodbye to?

The eagle's talons tightened on my shoulders, his signal we needed to get moving. When we'd left the Circle, it had been a joint decision. I'd never have altered our life so radically if he hadn't agreed.

"You got it, buddy," I said and constructed a spell that spit us out in the courtyard we'd recently vacated. What passed for daylight in wintertime Scotland illuminated puddles in low spots between paving stones. Nothing ever completely dried out this time of year, but I'd hit a brief respite between rain and sleet storms.

With Gwaihir still on my shoulders, I strode across the courtyard and into the house, ducking low so we'd clear the nine-foot lintel.

"I'll wait outside," he informed me and fluttered to the floor before turning and exiting through the still-open door.

For once, I didn't bother to check if the house had been disturbed. I hadn't been gone very long, and as keyed up as I was I'd have welcomed an opportunity to clonk someone over the head.

Taking the stairs two and three at a time, I hustled to my suite of rooms on the second floor. I hadn't removed my field pack since leaving, but I did now. Culling through it, I removed some items while adding others. So much for my healing herbal mixtures. They wouldn't have done Grigori a whit of good, but my heart had been in the right place.

I didn't plan on anyone laying eyes on me, but the place we were going had cameras. Most of them didn't penetrate magical warding, but some of the newer digitized infrared ones would pick up on heat emanating from our bodies.

I traded my khakis for black pants, and the rest of my clothes for a black shirt and black jacket. Tucking a balaclava and gloves into the pack, I stuffed my feet back into my boots and laced them. Back downstairs, I'd just settled in behind my computer when a flurry of squawks and hoots told me Tory and Ciara had arrived.

"Door's open," I sent as I ran through encryption codes to unlock my machine. You can't be too careful in my business, and I'd set all my computers to auto erase the hard drives if anyone but me so much as breathed on them.

Wings swooshed past as the eagles soared by. Gwaihir must be showing Tory the kitchen. I'd set it up so he could get food on his own via a special hatch in the front of the fridge. Not that he was spoiled or anything. In truth, he scarcely needed me to provide anything, but he enjoyed being catered to.

Ciara trotted close, taking up a position behind me so she could read the screen. I started to tell her to pull up a chair, but she already had. "Nice place," she said. "You'd mentioned other homes. How many do you have?"

"Four besides this one." My fingers were busy with the keys as I sought entry to the dark web. It would have the layout for the CDC. Not that I couldn't locate it via Google, but this search would be private and far more thorough.

She whistled. "Why so many? Aren't they a hassle to maintain?"

"Magic does it for me, with a boost from the Earth."

"Ha. For that to work for me, I'd need to build something underwater, which kind of defeats the purpose. Or not. Maybe I've finally been gone long enough, Poseidon wouldn't notice me in the ocean."

"Didn't take it well when you jumped ship?" I continued typing command strings to bust past supposedly impregnable firewalls.

"A bit of an understatement." She pulled her chair closer. Her alluring scent, almost like a drug, eddied around me. She'd donned clothing very similar to my own. Black from head to foot, with a hood pulled up to obscure her pale hair.

Schematics came to life on my screen, and I leaned in matching up the key to letters and numbers identifying areas in the breakout of CDC headquarters in Atlanta. Ciara bent so close our shoulders were touching. I could have turned my head and kissed her.

Could have. It would be a mistake. Either she'd retreat to

her "fucking men" stance and shut me out, or we'd end up in a clinch that would be counterproductive.

I'm used to denying myself anything akin to creature comforts, and this way I could nurture the illusion she was as taken with me as I was with her for a little bit longer.

"Werewolf wild-type virus isn't there." She stabbed an index finger at a list including botulism and anthrax and Ebola."

"Maybe someone felt uncomfortable adding supernatural viruses to the mix," I suggested.

"Or maybe it means it's not there." she persisted. "If we screw up and pick the wrong place, we won't get a second chance. Hell, they'll probably call in the FBI and lock the place down even tighter than it is right now."

A cacophony of shrieks came from the kitchen. Were they fighting over something? Mating? Fuck. I really had to get my mind off the sex track. Sending good luck vibes my bird's way, I turned my attention back to the screen.

"Do you suppose they're all right?" Ciara glanced toward the kitchen.

"Yeah." I stopped there, not wanting to float the possibility the birds were fucking their brains out. I flipped from screen to screen as one more slice of CDC operations flashed past. Now that I'd examined a few portions of the facility, it was simpler because each sector was laid out the same.

Ciara tapped the screen again. Normally, fingerprints on monitors drive me nuts, but I made an exception in her case. "Look at this," she said.

"What am I looking at?"

"The date. When did humans crack the werewolf code?"

"Um, in the 1990s, I think. There was a whole lot of hoopla around it since they don't believe in werewolves. Who was that scientist who pressed the issue?"

"Lockhart. She was almost turned. Escaped after they'd

bitten her but before the virus hit her bloodstream, so she got a saliva sample."

"The story I heard was she didn't get enough virus to turn her, but she's had a few unusual occurrences since then." The progression of events was coming back to me. Despite a promising career, she'd taken early retirement, and no one had heard from her in years.

"Aw crap," I muttered.

"Aw crap, what?" Ciara turned her blue gaze my way. It did odd things to me, made me long for a repeat of my earlier fantasy, except one where she was flesh and blood rather than imagination. Faithless dog that it was, my cock thickened. Like the original one-trick pony, it had a single go-to place.

The squawking from the kitchen had turned to cooing. May as well have had mourning doves in there.

"Lockhart turned into a werewolf. It took considerably longer because she didn't get much of a dose, but I bet you anything it's why she quit."

"Do you suppose we could track her down and talk with her?" Ciara asked in a thoughtful tone.

"She'd know where the virus was stored unless she destroyed it," I agreed. "But she'd have no reason to help us. None."

"She doesn't have a stake in this game anymore," Ciara pointed out. "There's also no reason for her not to help."

"Have you ever known any weres besides Grigori?"

She shook her head.

"Yeah, I didn't think so. They're not exactly warm and fuzzy. They pack up, stick together, and hate everyone who's not like them. They also have a strict set of rules about turning humans to maintain their food supply."

"What happened to Grigori?"

I shrugged. "Who knows? He was the first one I'd ever met, so when others who crossed my path were different, it was first a surprise and then an annoyance. I've made a point of avoiding them."

"I see. Perhaps this Lockhart gal is more like him, less like other weres."

I twisted my chair to face her. Our knees knocked against each other, doing absolutely nothing to quell my hard-on. "You're firing blind," I said bluntly. "We have no idea what she turned into. Or if I'm even correct about her turning at all. She could be somebody's grandmother baking cookies and knitting sweaters in a suburb somewhere."

"So, the question of the hour is if it's worth looking her up."

I nodded and returned to my scrutiny of the CDC schematics. It didn't take long to scroll through the final screens. "If they kept the werewolf virus, it makes sense it would be with all the other lethal viruses," I said slowly. "Surely, they wouldn't have built a separate bunker for it."

Ciara cocked her head to one side. "It's not on the list. Maybe Lockhart took it with her."

I snapped my fingers, recognizing truth in her words. "Brilliant! Of course. It's something any werewolf would do. They have a proprietary interest in total control of that virus."

"So, if you're right, and she was turned, she'd have cleared out her desk and any virus samples."

"If I'm right," I echoed and narrowed my eyes. "What do you want to do? Check out the CDC storage vault or hunt down Lockhart?"

"They're not mutually exclusive. The question is which we do first."

I was back to clicking keys. It only took a few seconds to identify Rhea Lockhart, Ph.D. A biochemist with a specialty in infectious disease, she'd graduated from Johns Hopkins in 1990, which meant she'd been quite new in her career when she'd had the run-in with the werewolf.

She appeared to have dropped out of her few professional organizations and off the map completely. The trail went cold ten years ago. No address, no driver's license, nothing at all to suggest she was even still alive.

Ciara had pulled out a phone. After scrolling and clicking, essentially duplicating my efforts, she said, "I checked a different database. No known address with them, either."

"Maybe not in those places, but I have an idea." I dialed up a different program on the dark web, one I pay good money for because they claim they can locate anybody. Usually, they're right. A few keystrokes later, I said, "Lookee here."

A long, low whistle trilled as Ciara shouldered me aside to take in the particulars. "She's not all that far from here."

"No. She's not. Makes this easy. We'll scope her out first, keeping in mind she has less than zero interest in being found. She's changed her name and everything else about herself."

"Yes, I noticed, but she kept the same initials. Sheesh, humans are such a bunch of dunderheads. Even the smart ones." Ciara entered info into her phone. Probably Rita Lowe's contact information.

The eagles waddled into the study, looking a little on the rumpled side. "Do we have a plan yet?" Gwaihir asked.

Tory flew closer to Ciara, landed, and proceeded to preen her feathers.

"Yeah, we have a plan. We're headed for Durness to find someone who might know about the werewolf virus. We believe the scientist who identified the virus may have turned into a were and fled, taking any samples with her."

"Find her and kill her." Gwaihir sounded positively feral.

I angled a pointed look his way and made my tone emphatic. "No killing. Not unless she attacks and gives us no choice. She might have the only clue to where the werewolf virus samples are."

"Her whole body is an incubator," Gwaihir said smugly. "Deliver her to Grigori. He can keep her captive and take what he needs from a living source." A satisfied squawk punctuated his words.

"Your bird isn't wrong," Ciara said.

"No, he isn't, but Grigori isn't in the habit of keeping prisoners. If it comes down to it, we can siphon some of her blood, and maybe the Circle healers can use it to grow more virus."

"Do you have needles and those little glass tube thingies?" Ciara asked.

"Nope, but I bet our biochemist friend still keeps a full lab tucked away somewhere."

"Why would she?" Ciara pushed upright from her chair. "Says here she runs a hardware store. No. Wait. Used to run a hardware store. It closed two years back."

"We'll wing it." I shut the computer down and stood. Ciara had slung a small bag I hadn't noticed before over one shoulder. "What's in there?"

"A few tools. Some things actually are smoother without magic."

Nodding agreement, I told her I'd be back in a minute and loped upstairs to collect my field bag. All the discussion had dampened my arousal, and my cock had retreated somewhat. Still thicker than usual, but no longer pressing uncomfortably against my trousers.

Maybe later, buddy.

Back in my living room, the scents of Ciara's magic surrounded me, dense and enticing. "Ready?" she asked.

"Yup. Coming with us?" I asked the eagles.

"We'll follow you," Gwaihir said.

"Tory?" Ciara skewered the bird with a stern look.

"It will be fine. We can find you," the smaller eagle reassured her bondmate.

I thought Ciara might pull rank. She didn't. Her casting swept us up, and I built a ward so we wouldn't scare the bejesus out of some poor schmuck who saw us pop out of thin air.

"Odd she didn't come with me," Ciara was saying. "She's never preferred to travel with another bond animal before."

"Were they eagles, like her?"

Ciara made a face. "That's it, huh? They've got a thing for each other."

Maybe more than a thing. Eagles pair bond for life, but I kept my mouth firmly shut. If Gwaihir and Tory forged something permanent, I could think of far worse fates than being in close proximity to Ciara for the months and years to come.

"I've got us warded," I noted as her transport spell faded and Durness's charming cobblestones and old buildings formed around us. People bustled this way and that, oblivious to our arrival.

Elbowing me, Ciara led the way between two shops. The uneven opening ended at a bricked-up wall, but it offered enough privacy to dismantle my warding. The same excitement that always grabs me at the front end of a project was in full bloom. I offered a grin. "Let's get cracking, shall we?"

CHAPTER 6

Her answering smile, savage and anticipatory, told me everything I wanted to know. We're in the assassin trade for a reason. Most of us are cut from the same mold. Adrenaline junkies, one and all, but we're the read deal. The ones who take off the gloves and don't play by any rules except our own. Maybe the birds weren't the only ones who might have a future together.

Durness was picturesque. A parish perched on the Irish Sea, it sported a collection of falling down buildings scattered among the intact ones. I'd never been here before, but there are hundreds of hamlets sprinkled through the Highlands.

"I can see the draw of this place," Ciara said. "It's wild and remote, an easy spot to drop out of sight."

"Plenty of game too. She'd have needed to settle somewhere her, ahem, unusual feeding habits wouldn't draw unnecessary attention."

A squawk from overhead told me the eagles were tracking us from far above. It was tough to estimate size when something was a hundred feet in the air, and Gwaihir could make himself appear smaller. Presumably, Tory had that ability as well.

"No addresses to speak of," Ciara muttered, peering at buildings we walked past. "Once I found her on the dark web, the only locator Google came up with was this township."

"Might not be too much of a problem," I replied. "Presuming she really is a were, she'll have positioned herself in the countryside, some distance from town. We should be able to track her with magic. How about if we stop in at that bakery?" I pointed at a once brightly painted sign that had faded from age and weather.

"Perfect. Tea, pastries, and maybe information."

"Exactly. Except I'd rather have coffee. You're Rita's long-lost, erm, best friend from college."

Ciara nodded enthusiastically. "Yes. And you're my brand-new husband. We're honeymooning and thought we'd look Rita up."

I made a grab for her hand. At first, she evaded me, but then she mumbled, "Guess we need to make it look realistic," and laced her fingers with mine. Her skin was calloused and firm. Clearly, she welcomed hard work, tasks where she got down and dirty. Something like an electric jolt traveled up my arm. Had she felt it too?

If so, there was no indication. Blushes didn't mar her fair skin, and her breathing didn't escalate like mine had. Warm sugar-scented air rushed from the bakery as soon as I pulled the door open. A few folks were seated at small tables, sipping tea and chattering animatedly. Ciara settled at a table in front of a window, and I strolled to the counter.

A short, plump woman swathed in an oversized apron nodded encouragement. Her gray hair was wound into a bun and pinned at the nape of her neck. Laugh lines spiraled out from very blue eyes. "Ye're quite the skinny one. What'll it be to fatten ye up?"

"Coffee or tea?" I called across the room to Ciara.

"Tea, please," she replied.

"Coffee for me, if you have it," I said and bent to examine the toothsome variety of pastries. It was a tough choice, but by the time a steaming cup of coffee and a pot of tea materialized, I'd chosen cinnamon buns slathered with gooey frosting, a brownie, and two decadent frosted cookies.

I paid with plastic. God bless credit cards. No more need to change money into local currency, but I did have Scottish pound notes. Not all that many, though, and I might need them to bribe someone.

Once I'd scrawled a signature—Richard Quinn—I stopped before picking up the tray with my goodies. "You look like you might be from around here," I ventured, stating the obvious. If her appearance didn't clinch it, her brogue did.

"Aye, born and raised. What is it ye're after, lad?"

"We've just married," I explained, lowering my voice to a conspiratorial note. "We choose this spot to honeymoon because my wife's dear associate from college is supposed to live not far away. She was one of her professors, and they haven't seen one another in a very long time. We were hoping to surprise her."

The proprietor was nodding and brushing loose strands of hair out of her face. "And will ye be offering up her name?"

I slapped my forehead with a palm. "It would help, huh? Rita Lowe. She does live in these parts, doesn't she?"

The woman's broad smile crashed and burned. "Aye, she's out thataway, but she's not the sort ye'd be wanting to drop in on."

I did my best imitation of total confusion. "Sorry, ma'am, but I'm not following you. And which way is thataway?"

Raising a floury hand, she pointed pretty much due south. "Maybe five kilometers and then a wee bit to the west off the main road." After a pause, she said, "None of my affair, but I'm betting college was a good bit of time ago. I hope your wife isn't disappointed. People change."

"Mmph. You wouldn't happen to have a phone number for her?"

"Nay. Don't want one. Your coffee will be stone cold, lad. Tea too. Best get back to your bride."

I recognized a dismissal when I heard one. Grabbing the tray, I wove through empty tables until I reached Ciara. We offloaded the items, and I ferried the tray back to the counter. The woman I'd spoken with was nowhere in sight. Clearly, she was done talking with me.

"I heard all that," Ciara said as she poured tea into a heavy white ceramic mug and stirred sugar into it.

"Sounds promising, all in all." I switched to telepathy. If anyone magical were about, they'd pick up on expended magic, but the odds were in our favor. Mages weren't particularly common, and mortals didn't believe in us anymore.

"It does. That gal was pretty spooked. I've never seen an expression change so fast."

"Yeah. She was definitely uncomfortable. Mostly, these isolated country types love to gossip, but she couldn't rid herself of me fast enough."

To maintain the charade I'd outlined, we chatted of this and that as we drank our beverages and chowed down on pastries. I'd bought too much, a definite failing of mine whenever I'm confronted with home-baked sweets, so I filched a bag from the counter and we took the uneaten yummies with us.

The woman who'd worked the counter must be the owner and also the cook. I saw her gray head through an opening into what was probably the kitchen, but she didn't so much as glance my way. In an effort to be considerate, I bussed our mugs back to the counter and met Ciara next to the door.

"Overstayed our welcome, did we?" she asked softly in a passable brogue.

"Maybe." I shouldered the door open, and we walked out into fading light. Days are short this far north this time of year. It probably wasn't much past three in the afternoon. "Main road out of town heading south has to be the one we're on."

"Not much choice," Ciara agreed as we set out at a comfortable jog that ate up kilometers. A glance skyward reassured me our bondmates were tracking our movements.

The occasional car blew past, but so did horse-drawn carts and people on horseback. One young woman drove a flock of goats from her horse with assistance from a couple of sheepdogs. We covered the roughly three miles in half an hour, but I started hunting roads to the west before we reached the three-mile mark.

Deploying a seeking spell would shave time off our search, but it would also alert Rhea we were nearby. I was about to ask the eagle if he'd seen anything when his voice scuttled across my mind, soft and low. *"Angle right, and head straight."*

"Cabin up against yonder cliffs," Tory added.

Ciara draped warding around us. Hopefully, we hadn't waited too long. While the eagles could escape notice, we stuck out like beached whales, maybe because our power wasn't subtle like the bond animals. They're part of the natural world, and as such they blend in better.

I saw smoke before I made out the cabin. Built from rocks, with a sod roof, it merged with the rocky cliffs behind it. The place had a deserted feel, as if its occupant either wasn't there—unlikely, given the smoke—or wanted the area to feel spooky enough to dissuade casual passersby.

"Do we need a cover story?" Ciara asked softly.

"Nope. She wouldn't believe us, anyway. We only have one move. Overpower her and see if she'll give up the virus samples she stole."

"What makes you so sure she hung onto them?"

"She's a scientist. They hate throwing anything out." I winced. Damn, I hoped I was right. She could have tossed the virus after stealing it, and then we'd be out of options.

Except her.

We were nearing the cabin. I waved a hand to my right. Ciara nodded understanding and moved to circle behind the place. We'd burst through both entrances, grab the element of surprise, and corral our quarry.

If things went well.

I built my own ward and continued toward the front porch. As I'd gotten closer the place, which had appeared ramshackle, was actually solidly constructed. Wolf prints and the odd footprint dotted the dirt. Rhea had managed to frighten the neighbors so thoroughly, no one dropped in for tea and crumpets.

Or bloody carcass remains.

But she wasn't exactly on a beaten path to anywhere. Miles of wilderness stretched in every direction. Although this location was remote by UK standards, if she'd truly wanted to lose herself, she'd have been better off in Nevada's hinterlands— or the Arctic.

"Three. Two. One," I counted down so Ciara could match her entry with mine and bolted up the front steps and through the door. The werewolf would sense a wee bit of expended magic for my telepathy, but by the time she jumped up to investigate, we'd have her.

Magic at the ready, I had a cage in hand, ready to drop it over the were's head. Ciara burst inside from behind me. "No back door," she said.

The birds crowded in after us.

I stared warily about, but the one-room cabin sure looked empty. One side had a curtained off alcove. The curtain was drawn back revealing a neatly made bed. No secrets there. I smelled werewolf, but I would. This was her den.

"She has to be here," Gwaihir insisted.

"We didn't see her leave, and we would have," Troy agreed.

"Ssht," I told the birds. It was time for plan B. "Rhea Lockhart," I began, "we're not here to hurt you. We know what you are, and we won't blow your cover. A close associate of ours had a run in with demons. It's killing the virus that made him a werewolf. You're who isolated the virus, so we were hoping you still had the samples you confiscated from the CDC when you quit working for them."

"What?" Ciara sneered. "She'll just crawl out of some cellar and hand them over?"

"You never know." I made a slight shrugging motion. The birds shuffled this way and that, nostrils flaring as they scented the air. The cabin was extremely tidy. Everything had a place; Rhea was into putting things away.

Not many humans would choose such an isolated life. It made me even more certain she'd been turned. Terrified, she'd covered her tracks, buried who she'd been, and begun anew. Or tried to.

Ciara had begun a systematic examination of the cabin. The second hooked rug she pulled aside exposed a trapdoor. "Not especially original," she muttered and tugged it up and out of the way.

Before she bolted down the hole, I said, "Hold up."

"Why?" A pair of blue eyes bored into me. "She already has a head start."

"If the tunnel leads outside, yeah, she does. But it might end in a cave, in which case she's cornered."

"Who cares? Christ, Quinn, I never took you for a pussy."

Her words stung. No one calls me a coward. No one.

Ciara started down the ladder. I dove across the room and grabbed hold of her arm. "We are not here to kill her, or to terrorize her. Unless we have to."

Ciara stopped trying to rip her arm out of my grip, a losing proposition on her end unless she blasted me with her sea-linked power. It would be strong here because of our proximity to the ocean.

"We'll be outside," Gwaihir squawked.

"If the tunnel led outside, we'll see her," Tory added.

The reek of werewolf wafted out of the hole, filling the cabin. A low growl made the floorboards vibrate. "She's down there," Ciara said. Twisting, she repositioned herself so she sat on the edge of the trapdoor opening, legs dangling into darkness.

"Yes, and she's frightened, so the wolf took over. She never learned to control her other side."

"Doesn't that come with the territory?" Ciara sounded surprised.

"No. Unless she had other weres to teach her, she'd be on her own. Grigori told me quite a bit about his past back in the days when we sat around fires at night."

"Never thought about it before, but I guess there weren't always guild houses."

"No. There weren't," I began, but another growl, louder this time, vibrated from beneath the cabin.

An idea was shaping up. I've always flown by the seat of my pants in the field. All my planning happens beforehand, but it's subject to change. "Come out," I suggested peppering my words with the lightest of compulsion spells. No reason to spook Rhea further. "The werewolf I told you about, the one who's dying and needs virus, would be willing to teach you to control what you are."

Ciara's eyes widened and she mouthed, "Bullcrap."

I was firing blind. For all I knew, Grigori would tell the poor creature hunkering under the floorboards to pound sand, but he had a compassionate side, and if he didn't have the stamina to teach her, my bet was he'd point her in the right direction.

"Come out," I repeated my suggestion with a tad bit more compulsion. "We can help you find your human form again, and—"

A cacophony of growls and snarls cut me off.

"Let me try," Ciara said softly. At least she wasn't fighting my lead—or taunting my approach.

"Go for it," I mumbled.

After kindling a mage light, Ciara climbed down the ladder. I whistled for Gwaihir before following her. He'd understand what I meant, that the action was here, not out-of-doors.

"I'm a sea wizard," she began. "Quinn is an earth wizard. Our power is similar but from different sources. Each of us grew into our magic because others taught us. You're a highly educated woman, but nothing you ran into in college or graduate school— or the world—would have prepared you for your transformation. There are materials you could have studied, but they reside on the dark web. Not everyone knows how to access it, but even if you did, most are deeply encrypted and require keys to open them."

"Go away," rattled through my mind in a low, guttural snarl of a voice.

"We want to help," Ciara responded.

"We do not need you. I am in control."

Yup. There it was. The problem, with a capital P. For any iteration of shifter, the animal was never in control, sometimes in ascendency, but never in control. We needed Grigori. The intricacies of werewolf culture weren't part of my lexicon. I sat on the floor across from Ciara. Of all the times for Grigori to be incapacitated, this topped them all.

I changed topics. "Did you take the virus when you left the CDC?"

A strangled, *"Yes,"* in a different voice told me Rhea was struggling to assert herself. And failing.

I tapped Ciara on the shoulder, got to my feet, and headed for the ladder and the trapdoor. The birds were on the porch. I waited for Ciara to join me and draped a sound shield around all of us. "We have a couple of choices," I said pitching my voice very low.

"We could hunt for the virus and leave," Ciara said, in equally hushed tones.

"We could appeal to the werewolf," I added, "or go into the cellar and disable her. Then Rhea regains ascendency."

Ciara shook her head. "Wouldn't work. The wolf will jump back into the driver's seat. I've known shifters whose animals slipped the noose and went on rampages."

I had too. Those situations never ended well. Usually the shifter in question ended up dead. It effectively severed the bond. The part we'd always missed was corralling the animal to make certain it never bonded with another mage.

"We could knock the wolf out and teleport her to the guild house. Let Grigori take over."

"Is he strong enough?" Gwaihir cut in.

With an infusion of virus, he would be.

"Okay, this is what we're doing," I said, my resolution to include Ciara in every decision sacrificed on the altar of expediency. "Gwaihir and Tory will locate the virus samples. My bet is they're in padded cases inside metal boxes, probably buried underground to keep them cool. Once you find them, return to the guild house."

"What will we be doing?" Ciara asked.

"What else?" I smiled crookedly. "Going nine rounds with a pissed-off werewolf. Or only one if we get lucky and disable her quickly. Then we net her and transport her to the guild house."

I'll never know what the were did to mute the clack of claws on the cabin's wooden floor, but the beast flew out of left field, shredded my sound shield, and landed on Ciara's back, knocking her flat.

CHAPTER 7

Tory spread her wings and latched talons into the wolf's beefy shoulders. This werewolf had a shaggy red pelt with golden markings. Careful not to hit Ciara or Tory, I leveled magic at the wolf's chest. Rather than lethal, I'd set my power more to a stun level. It didn't even slow her down.

Ciara writhed and bucked beneath the wolf's weight, but couldn't budge her. The distinctive briny scent of her magic, rich with salt and minerals, filled the air. Water cascaded onto the wolf, buckets of it, soaking the animal to the skin. Tory kept up a steady barrage of pecks, trading sides of the wolf's head. Blood formed rivulets visible through her dense fur.

It gave me an idea, and I scooped some blood onto a finger, breathing the wolf's scent into myself and mixing a spell around it. Gwaihir attacked from the front, aiming his sharp beak for the wolf's eyes. *Do not blind her,* I sent, shielding my telepathy as best I could.

"Why not?" my bondmate demanded.

"Because you might blind Rhea too." I had no idea how deep the

connection between the two ran, but I was certain Rhea was a reluctant recruit. She'd retreated to this remote location to avoid revealing her shame to the world. Must have been quite the downfall. From respected researcher to hermit. The cabin was comfortable but lacked electricity. If she had a generator, I hadn't stumbled across it.

The werewolf roared fury, jaws snapping too close to Gwaihir for comfort. I went back to the spell I'd concocted with her blood. An axe sat on the porch. Grabbing it I swung hard enough to connect with the side of her shaggy head. A solid *thwack* told me my aim was true. It didn't knock her out, but it bought me a bit of time. She shook herself before lunging at me exactly as I'd hoped she would.

Illusory water still cascaded from nowhere, soaking everything in its path, including me and the birds. The small cage I'd fashioned from werewolf blood was done. I slapped it over her nose and mouth when she dove toward me, effectively trapping Ciara's water, and hopefully cutting off the were's access to oxygen.

Chanting like a madman, I told the cage to stay put. The next few minutes were nip and tuck. The were yanked at the cage with both front paws, but her attention had been diverted. Ciara rolled out from under her. The birds each took a paw, pecking the shit out of them and impeding her efforts to dislodge the cage.

More blood oozed and rolled right into my cage, strengthening it. Rhea might be an unwilling participant, but this wasn't the brightest werewolf on the block, either. A way out of blood-borne spells existed, but the were's window of opportunity was rapidly fading.

Bloody bubbles oozed around my cage. The were fell onto her side, still tugging weakly at my contraption. I'd used her own power against her, and she'd been inept enough to let it happen. I waited for the wolf's body to cede to Rhea. Didn't happen.

Ciara stood next to me and called off the flood. Fury wafted from her, and she shook her fist at the flailing were. "If I wasn't worried about killing them both, I'd finish her now." Tory squawked agreement.

The birds had left off pecking, driven by a sense of sportsmanship. When your enemy was down, you didn't keep after them unless you aimed to kill. I'd told my bird not to blind the werewolf; he remembered we weren't going to kill her, either.

I stood over the were and mixed earth with what remained of Ciara's water until she stopped moving. I waited to make certain we had her solidly unconscious before I removed the cage. Bloody water streaked the ground.

"Why didn't the woman materialize?" Ciara asked and cobbled a teleport spell together.

"No idea." I fed power into hers after winding bands around the were. If I'd guessed wrong about how deep her trance was, I didn't want her interrupting the transport casting with competing magic.

"We'll hunt for the virus," Gwaihir announced. "Meet you at the guild house."

Tory had been flying in small circles. She landed on a root cellar door and pecked through the latch. Gwaihir lifted it with his beak.

"Do you figure they need help?" Ciara's spell eddied around us.

"If they did, they'd ask."

Ciara kindled her spell, and we dropped into darkness. I added magic to her casting to hurry things along. "Is there a way to separate the woman from the wolf?" she asked.

"Don't know the answer to that, either. I'm banking on

Grigori to sort this out. He can tap into the were's blood. It should boost his failing virus population before our birds return with the virus samples. Besides, they're years old and haven't been stored under anything like proper refrigeration, so they might not be any good."

"I'd wondered about that," she murmured.

The werewolf lay between us, trussed like a stuffed pig. I hadn't wanted to take any chances, and so far she hadn't twitched as much as a whisker. "Are you all right?" I asked Ciara.

"More humiliated than injured." She smiled ruefully. "Been a long while since another supernatural caught me off guard. I don't understand how she could have snuck up on us."

"She's a weird blend," I agreed. "Strong enough to totally annihilate the woman, but not savvy enough to sidestep my blood casting."

"So that's how you did it," Ciara said. "I was facedown and couldn't see much."

The were made a grunting sound, low and feral. I chucked more power at the binding spell. Between Ciara and me, we could probably control her, but it would be simpler if we didn't have to.

"Whatever we have with her"—Ciara nudged the werewolf with a foot—"Grigori will need a more permanent solution to his, erm, problem."

"What makes you think there is one?" I asked.

She made a small shrugging motion. "There has to be. Otherwise, Grigori will be shackled to infusions of virus forever. Whatever's killing the werewolf virus in his body will attack any new virus too."

"Do you know what happened to him?" I asked.

"Nope. Wasn't there. But I heard plenty from those who were. Demons had been running amok. They targeted the

Circle because a few of ours ended a bunch of them. Aidyrth was part of it. And Mae and her hawk. And many more. Aidyrth's new bondmate had the idea of crafting explosives and blowing up several sections of Hell. It worked quite well, but Grigori was captured. He'd taken the location closest to Hell's center, and demons caught him mid-shift."

"Aidyrth the dragon?" I sought clarification. It was an unusual name, but there could be more than one of them.

Ciara nodded. "The same. She rescued Grigori. He bounced back quickly, and for many months we were certain he'd escaped unscathed." She scrunched her face into a frown. "I'm positive he noticed weakness long before he told any of us about it."

"By the time he did, whatever was wrong had progressed beyond the White Faes' ability to intervene," I muttered.

"Something like that. Hang on, we're almost back to the guild house."

I thought about what she'd said. In my days with the Circle, bombs were considered cheating. For Grigori to suspend one of his closely held beliefs to embrace a new strategy was significant. Perhaps there might be enough latitude for me to carve out a niche for myself, and—

I cut my train of thought off at the roots. The only reason I was considering returning to the Circle was Ciara. She fascinated me, and I had no idea why. Neither was she sufficient reason to upend my life.

Our captive writhed feebly, pushing against her bonds. "Are the dungeons still usable?" I asked.

"They are. Should we chuck her in a cell?"

"Best place I can think of. Grigori can assess the problem without running any undue risks."

Ciara placed a hand on my arm as the courtyard shaped up around us. "You're worried about him, huh?"

"I am, but he's never been one to take being mollycoddled—by anyone." I stopped there. I'd been alarmed by Grigori's appearance, worried enough to commit to time in the guild house library researching werewolves, a topic about which I knew painfully little.

"I'll leave her in one of the cells," Ciara said. Before I could protest I'd take care of that nasty job, she and the werewolf were gone.

I headed for the front door, taking the stone steps three at a time, and calling for Grigori with my mind voice. I expected him to be in the foyer or the great room, but that was the werewolf I remembered and not today's reality. I met him on the landing between the first and second floors making his way slowly toward me.

Pity or compassion aren't go-to places for me. No one would ever accuse me of being kind, but Grigori's bearing smote me. He tried to straighten the slump to his shoulders; vertebrae cracked, and a low growl rolled from his mouth. As before, he was in his wolf form. I'd assumed the human one took less effort to maintain, but I must have been wrong about that.

He fastened his amber eyes on me but didn't say a word. To save him from descending the last flight, I settled on the landing and said, "We found the researcher. She'd been turned, but something is wrong with the pairing."

Grigori growled again. *"Get on with it,"* rolled through my mind. Finally, a glimmer of the Grigori I remembered. I took care to shelve my concern. He didn't need anything from me except results.

I nodded tersely. "The were is in control. The woman is clearly horrified by what's happened to her. We found her in a rustic cabin in the Northern Highlands. Well off the beaten path, with no electricity or running water. She's apparently been there since she left the CDC."

I stopped long enough to take a measured breath before continuing. "She broke free of the wolf long enough to tell us she'd stolen the virus samples when she quit her research job. Erm, she didn't exactly use the word stolen, but how else could she have removed them?"

"Did you find them?" Grigori's voice was rough and raw.

"The eagles were looking. Assuming they were successful, they should have returned by now." I stopped for a moment before adding, "Those samples have been without refrigeration for years. I have no idea if they're still viable."

Grigori laid his head on his huge paws. He's never been one to want sugarcoating, but his disappointment was palpable.

"Hold on," I said. "It's not all sketchy news. We brought the werewolf back. Even if the virus samples aren't usable, our healers can draw blood from her and create an infusion to boost your virus population."

Grigori pushed upright. It cost him, but he moved more quickly than I'd have thought him capable of. "Where?" he rasped.

"Ciara took her to the dungeons."

Power flickered and flared around Grigori. And then it sputtered and died. Before he tried again, exhausting his slender stores still more, I draped a quick teleport spell around us and aimed for the sub-basement.

My spell spit us out close enough. We were in one of many combat practice rooms outfitted with technology something like *Star Trek's* holodeck. Grigori had constructed them to assist newly bonded pairs as they learned to work together.

I slapped my palm on the reader next to the heavy door. Surprisingly, the mechanism remembered me. Either Grigori never reset anything, or I'd made the cut when he erased the central computer's memory of those he'd banished from the Circle. Or those like me who'd left on their own.

How had he known I'd be back? Was prescience part of his magic?

The moment the door to the arena opened, I heard howls and outraged barks. "Looks like she woke up," I muttered.

"You're fortunate whatever spell you employed kept her quiescent for the trip here," Grigori replied. "Female weres are in a class by themselves."

I filed it away, more determined than ever to carve out some time in the library so I could fill in the gaps in my understanding of werewolves.

Ciara stood on the far side of a stout iron grating, arms folded across her chest. The splooshing of water was followed by, "If you don't quiet down, I'll drown you."

Grigori chuckled and tapped into my magical center. I opened it willingly to him, not sure what he had in mind but trusting him with my life as I always had. I hadn't left the Circle because of him, but because of me.

His human body took shape where his wolf had been. Thinner than he'd been, Grigori still cut a striking figure with his six-foot-five-inch height, broad shoulders, and flame-red hair streaming down his back. His eyes weren't as deep a blue, but they hadn't lost their penetrating aspect. Swathed in a black robe woven with silver strands, he'd selected clothing mirroring the colors in his pelt.

I kept my magic available to him, aware he was drawing on it to maintain himself in this body. He pinned his implacable glare on the caged werewolf and said, "Stop that. You bring shame on our kind."

Not sure what I'd been expecting, maybe hisses and more outraged yowls, the werewolf did none of the above. Instead, she stopped dead and dropped her head. Next she tucked her tail and pinned her ears back, looking for all the world like a submissive canine.

"Better." Grigori spat the word. "Withdraw. I would meet your human half."

"We're fairly certain she doesn't get much airtime," Ciara said, her tone dripping censure.

The werewolf quivered but nothing changed. Finally, she growled, "She doesn't wish to come out,"

Grigori took a step closer, either studying the problem or intent on intimidation. "Who is in charge?" His tone was milder, invitational.

"Me," the wolf croaked, falling into the trap Grigori had baited. She immediately switched things up and added, "Neither of us."

"Which is it?" Grigori persisted.

"She knows nothing," the wolf whined. "She didn't welcome me, didn't understand the honor I bestowed on her, and—"

"Enough," Grigori roared. "Withdraw. I would speak with her myself."

This time, the wolf form shimmered and shuddered. When it settled, a woman with tangled, gray-streaked blonde hair lay prostrate on the dungeon floor. She pushed to her knees and then stumbled to her feet. I pegged her for around fifty when she'd been turned. Lines creased her forehead and spiraled out from hazel eyes. Medium height, she was far too thin and appeared to be strung together with piano wire. Her skin held an unhealthy translucence. Patched Levis hung off her hipbones, and a cable-knit cream-colored sweater swathed her torso. She was barefoot, but she probably didn't need shoes since she spent most of her time in stasis waiting for the wolf to weaken enough for her to break through.

She took an uncertain step nearer Grigori, as if she'd forgotten how to walk. "Awk, Christ. You're another one, aren't you?" she croaked.

Instead of answering, Grigori asked, "Are you capable of hanging onto your current form?"

Rhea shook her head.

"Didn't think so," Grigori said in as supportive a tone as I'd ever heard him use. "I would open your cell, but I don't wish to engage in battle with your sister side."

"Not my sister. Not now. Not ever," Rhea gritted with a surprising show of spirit.

Grigori grabbed a three-legged stool from near the wall and plopped onto it. "If your transformation had been more normal, you wouldn't loathe what you've become. How about if you tell us what happened?"

"It won't let me." Rhea's tone was dull, defeated.

"I am stronger than she is," Grigori said. "Furthermore, she recognizes me as superior to her. Like all canids, werewolves have a pack structure. Let me worry about your other half."

He was sucking power from me to keep himself in his human form. I tapped into Ciara to give him more time. At the rate he was extracting magic, we might need a few more Circle members to assist. The other werewolf recognized Grigori as dominant, but she didn't understand how depleted he was. If the truth leaked out, we'd lose our advantage—and probably the woman standing shakily in front of us would vanish forever.

Grigori understood the situation better than me. He siphoned less and less until he found a balance point, one where he could maintain the status quo and not risk draining me.

"We're back," Gwaihir's voice ran through my head.

"Did you bring the virus?" Grigori asked my bondmate.

"We did," he replied.

"Take it to the White Fae," Grigori instructed.

Rhea apparently picked up on telepathy, courtesy of her association with the werewolf because she said, "You went to a lot of trouble for nothing. I stole the werewolf virus to make damn good and sure no one would ever have to deal with the hell I fell into. But it's been sitting around for years. I would be shocked if it retained viability."

"Why didn't you destroy it if you felt that way?" Grigori asked.

"She wouldn't let me," Rhea replied bitterly. "I finally gave up and left it alone knowing full well the samples would die on their own."

The same spotty glistening that had presaged her transformation drove her to her knees. "Nooooo," she shrieked. "I'm sick of you, I'm—"

Words turned into a snarl; claws formed where fingers had been.

"Can you do something?" I asked Grigori.

"Maybe." His reply was terse. The draw on my power intensified tenfold. Lightning crackled from his outstretched palms encompassing the partially shifted werewolf in her cell.

CHAPTER 8

"This should help," Ciara said as the briny smell of the sea filled the stone dungeon room. Borrowing a page from her, I added dirt to her illusion. If the werewolf was convinced we were intent on burying or drowning her, she'd behave better.

Maybe.

She sure didn't appear to give a fuck about the woman she'd turned. How had it happened? I wanted to know too. The transformation slowed but didn't reverse itself. One front and one hindfoot were lupine, and the shaggy red pelt had begun to sprout.

"You will cede to the human," Grigori ordered in stentorian tones. "Do. It. Now."

"Or?" The werewolf snarled

Ciara nudged me. We upped the ante on our water-dirt combo. It formed a thick, soupy mud that coated the misshapen creature, part wolf, part woman. Once I knew more about the circumstances binding them together, I might feel sorry for her.

Minutes ticked past, several of them until the wolf part of things shrank to nothing, leaving Rhea huddled and shivering, hands around her drawn-up knees. She looked up at us, not even trying to get to her feet. Ciara and I withdrew our combination of earth and sea power.

"I don't get it," Rhea muttered. "Why am I suddenly neither wet nor dirty?"

"Cheap parlor tricks," I said and offered an engaging smile. I'd meant to lighten the mood, but she didn't take the bait.

"If you kill me," she said in a surprisingly strong voice, "will it kill that thing too?"

"No," Grigori replied. "Even worse, catching her would likely prove beyond us once you were dead."

Rhea shook her head and rolled to her knees. From there, she stood and clasped her hands behind her. "Not the answer I was hoping for."

"How were you turned?" Grigori asked pointblank.

"I wish I knew." Another head shake was followed by a shaky breath. "I had this theory about a wild-type virus, one with multiple RNA variants, being behind both vampirism and werewolves. My colleagues thought I'd gone off the deep end, so I limited my research to late evenings when I had the labs to myself."

The drag on my power lightened up. Grigori was titrating what he took again. We'd be okay—unless the werewolf made another cameo appearance.

"How'd you get interested in something that esoteric in the first place?" I asked Rhea.

"One of my cousins turned into a vampire." Rhea winced. "Everyone believed she'd vanished, run off and maybe become one of the many gruesome statistics common in big cities. I thought the same until she came to me one night and told me what had happened. We were closer than sisters, and what was left of the human part of her probably missed me."

Breath rattled from Rhea. "I only saw her the once. She said it would be far too dangerous if any of her new...kinsmen discovered she'd spoken with me. Before she left, I asked if I could examine a few drops of her blood.

"It was the beginning of the journey that landed me where I am now. I was distraught over what happened to her. She claimed it was permanent, but maybe if I culled through her blood, I'd find an antidote."

Rhea licked at dry, chapped lips. "What I found was the weirdest virus ever. Viruses only have RNA. They hijack their host's cells to replicate themselves. But most viruses have only a single type of RNA. The ones I found in my cousin's blood had three. It got me to thinking."

"You played a dangerous game," Ciara said.

Rhea nodded. "I looked over my shoulder for a year after Melody's visit, but nothing ever happened. I relaxed a bit after that. My cultures of vampire virus were coming along nicely, so I asked the same question any researcher would."

"What other supernatural creature requires warped viruses?" Grigori muttered.

"Exactly. I discovered the dark web. Eh, discovered is too strong a word. I'd always known about its existence, but not how to access it. Once I fixed that little problem, I entered a shadowy world, one most people would have a hard time believing existed."

"Not us," I said brightly.

"Aye, it's where most of us live. Our go-to place for information," Ciara added.

"It's also like sifting through dross looking for bits of gold," Rhea said sourly. "For every would-be shaman, witch, or sorcerer trumpeting their powers, there's scarcely anybody with true occult connections."

I leaned closer. "How could you tell the difference. It's sometimes not easy for us."

She made a wry face. "Let's just say I wasted a lot of time, but I finally followed a lead to a sub-lead to yet another and found a pack of werewolves. The guy who clued me in to them turned out to be part of them, and—"

Ciara angled a pointed look my way before saying, "The whole thing was a trap, and you walked right into it."

"Lamb to the slaughter," Rhea agreed and rolled her eyes. "All I sought was a tiny bit of werewolf blood. I wanted to compare and contrast it with the cultures from my cousin."

She stopped, maybe to organize her thoughts. When she began talking again, her words were halting, and she'd dropped any pretense of joking about her gullibility. "The pack hung onto me. Escape wasn't possible; the cave where they dumped me had only a single entry point, and it was barred and guarded. I was cold, hungry, desperate. I assumed I'd signed my own death warrant, and after a few days I started looking for ways I could hasten the inevitable."

"They were grooming you," Grigori muttered.

I'd always wondered why he was the only werewolf in the Circle of Assassins. At first, I'd figured it was accidental, that werewolves weren't natural assassins beyond their immediate food needs. Apparently, I'd totally missed the boat.

"What do you mean?" Ciara asked him.

Grigori narrowed his eyes. "Vampires give their recruits a choice. They drain them to the point of death before offering eternal life from a streaming wrist. Those who are strong enough—or sunk deep in horror—find the wherewithal to refuse. The others become newly turned immortals.

"Werewolves live by a different code. Most packs have strict quotas on adding new members. If they didn't, obvious issues would ensue around insufficient food for everyone. The entire pack must agree by unanimous vote before a mortal joins their ranks."

"Wasn't I the lucky one," Rhea gritted.

"By their way of looking at things, you were," Grigori replied in bland tones. "To those like me, the greatest honor of all is inclusion in a pack."

Rhea stared right at him. "Where's yours?"

"I walked away long ago. My situation isn't relevant to yours, though. You were their prisoner. What happened then?"

"You already know," she mumbled and dropped her gaze to the stone floor. I didn't blame her. Holding eye contact with Grigori was a challenge for all but the strongest mages in the Circle.

"Maybe, but I want to hear your version."

"I grew weaker. Not being offered food or water does that. One night when I hovered so close to dying I prayed to whomever might be listening to hurry things along, this wolf came to me. She lay next to me. I wanted to scoot away, but she was warm, and I was so cold my bones had turned to ice.

"She licked my neck, gentle as anything. I let myself relax. If she was planning to make a meal out of me, she'd have led with her teeth, right? I felt a twinge in my shoulder, but nothing too terribly painful. After a time, the wolf left. I felt better, stronger, but I didn't understand how it was possible.

"With the dawn, the man who'd lured me entered the cave and released my bonds. He blindfolded me and led me back to my car, except it wasn't in the same place. He, or someone, had moved it. By the time I fished my keys out from under a floormat, he was gone."

Breath whooshed from her. "I drove home, showered, opened a few cans for a meal, and fell on my face. After I was finally awake again, it didn't take much digging to discover I'd been gone for ten days. My phone was full of calls and messages. My colleagues were worried about me, frantic I'd become another statistic."

Rhea shook her head. "For the next couple of weeks, I didn't notice anything special."

"Until the next full moon," Grigori said.

"Of course you'd know." A resigned note sat beneath her words. "Yes, the next full moon was my first transformation. I was trapped inside the wolf. Nothing I did made the slightest difference. I assumed I was lost forever. No one was more surprised than me when she left and I was myself again.

"I didn't trust it to last, though. My blood held the key to my question about werewolves and if the mutant RNA was linked with vampires. I started samples cooking, found the place in the north of Scotland, and planned my exit from the CDC. I've never had many friends, so I was spared skirting explanations."

"How many times did the wolf take over before you dropped out of sight?" Grigori asked.

"Three, and the last visitation, or whatever you call them, stretched for many days. It was when I understood I'd overstayed my welcome and pulled the pin on my escape plans. I figured I'd be safe enough on the plane. By then I'd done what research I could on the dark web, and I trusted the wolf would only show up when we were alone. I'm close to immortal, but there are those who know how to kill werewolves.

"I was banking my sidekick wouldn't want to risk it."

"Did she ever talk with you?" Grigori asked.

Rhea shook her head. "I tried talking with her. Begging. Pleading. All I was ever met with was silence. The first couple of months in Scotland were quiet. She took over when the moon was full, but then retreated. I was beginning to think I'd made a good decision."

"She was testing you," Grigori said. "Assessing your strengths. And your weaknesses."

"She pegged me as a complete wuss, which I'm not," Rhea retorted. "But neither was I strong enough to wrest control of my body back from her. Once she figured that part out, I was lost. More and more days were spent in wolf form until I retreated into myself and stopped caring. About anything."

"It's not the way the bond is supposed to work." Grigori sounded tired.

Knowing I might incur his wrath, I said, "Maybe it's enough for today."

"We're getting there," he said. At least he didn't snarl and tell me to shut up.

"Is there a way to keep the wolf quiet?" Rhea asked.

"There are ways to subdue you both," Grigori said. "Whatever we do to one of you will affect the other."

"Do it," Rhea said firmly. "I could use a break."

A trio of White Fae entered the room. Grigori might have summoned them, or their appearance could have been fortuitous. Power shimmered around them turning the air a pastel violet. One stopped next to Grigori and laid a hand on his neck. I sensed the shift in him as his magic strengthened. Maybe the virus samples Gwaihir and Tory had rescued weren't as defunct as Rhea had predicted.

Grigori cut his connection with Ciara and me. "Take this woman to the infirmary," he told the Fae. "Do not let the werewolf come forth."

"She will be placed deep in trance," one of the Fae warned.

"I welcome it," Rhea said.

Grigori placed his hand on the cell's locking mechanism. I heard his telepathy when he told the other werewolf, *"You are badly damaged. By the bonds that connect our kind, I shall attempt to restore you. If I fail, your life is forfeit."*

Even though I listened closely, I didn't hear a response.

The cell door creaked open, and the White Fae hustled inside, surrounding Rhea. In the space between two breaths, they were gone.

"Are rogue werewolves a thing?" Ciara asked.

I winced. I'd have dressed my question up a bit, but she cut to the chase.

"Not for those from my bloodlines," Grigori replied. "There are newer strains of werewolves who adopted different rules." He set his mouth in a tight line. "No matter how far or how fast you run, you cannot escape what you are. The modern rulebook has failed time and again because it didn't take werewolf essence into consideration. We must have a bond with our human half. We are two sides of the same coin. Or perhaps opposite ones.

"Nonetheless, we are shackled together, and we share everything. My wolf is my closest friend, my confidant, my soulmate. It's why werewolves rarely mate. Our other half is our mate. We require none other. Rhea's wolf made no attempt to build a bond with her. Consequently, Rhea hates her, and my bet is the wolf feels trapped.

"That's what I'm banking on, and the angle I will work when I try to convince the wolf to sever the bond."

"You can do that?" I asked. "Walk away as if it never happened? Vampires can't."

"Because it's a permanent alteration. And there's only one of them. Where once was a mortal, now stands a vampire. Werewolves maintain our dual natures. There is a dissolving ceremony. Normally, it leaves both wolf and human scarred, but that's assuming they developed a closeness, an interdependency."

"Never happened for that pair," Ciara said.

"We shall see how this plays out." Grigori stretched his arms above his head and rotated his torso. "I feel better than I have in months. Wonder how long the effects will last?"

"When they fade, the healers can hit you up again," Ciara said.

"Meanwhile, we have paybacks to plan, demons to slay, and an entire underworld to sabotage." I grinned broadly, entranced by the possibility of endless carnage.

Grigori slapped me across the back. "I've missed you, Quinn."

A smart-aleck comeback died on my lips because I'd missed him too. Not the Circle of Assassins, but him. Something pure and decent hovered beneath Grigori's lethal tendencies. He had ethics. Standards. On more than one occasion, I'd asked myself what he would have done and patterned my response in kind.

"Don't spread it around," I said, "but the feeling is mutual."

"Erk, the testosterone is choking me." Ciara made a gagging noise.

"How about if you get Quinn settled?" Grigori said.

"I can find my way around," I told him. "Hasn't been that long since I've been here."

"Fine. Have it your way." Power swirled around Ciara before she vanished. Something warm, earthy, and elemental left with her. I struggled against calling her back.

Grigori turned his blue gaze on me, looking through me as usual. "Do you not like her?"

The answer was too complex to even try to put into words. "I'm going to the library. I'll be there for a while."

He didn't pursue his line of inquiry regarding Ciara. "Anything in particular, or more of a general knowledge brush-up?"

I offered a jaunty grin. "Werewolves, my man. I'm going to peel back the secrets and find out all about you and your kind."

He nodded solemnly. "Excellent. Research the dissolving spell while you're at it. If luck is with us, we'll need it soon."

"What will happens to Rhea afterward?"

He shrugged. "I'll be as careful as I can scrubbing memories of her time as a werewolf and send her back into the world she left."

"She got a raw deal."

"Christ, Quinn. No one knows that better than me."

"Any way of rehabilitating her werewolf?"

"A very good question, but unfortunately not one I have an answer for."

I turned to go. "Who knows. Maybe I'll find something on that topic in the library."

"If you do, bookmark it and call me." Grigori's words chased me as I sprinted for stone stairs at the far end of the sub-basement.

As I retraced familiar hallways and stairs to the library, I chided myself for how I'd handled Grigori's offer of Ciara to help me settle in. I didn't trust myself around her. Not for a nanosecond. And not anywhere near a bedroom. Until my cock stopped springing to attention the moment I caught her scent, I'd do well to steer clear. It was just now retreating from its engorged state.

I didn't need female complications. My life was difficult enough with just me to worry about. Not that Ciara couldn't take care of herself. I was the problem. I turned into Sir Galahad the moment a woman entered my life, and became her self-appointed protector.

That approach was dead on arrival with Ciara, but I didn't have a plan B. Better to not even open that door than to fall over both feet and stuff them into my mouth right next to my bloated dick.

I pushed through swinging doors into the guild house library. It had always been my favorite room in all the guild houses. This one had twenty-foot ceilings with shelving that began at floor level. Books and scrolls spilled from the overstuffed racks. Long wooden tables with benches on both sides ran the length of the large chamber. At the moment, I was the only mage here.

Clearing my mind of everything except a need to know the whole shebang about werewolves, I sent power spinning outward with instructions to find source documents relevant to my search. More efficient than any card catalog, books and scrolls wriggled in their spots on the shelves, inviting me to plumb their secrets.

CHAPTER 9

I was on my third cup of coffee, or maybe it was my third pot. Ragged stacks of crumbling pages surrounded me on all sides. It wasn't readily apparent, but I did have a filing system. Items Grigori might want to review sat to my right. Documents I'd skimmed that weren't especially relevant were on my left. Ones that skirted the two camps were piled in front of me.

Wings swooshed as Gwaihir flew into the library. After a few circles, he landed on one of the few spots not littered with my research. I stopped reading, holding onto my place with an index finger, and glanced at him. I started to ask where Tory was but didn't. If they were becoming an item, I didn't want to know. Gwaihir would leave the guild house when I did, more or less. In the meantime, I needed his full and complete attention.

Having him pining for Tory wouldn't play well over the long haul. Eh, maybe I was reading too much into it. Or I was jealous he'd managed a feat that was proving beyond me. Never mind I'd given up before I even tried. I needed to pull my head out of my ass and focus. I'd barely met Ciara, and she'd taken up residence under my skin.

Rather than asking anything personal, I settled for, "How's it going?"

"We left the virus with the White Fae. From the looks of things, it helped Grigori."

"My take too." I nodded. "I was there when they dosed him with it. From my vantage point it appeared to be a magical infusion that soaked through his skin."

"It's a stopgap." Gwaihir's feathers rustled as he rearranged them. "What happened with the other werewolf?"

I narrowed my eyes, reconstructing events. "She seemed to recognize Grigori as her superior. She made one bid to take over but retreated when he pressed her." I swept an arm to encompass my reading materials. "I'm researching their social structure and other relevant items I come across."

"What's next for us?"

The question was out of character. Gwaihir usually picked his path, making sure it coincided with mine at key points. Some bondmates were joined at the hip, but that had never been our modus operandi.

"Not sure. Grigori summoned us for a reason, and it sure as hell wasn't to bail him out."

"Do you know why, exactly?" my bondmate pressed.

The message coded into the crystal scudded through my mind. Gwaihir had been off hunting with Tory when I'd first heard it.

"I do. I'd responded to a posting for our next job, but Grigori was the one who placed the ad with inducement spells woven into it."

"So, he meant to get your attention." The eagle mimed a whistling noise.

"He did, indeed. Anyway, here's what was coded into a

chunk of quartz: *I wouldn't have placed that job post on the dark web keyed to your energy, except a task lies before us. It's huge and daunting, and the Circle needs your help. I'm hoping you'll consider carving out a month for us. We will pay you well. The amount is negotiable, and we can firm it up once you accept."*

"Interesting. First time I heard the details," the bird squawked.

"It is intriguing and in all our interests to have Grigori in fighting shape." I didn't elaborate, but his skills truly shone in the tactical department. If the task ahead was "huge and daunting," he was the logical one to map out our attack.

"We need to deal with the other werewolf before we tackle huge and daunting," Gwaihir said. "She's a loose end, and we can't very well dump her in the dungeon while we leave for days or weeks."

"Sure we could—so long as we managed to separate Rhea." I shook my head and dragged a couple of scrolls front and center. "Let me get back to this. I need information so we can put that part to bed."

"I'll be outside. With Tory."

He'd brought her up, so I dove in. "Hold up a moment. You know her, right? Does it run deeper than that?"

"Of course, I know her. All the birds from my line are acquainted. What do you mean?"

I leveled my gaze his way. "The two of you were mating."

The eagle shrieked laughter. Once he stopped hooting and cawing, he said, "So? Nothing you don't do from time to time."

His words earned a rueful grin from me. "Touché. But don't eagles, erm, mate for life?"

"And how do you suppose that would work?"

"Probably not very well, given our bond."

He fixed his dark gaze on me. "You have been to my world. Not all my kinsfolk choose to bond with a mage. Many of them keep to themselves, much like our dragon friends." He stopped for a moment. "It's off track, but the one I feel sorry for is the unicorn. Not only is she all alone here, but her kin have cut her off. They have even stronger feelings than dragons about trafficking with mages."

"It is way off topic, but are Rhiana and Dorcha still in the Circle?"

"Off and on, like always."

I dragged my attention back to the scrolls. Rhiana was an elemental mage. Loosely related to those like me who'd mastered one of the four elements, she was far older. Rhiana had formed from air and fire soon after Earth spun out of the sun. Mages who came after her, like me for instance or Ciara, didn't hold a tenth of her power.

Gwaihir flicked a wing my way and flew from the library. The door opened for him courtesy of a shot of power. I raised my coffee cup to my mouth only to find I'd drained it. The nearby pot was empty as well, but I'd be damned if I'd allow myself the luxury of more until I was done rustling through the stack of source documents.

The next scroll turned out to be pay dirt. It contained a separation spell for werewolves and also instructions to snare the wolf so it didn't escape. Apparently, our problem werewolf was far from the first if someone had felt the need to memorialize instructions like these.

I got up to make more coffee and asked Grigori to meet me in the library. The dark, fragrant brew dripped through an early version of today's coffeemakers. I've always been almost the only one in any guild house who preferred coffee to tea, and so I made certain to pack beans in my duffel.

Back in wolf form, probably to conserve his magic, Grigori padded into the library and said, "Still like that shit, eh?"

"The bigger question is why you don't?" I filled a mug and

hustled back to my workspace. Grigori stood where I'd been sitting, his big, shaggy head right over the open scroll. With more delicacy than I'd imagined him capable of, he hooked a claw beneath the fragile vellum and moved to the next panel.

Books are a huge improvement over scrolls. I'll take pages any day over one long sheet that insists on rolling up and obscuring what I'm studying. I stood quietly, sipping my coffee, as Grigori moved from panel to panel. He'd read beyond my stopping point, which meant he'd uncovered additional information.

The air around him developed a liquid aspect, and he morphed into his human form. I've never understood how he emerges fully dressed. Other iterations of shifter usually strip before they invoke their animal bodies to avoid destroying a set of clothes.

As I thought about it, Rhea had been dressed too. Maybe it was something unique to werewolves.

Grigori shook himself. He'd changed out of the robe at some point and was clad in black denim pants, a cream-colored shirt with long, flared sleeves, and black boots. Rather than cascading down his back, his red hair had been gathered into a neat queue.

He turned to look at me. "We'll need a few ingredients, but this might work."

"What do you mean, might?" I sputtered. "Whoever wrote that didn't sound at all tentative."

Grigori's generous mouth spread, forming a rueful grin. "Have you ever read a magical primer where the author added cautions to the mix?"

"Um, yeah. I have, but they were far more modern than this one."

"Sign of the times, brother." Grigori moved to where he could clap me across the back. "Sign of the times. Everything anyone purchases these days is rife with warnings. Back when that"—he angled a glance at the table—"was penned, no one was worried about their reputation. Or lawsuits, either."

Laughter bubbled from me. "True enough. What are the risks, assuming we can get hold of zephyr dust, a puffer fish, and all those other esoteric components?"

His smile vanished. "Significant. We could kill them both if the werewolf puts up too much of a fight." Forehead creased with lines, he continued, "Any type of separation casting creates massive pain. No way to lessen it because both parties need to be awake. Usually, the wolf is in ascendency, but since I don't trust her, we'll have to work with the woman."

I thought about Rhea. "She's already asked us to kill her, so she'll probably sign up for anything that will rid her of the wolf. I'm still working on how this happened in the first place. Most werewolves wouldn't want to saddle themselves with a reluctant recruit, someone who'd make their lives miserable."

Grigori raised a russet brow. "Oh? And how many of us have you known well enough to make that assessment?"

"Point taken."

He returned to the place I'd been sitting, withdrew a sheet of paper and a pen from a drawer, and started a list of the items we'd need. As he wrote, he said, "Very few of us have embraced change. We are an ancient race. Much like dragons and elemental mages, we prefer to keep to ourselves and cling to the way things have always been.

"How that translates to Rhea Lockhart is the wolf assumed she'd get with the program, that she'd recognize the honor bestowed upon her and be grateful. When it didn't happen, the wolf forced her will on Rhea and simply took over, assuming sooner or later the mortal would come around."

"What about the rest of her pack?" I asked. "When Rhea found her, she was surrounded by other werewolves."

"They'd have counseled the wolf to bide a bit, see how the tides flowed. When Rhea panicked and moved to a remote location, the wolf erroneously assumed it was so they could be more open about their liaison." Grigori exhaled noisily. "I wasn't there, but my guess is Rhea's continued contempt and disgust spurred the wolf to press to the fore and remain there."

"So she can't be very happy with the status quo, either," I muttered.

"Probably not. I considered leveraging that angle, but it will take more time. The casting outlined in the scroll will be far quicker and cleaner."

"Assuming it doesn't kill them." I didn't care about the werewolf, but I was invested in Rhea sustaining as little damage as possible. She'd been through enough.

A trio of White Fae flew into the library, gossamer wings beating so quickly they were a blur. Grigori handed the list to one of them, and she landed long enough to skim it.

"How is the werewolf doing?" I asked.

Another of the Fae twisted her ethereal features into a frown. "Fighting our herbs and our power, but we've managed to keep her unconscious."

"Is she still in her human body?" Grigori asked.

The Fae with the list nodded tersely. "One paw tried to punch through. We smothered it with a belladonna and valerian wrapping."

"Belladonna?" Curiosity rose to the fore since it was poison to every manner of creature I knew—and one of my favorites in the field. Unlike cyanide, its scent was simple to disguise.

"Aye," the Fae concurred. "No one likes it, but the werewolf was never in any danger."

"How soon can you fulfill the list?" Grigori broke in.

By now, the other two White Fae were hovering around the

one with the list. They made little clucking sounds, but one said, "Give us three hours."

"Done," Grigori said. "Meanwhile, we will make preparations."

"Guess they have their own version of a dark web," I joked once they'd left.

"Their sources are far more efficient," Grigori noted.

"Can we cover a couple of things before we launch the preparations you referred to?"

"Of course."

"Why is your werewolf experience so different from hers?"

"What's the second topic?"

I assumed he didn't plan to address the first one, so I said, "When Ciara fetched me, she alluded to a significant task. You didn't call me back here to help you."

"How do you know?" Understated humor ran beneath Grigori's question.

"Because you have too much pride." He'd asked, and so I was blunt.

He tilted his head at a thoughtful angle. "You're right about the pride part, but I know you too."

"What's that supposed to mean?"

"The reason I sent Ciara to fetch you is valid—and deadly serious. Worlds hang in the balance, but I also hoped you'd find a way to get me back in the game. And you did."

I scowled. "My solution was far from rocket science. The question is why nobody else came up with it first—particularly you."

"I was hanging on by a thread. My dearest companion was dying. It's simpler for me to be in my form, but I maintained the wolf body to encourage him to stick around, to not give up."

It was a solid entry point, so I rephrased my earlier

question. "How come your wolf is a trusted friend and Rhea hates hers?"

"Think about it," Grigori countered. "Different times spawn different types of humans. I sprang from an era when magic was revered, valued. Werewolves were powerful, and I sought them out, determined to become one."

"Talk about a different mindset," I muttered.

He nodded. "All Rhea wanted was blood for her agar plates. I craved the real deal, all of it. The power and the magic and the respect."

An idea began to percolate. Grigori would cut me off if he thought I was full of shit. "How about a first step, something we do before we bring in the heavy artillery and strip out the wolf?"

"I'm listening, but make it quick. Three hours isn't all that long. We have work ahead."

"From where I sit, Rhea feels like a victim, but the wolf does too. It assumed Rhea would appreciate it, become a viable part of a partnership. When it didn't happen, the wolf probably was uncertain how to proceed. Rhea's fear and anger were toxic, so the wolf took over to avoid dealing with her."

"I already figured that part out. What are you proposing?"

"Take a few minutes. Talk with her. Tell her the good parts about being a werewolf. So far, her entire mindset is focused on the bad parts, the loss of control, mostly. She's in her fifties, which is nothing to us, but by human standards, she's at the top of her game vocationally. Or she was before she got scared and ran away to hide her shame."

Grigori set his mouth is a tight line. "I'll give it a shot, but it's a waste of time."

"Not the attitude to go into this." I leveled my gaze his way.

"What is?"

"The procedure laid out here"—I flicked the scroll—"isn't

without danger. And it's permanent. She doesn't get a do over if she decides she made a mistake."

"But she can reclaim her life."

"Maybe. Assuming you don't erase too many of her memories. Hell, Grigori, you know how mind wipes go. She might have to learn to add all over again. Not all brains are organized the same way, and when you go mucking around in the hippocampus, you could turn her into a vegetable."

"Give me a little credit," he huffed.

"I'm giving you plenty," I retorted, "but this is me you're talking to, not a new recruit. I've dicked around with people's memories. It's far simpler to plant memories than to remove them. While we're at it, you're pissed at Rhea's werewolf. It's not productive. From her perspective, the rulebook changed, and she doesn't understand what went wrong any more than Rhea does."

He started out the door. I loped after him. "You're done talking," he informed me.

"Thought we'd do this together," I said.

He stopped moving and flashed around to face me; fury streamed from him. "When did you stop trusting me?"

"That's not it at all. I feel responsible since I rousted Rhea out of her hideaway. Besides, if things don't work out, it may take two of us to force her back into her trance state."

He raked me with something hot and thorny that tested my words—and my resolve. Apparently, I passed because he started moving again and didn't protest when I trotted by his side.

We hurried along corridors on our way to the infirmary. "What would have happened if Ciara and I hadn't intervened?" I asked, curious if I'd set bigger wheels in motion than I thought.

"The wolf is well on her way to going rogue."

"And that means what?" I pressed.

"Like all shifters, the werewolf bond was designed for the human to be in control. In this case, the wolf took over. Eventually, the pressure of making all the decisions would have eroded her mind. She'd begin making reckless choices. Sooner or later, she'd get into major trouble and try to return to her pack. They'd take one look at her, know she was beyond salvage, and end her."

"No judge? No jury?"

"What do you think?" Grigori pushed through the door into the guild house infirmary. On the second floor, it was at the end of the building and ringed with crystalline windows. Light came alive in the cheery room, the illumination mingling with magic from the White Fae.

Rhea lay on a raised platform beneath the largest window. Far from quiescent, she writhed and moaned. A translucent canopy had been draped over her. It pulsed with a combination of energies: hers as the wolf struggled against its bonds and White Fae as they did their damnedest to contain things.

One detached herself from the group ranged around the head of Rhea's pallet. "I was told we had three hours," she said.

"We are here for another reason," Grigori told her. "Can you rouse her?"

The healer narrowed her silver eyes and settled to the ground in a flutter of silver-edged wings. "We can, but 'tisn't wise. Additional power will be required to force her back under if events spiral out of our control, which they will. Rather quickly too." Her voice was low, musical, and held a worried note.

"Let me worry about that," Grigori said.

I'd edged nearer the pallet. Spots of color dotted Rhea's cheeks; she was panting and agitated. From time to time, the wolf took shape around her, retreated, and tried once more.

Grigori joined me. In a shower of sparks, he reclaimed his

wolf form. Raising a front paw, he cleaved through the shroud around her and strode forward.

Before I could link with him, or share magic, or do much of anything, the body on the raised platform shrieked, a doleful haunting sound I'll hear in nightmares forever. Amid ripping, tearing noises, the wolf sprang for Grigori. It wasn't fully formed, which made its attempt all the more pathetic. Saliva spooled from lolling jaws. Teeth clacked together, taking a chunk out of its lolling tongue.

Beneath the howls, Rhea hurled curses. Crap. Maybe my bright idea wasn't all that great after all. I started to push power, aiming at containing the renegade werewolf, but Grigori flipped the partially formed wolf onto her back and plopped his foreleg in the middle of her chest, holding her easily.

"You will listen to me. You will not fight."

"Or?" the other were snarled.

"Or I shall end you. Are we clear?"

The were angled her head, working to get her jaws around Grigori's leg.

"If you do that, we're done." Grigori's tone was mild, but I knew him well. He'd annihilate Rhea, considering her collateral damage. In full werewolf mode, he expected the wolf beneath him to capitulate. Anything less, and he'd make good on his threat.

CHAPTER 10

White Fae had pressed in on both sides of me, forming a ring around the pallet. A minute ticked past, and then another. Finally, the prostrate were dropped her head to one side.

"Better," Grigori snarled, showing a mouthful of teeth. "None of what I have to say is up for discussion. You will listen, and at the end, you will indicate yes or no. If the answer is no, the Fae will snare you once again, but not for long. I have the spell in hand to separate you from Rhea Lockhart. Once it is complete, I shall return you to your pack to face justice."

"Separate us. Do it now," Rhea yowled. "I don't care what you have to say."

"You will listen," I admonished her. "There's a price to the magic, and it involves your memories. You know too much. We cannot leave any trace of us or your tenure with the werewolf, and—"

"Quinn!" Grigori's tone was pointed. "Shut up."

I raised a hand, palm outward. "Sorry. Didn't mean to steal your thunder."

"You've experienced the worst of the shifter bond," Grigori told the joined pair. "If the experience was always like yours, no one would ever deign to share their essence with an animal. I wouldn't be here talking about this, but Quinn wanted to make certain we turned over every stone before taking steps to dissolve the magic binding you together."

"I still want out," Rhea muttered, her words garbled since she was forcing speech through the wolf's mouth.

"I'm sure you do," Grigori replied. "If my initial years with my wolf had been anything like yours, I'd have done damn near anything to pull the plug. I wanted the bond, sought it out, but times were very different a thousand years ago."

"You can't be that old," Rhea sputtered.

"You know nothing," her werewolf retorted.

"Because you never took the time to teach her," Grigori admonished. "By the great wolf, Fenrir, how could you have expected her—a product of the twenty-first century—to welcome being saddled with your presence?"

"The others said she'd come around."

"What others? What pack do you come from?"

The wolf shrank into a ball around the foot Grigori still had dead center on her chest.

"You may as well tell me," Grigori said. "I can mine the information from your memories easily."

"The Morak," she growled after a lengthy pause.

I'm not as good at reading Grigori's expressions when he's a wolf, but surprise registered on his lupine features. "But they were banished," he said.

"After a while, we came back. Delta world had no game. We were starving, and—"

"Stop!" Grigori bellowed. "You know the rules. If your pack had need to change anything, your alpha was to contact the werewolf council."

"He said he did."

Power flowed from Grigori as he checked the truth in her assumption. A low snarl rolled from him. "I see. He lied to you, but perhaps not all of you. Is Suni still your alpha?"

"Uh-huh."

"Still mated to Ara?"

Another grunt that might have been assent. My knowledge of werewolves was expanding by leaps and bounds. Still, nothing I'd read suggested they had a central council, or that they banished rebellious packs to distant worlds. Maybe no one was willing to commit that type of thing to paper. Clearly, Grigori led at least two lives, one of which I knew nothing about.

"What'd they do wrong?" I asked.

"You are not pack," he growled. I took it to mean I wasn't entitled to know. Eh, not all that important.

He turned back to the wolf cowering beneath his foot. Something must have motivated him because he withdrew his paw and barked, "Sit up."

The red-pelted wolf obeyed immediately. Her ears were pinned back, and her shoulders slumped. I'm not an expert on canid body language, but everything about her screamed defeat.

"Do you want to start over with the woman?" Grigori asked.

The werewolf whined. "I do, but how can I? She hates me. I know her thoughts, and they're...ugly."

"Rhea, do you wish to start over?" Grigori asked.

"No! Why would I? I want my old life back."

"It might not be possible," Grigori cautioned. "Erasing memories can be a crapshoot, particularly if I err on the side of caution. Caution on my side, that is."

"You don't have to. I won't say anything."

"Can't take that chance. There are benefits to being joined

with a werewolf. So many, they were sought-after companions, and—"

"Yeah," she mumbled. "A thousand years ago."

"Silence," he bellowed. "You will hear me out and not interrupt. Immortality and magic are the benefits. When the partnership works the way it was designed, both you and your wolf agree who will be ascendant. Except during the full moon when it's the wolf's turn to shine."

One of the Fae from the library glided near. "We found everything, Master."

Grigori glanced at her. "Well done, Marion."

"Do you wish me to begin decanting the infusion?"

Grigori turned his attention back to the werewolf. "Cede to the woman. Do it now."

With more alacrity than I'd have predicted, the wolf faded, leaving Rhea in its place. Grigori shifted forms too. "Once we begin this process," he told her, "we shall see it through to its end. It is painful and permanent. I will do my best to leave you more or less intact, but I make no promises."

"But if I stay like I am," she wailed, "I'll be stuck hiding away from everybody forever. Look how you live. You're not exactly part of the modern world."

"You know nothing about me," he replied. "Nothing. My life and what I do is not up for discussion. Yours is."

Rhea cocked her head to one side as if she were listening to something. Twin furrows formed between her brows. "Do you really run an international group of assassins?"

"I do, although your wolf shouldn't have told you that." He paused, maybe to decide what to say next. "Being a werewolf isn't shameful. Most of our kind live side by side with mortals, with no one being the wiser. You would have a pack affiliation, but it will not be the Morak. Once the council discovers they returned to Earth without permission, they will be banished again. This time, we will ensure they stay gone."

"The wolf says she'll have to go with them. What would that mean for me?"

"If you remain bonded, I will petition the council to reassign you to a different pack. It's an unusual move, but these are unusual circumstances."

The furrows between Rhea's brows deepened. "She's begging me. Why did she never talk with me before?"

"She says she tried, but you didn't listen," Grigori pointed out.

"All she did was lecture me, berate me for not being appreciative she'd chosen me," Rhea protested.

Grigori rocked back on his heels. "We're out of time. What'll it be?"

"Will you help us?" Rhea asked. "The wolf is really different than she's been."

"Maybe it's because you're more open. Not being frightened half to death makes a huge difference." Grigori's voice was gentle. "I cannot help the two of you, but what I will do is make certain you go to a pack that will assist you. The council will work things out, but I will facilitate it."

"Does this mean I can go home?" Rhea asked.

"Eventually," Grigori told her. "Do you still have a home in the States?"

She nodded. "I do. It's been sitting empty for far too long."

"It's a good long-term goal," I cautioned her. "Expect to spend time, maybe quite a bit, learning about your new power. You're still thinking like a human. Once you begin thinking like a werewolf, you'll be ready to rejoin the world. If you still want to. Many of us don't."

The Fae, who'd been hovering, withdrew. She had her answer about the infusion. It appeared we wouldn't need it.

"Best of luck to you both," Grigori said and turned to leave.

"But you can't go," Rhea protested.

"I have to," he said and kept walking.

She sprang after him and grabbed his arm. I expected him to spin and cuff her. He didn't. "What?" he growled.

"I heard everything, even when the wolf had my body, or our body, or however the nomenclature goes. I can make you stable preparations of the werewolf virus and leave instructions for how to keep it going in perpetuity."

"Tell the Fae who tended you," Grigori said and vanished.

Rhea's eyes widened. She laid a hand over her heart. "Christ. There's a lot to get used to."

"You don't know the half of it," I told her. "Be kind to your wolf. She's suffered as much as you have."

A group of White Fae surrounded Rhea, herding her back into their domain. I considered tracking Grigori down, but he was probably up to his ass in werewolf business. Ciara saved me the trouble, shimmering to corporeality a few feet away.

"The story had a happy ending?" she inquired.

"Maybe. We're not near enough the end to know for certain." I started for the library. "Walk with me."

She raised a blonde brow, and, as we walked, I outlined what had transpired, followed by, "Did you know werewolves had a council? Vampires don't."

"Yeah, but they're nothing alike," she said.

"Mmph. I suppose not since Vampires are dead. Why didn't Grigori consult his own council when he started fading?" I asked.

We'd reached the library. Ciara turned, crossed her arms under her breasts, and sent me one of those you've-got-to-be-kidding looks women have turned into an art form.

I cleared my throat. "I wouldn't have asked if I knew the answer."

"Werewolves maintain a strict hierarchy," she began. "He could have asked for assistance, but he'd have lost status. A whole bunch, especially considering he doesn't have a pack affiliation. None that any of us have determined, anyway."

Unsure what him being part of a pack—or not—had to do with anything, I shouldered into the library, holding the door for Ciara. She strode through murmuring, "How chivalrous of you."

The sarcasm was unmistakable. "Fine. Next time open your own goddamn door." I hurried to the place I'd been ass deep in scrolls.

"Sorry. Sometimes I'm too bitchy for my own good," she said and settled next to me on the long bench.

I shuffled through scrolls, determined I'd mined everything useful out of the one I'd shown Grigori, and opened another. The scent of the sea was followed by a sound screen settling around us.

"Grigori doesn't like it when we talk about him," she explained. "I'm making certain no one listens in. Do you know why he left his pack? How it happened?"

I shook my head. "Always figured it was none of my business. In truth, I didn't know werewolves had stuck with a pack structure. He's the only one I've ever known well. I've run into a few over the years, though."

"Everyone has," she inserted.

"Yeah, well, it hasn't been the best experience. Once I catch their scent, I give them a wide berth. Unless they're my target-du-jour. In that case, all bets are off."

She twisted and draped a long leg over both sides of the bench so she faced me. She'd changed into dark-blue leggings and a knit tunic in shades of violet and cream. Both clung to her curves, showing off breasts and hips. Her backside was faced away from me, but I didn't need to see her ass to remember its high, tight swell. A heavy silver chain spanned her neck with a trident dangling from its links.

Damn it. There went my cock again. So long as I stuck with my current position, feet beneath the table, it shouldn't be too noticeable.

"You were one of Grigori's first recruits," she said.

"That I was."

She made a slight shrugging motion that accentuated her assets. "Not sure what I assumed," she went on, apparently unaware of the effect she had on me. "Maybe that the initial bunch of you were close enough to trade secrets."

I blew out a breath, working to think about something other than peeling her clothing off layer by layer and worshipping the warm flesh beneath. "Back then, we were all men," I pointed out. "We prefer to keep our distance. Knowledge is power, and—"

She flapped a hand my way. "I get it. By the time I showed up, the Circle was more intimate, a bastion against the modern world. One of the attractions—for me, at least—was being with other mages. And not being under Poseidon's thumb."

I flicked a finger at her pendant. "You still wear his sigil."

"Aye. To remind me to seek out positives when my entire existence is swimming in shit." She shook her head. "What I meant to say is Grigori was given an ultimatum."

"By whom?"

"His pack, who else?" A small headshake suggested she still thought I was dumb as a post, but she didn't say it. "He had to choose. If he continued running the Circle, it had to come under pack jurisdiction."

Understanding slapped me, and I smiled. "How like Grigori to tell them to take both options and shove them. He walked away, didn't he?" After Ciara nodded, I went on. "Took a while before he picked up the werewolf banner again, didn't it?"

"Centuries, and then he finessed it via the council. As far as his pack is concerned, he's dead, stricken from their records, or however they keep track of who's in and who's out."

Interesting. I turned back to the scroll, but Ciara's information filled the gaps in what I'd been searching for, so I rolled it back up and secured it with a strip of leather. "Do you have details about the mission ahead of us?"

"Which one?"

"The reason Grigori sent you to roust me out of my home. You alluded to something huge and daunting."

She nodded. "I was instructed to use those words."

With all our conversation, my cock had retreated to a semi-rigid state. I mimicked her posture, straddling the bench so I faced her. "Not exactly what I asked. If you know more, now would be a good time to tell me."

"So you can decide if you're going to remain?"

I shook my head. "Not at all. I'm committed to whatever this mystery mission is, and I'll stick around to see it through. If Grigori's estimate is a month, it must span several worlds and require a coordinated approach."

She crossed her legs, propped an elbow on one, and rested her chin on it. "I've told you what I know. Grigori's played his cards quite close to the vest on this one."

"Does he suspect traitors in our midst?" I kept my voice low despite the shielding around us. The smells of a restless ocean ebbed and flowed, reminding me of the sea's many moods. From gentle waves to pounding hurricanes with not much of a transition zone.

"Don't know about him," Ciara said, "but I've wondered about that for a while now."

"Say more."

"Nothing I can put my finger on. Not exactly. But I've

suspected perhaps Grigori wasn't poisoned during that demon attack, but more recently."

"As in when his symptoms actually began?" She nodded, and I considered her suggestion. "It makes more sense," I muttered.

"Aye, it does, indeed," she replied. "I never bought into the whole delayed reaction thing. Particularly since the cure was so quick. He started looking better as soon as the healer dosed him with more of whatever it is that makes him a werewolf."

"Good news, then," I said.

She scrunched her face into a grimace. "How? In what universe is housing turncoats good news?"

"Means we can find them, root them out, draw and quarter them, and be done with that side of things."

"Do you think Grigori hasn't already tried?"

I thought about it before answering. "We've had problem mages from time to time, but none of them were stupid enough to turn their malevolence his way."

"First time for everything," she muttered.

"Yeah, but much as Grigori had too much pride to lay himself bare before his council, the same selective blindness might mean he's not looking at what's right in front of him." I hesitated a beat. "Have you, erm, floated your theory elsewhere?"

"Do you mean have I confided in anyone?"

"Uh-huh. Like you're doing right now."

"Nope. I'm pretty new by Circle standards. I'm still earning my chops."

The phrase was so modern it made me smile. "What better way to earn them than uncovering a plot against the Circle's founder?"

"What if I'm wrong? Then everyone will hate me, and I'll have to leave."

I placed a hand on her thigh. It was so close, and her scent so alluring, I couldn't resist. I expected her to push it away, or slap me. Neither happened. I took it as a win.

"What if you're right? You'll be a hero."

She snorted. "With a fucking target painted on my back." She exhaled noisily. "If there's a coup afoot, someone trying to either take the Circle down or alter its leadership, it's probably a two-pronged effort."

I nodded. "Mages outside the Circle and a few who've infiltrated. It makes sense."

"I might be new to the Circle, but I've been an assassin—and a spy—for a whole lotta years."

I leveled my gaze at her. "Why trust me?"

Spots of color dotted her cheeks, but she met my gaze. "Tory adores your bondmate. Eagles have solid instincts. They don't get caught up in petty squabbles like some of the other bond animals."

I smiled. "The friend of my friend is trustworthy?"

She grinned back. "I thought that saying was the enemy of my enemy is my friend."

"Eh, I took a bit of poetic license. Actually, I'm honored you confided in me."

She laid a hand over mind and squeezed lightly. Her touch was cool and inviting, but I resisted the impulse to turn my hand over and lace my fingers with hers.

"We can do more digging," she suggested.

"We could, but we're going to bring this to Grigori."

She snatched her hand back. "I told you that in confidence."

"Why do you want to keep it a secret from him?"

Her gaze skittered off to one side. "Not sure. I'd like to be more certain than I am before I give voice to conspiracy theories."

"How certain?"

She frowned. "Maybe 75 percent."

"And where are you now?"

"Hovering around the fifty mark."

"It's good enough." I made a grab for her hand, and she didn't pull it out of my grip. "You trusted me. Don't stop now. Grigori may have already considered your theory. He could have his eyes on some of the Circle, or maybe he discarded the idea. Regardless, we need to talk with him." I let go of her, stood, and walked some of the scrolls to their spots on lower shelves. The upper ones required a magical boost one at a time.

By the time I returned to my spot, Ciara had shelved the other books and scrolls. "Full of surprises, aren't you?" I said.

"Whatever do you mean?" she asked, playing dumb.

I made another grab for her hand, but she eluded me this time. "You've been researching werewolves on the Q.T.," I informed her. "You knew exactly where those source documents belonged."

The corners of her mouth twitched into a smile. "Our secret?"

Secrets crafted small intimate places between two people where no one else was allowed to tread. Between the brine and musk of her scent and her request to keep her investigation private, my resolve to keep my distance crumbled. I wrapped my arms around her and covered her mouth with my own.

CHAPTER 11

The sharp sting of the slap I anticipated never happened. I'd expected her to stiffen and exit my embrace. Instead, she leaned in, molding her body to mine. She felt divine pressed against me, an exotic blend of ancient and modern. No matter what the era, some things never changed, and the heady rush of arousal was one of them.

I threaded my fingers into the silk of her hair, soaking in the exquisite shape of her skull as I cradled her head. Our mouths were glued together, tongues playing as we kissed, bit, and teased each other. Lower, against my chest, her nipples had formed peaks. I wanted to reposition a hand, sandwich it between our bodies and touch one of her high, firm breasts, kneading the nipple until she moaned.

Wanted to but didn't. We swayed against each other. I'm certain she noticed the swell of my erection prodding her belly. How could she not? Power flickered around us as we drank each other in. What was wrong with me? Presented with a willing woman in my arms, I should scoop her up and take her to bed.

I'd never had any scruples about dipping my pen into

company ink. Most of my liaisons had been with partners I'd met on the job. Where else would I come across lovers? I don't frequent bars, and all the singles clubs and Internet dating apps gave me the creeps. All I was usually on the prowl for was a one-night stand. The porn sites filled in nicely, but the couple of times I'd used them, the women hadn't even pretended to be interested. Society lost something when old-time courtesans fell out of favor.

Ciara wound her arms around my shoulders and broke our kiss. She touched my mouth with the tip of her tongue and said, "You're a million miles away. Did I do something wrong?"

"Not at all."

"Then what is it?" She angled her head to one side and raked me with a speculative glance. "You kissed me, but then your attention wandered."

The corners of my mouth formed a smile. Skirting the wandering attention issue, I replied, "I kissed you because you're irresistible. I've been thinking about what your mouth would feel like ever since you showed up at my house."

"Only my mouth?" she teased.

I moved my hands slowly down her shapely spine until I cupped her ass. "Not just your mouth. All of you, but we have work to do. A lot of it."

"No one will miss us for the next half hour." Her lips glistened from our kiss. Her eyes were warm and inviting, and her ass to die for. The same question that had popped up before tormented me. What was stopping me?

"Probably not," I agreed and blundered through what would surely sound lame. "There's something different about you. Something special. Maybe it's because our magic is so similar. Maybe it's something else, but I don't just want sex."

"It would be a start." She prodded my erection with her hips. "Your buddy agrees."

Letting go of her rump, I left one arm behind her back and cradled the side of her face with a hand. "It isn't that I don't want you. I do, so much it's taking everything in me to hold back. Under other circumstances, I wouldn't hesitate, but I don't understand what I'm feeling. Part of me—a big part—is screaming I'm a fool for not following you to your chamber, or one of the vacant rooms in the guild house."

"And the other part?"

"Wants to do things differently. So we might maybe have a chance." I smoothed a thumb over her cheekbone. "All my non-relationships have begun in bed. I bet yours have too."

"That's a quantum leap, my dear. You're assuming I've had the odd love interest."

"Have you?"

"I'll show you mine if you show me yours," she joked.

"Fair enough. It's been over a year since I've had a woman in my life, but she and all the others who've crossed my path were transient by design."

"It's the life we lead, isn't it?" She'd fastened her gaze on me, eyes liquid with interest.

I nodded. "I can't tell mortals the truth about what I do. Trysts with them have to be brief and end long before they start probing about anything personal. Most mages are, well, you know how few of us form lasting bonds."

She nodded back. "I do. I had a lover, one of the Selkie. It lasted a very long time, but once I left the sea and Poseidon's court, we had nothing in common. We tried, but it was never the same." Sadness tinged her words.

"I'm sorry," I murmured, feeling shallow for my lack of commitment. At least Ciara had made a good-faith effort. I'd been too self-absorbed and had hidden behind one excuse after the next.

"There are a few couples in the Circle," she went on. "It

pleased me since the bond animal attachment takes up so much psychic space."

"Did you worry Tory wouldn't want to share you?"

"Yes, but it was silly of me."

"Not at all. The Circle of Assassins was something new for you. So was having a bondmate."

My body was alight with her nearness. To reduce the temptation to crush her against me once more, I took a step back, untangling my arms from her body. She let go too. "You're a pretty man, Quinn."

"You're the pretty one. Let's see where things go between us."

"Nicest brush-off, ever."

"But it's not. I hope we'll figure things out." My words understated the longing surging through me, but I wouldn't offer false hope. I'd never been good partner material. Preoccupied with work, I couldn't remember the last time I'd taken a break longer than a few days.

The scent of the sea grew stronger as her power eddied around me, maybe testing my words, or my integrity. When she smiled again, it was soft and genuine. "Me too. If you're still set on sharing my half-baked theories, we should find Grigori."

"I'll ask him to join us in the grove."

"Good call. He won't like hearing my suspicions."

"Yeah," I agreed. "And we sure as hell don't want anyone else to listen in." Because I couldn't stand to be this close and not touch her, I reached for her hand. She laced her fingers with mine, and we stood like that for a few seconds before moving apart again.

"See you in the grove," she said and walked out of the library.

I sorted where Grigori was and headed for the nearest

staircase. My initial bent had been to use telepathy, but it could be intercepted. Better to take a few extra minutes and be safe. If the Circle had been infiltrated, whoever was behind it was skilled. They'd have to be to make it through Grigori's vetting process.

Mages couldn't stroll into the Circle. The Circle reached out to the few they were interested in. I didn't care for the direction of my thoughts because they pointed to a coordinated effort that had begun long ago. If Ciara's concerns held weight, a group of mages had positioned themselves to catch Grigori's attention.

It took far more than a single kill. Grigori assessed everything about potential recruits including their style, how they comported themselves when they weren't on assignment, any connections that might pose potential risks to the Circle's anonymity, and how they'd fit in. Some mages, like Loren, the other earth wizard, had turned into prima-donna problem children, but they hadn't shown their true colors until after being inducted.

Or maybe being in the Circle had inflated Loren's sense of self-worth, making him insufferable. It was a chicken-and-egg problem; one I'd never bothered to sort, mostly because it was probably different for every mage who developed stick-up-their-ass tendencies.

The Circle had been good for me for a long while. I'd appreciated the companionship, but the allure of running my own operations had proven too much to refuse.

The door to Grigori's rooms was shut, usually a sign he wanted to be left alone, but I knocked anyway. After waiting a discreet interval, I knocked again.

"What?" rumbled through the stout oaken door.

"You're needed." I kept my message simple and vague. It could mean anything.

Grigori yanked the door open and gestured me inside. I shook my head. "I'll be in the grove."

"Can it wait?"

"Not for very long."

He set his mouth in a tight line and nodded before pulling the door closed again. I retraced my steps, building an invisibility spell as I moved through the guild house. By the time I pushed through the substantial front doors, my casting was complete. In some ways, it was a waste of time and magic since everyone here could sense my power even through an illusion.

Still, it made me feel better. I could have teleported to the grove, but everything employing power leaves tracks. Besides, movement soothed the ragged places dogging me. Between Ciara's unsettling revelation and replaying holding her against me, I welcomed the simple slap of my boot soles against dirt. Running was something I had control over.

A snort burst from me. Control could be my mantra. It was what had driven me from the Circle, what had kept me a loner all the long years of my life. At the slightest whisper I might not be in command of every smidgeon of every event, I muscled up and forced outcomes to bend to my will.

So far, I hadn't failed, but there'd be a first time. And a second.

I slowed to duck between two stout white oak trees and dismissed my invisibility spell. Several trees formed a circle and provided a private place for Grigori to dish out assignments. In some way I'd never been able to ferret out, the trees were linked to his power.

"Is he coming?" Ciara glanced up from where she leaned against a tree.

"I believe so."

"Did you speak with him?" she pressed.

"Yup and asked him to come here. He wanted to know if it could wait, and I said not for long."

She blew out a breath. "Are you certain this is the right path?"

"Yes. If I were in his position, I'd want to know."

"Me too, but he's not like either of us," she murmured.

"What do you mean?" From where I sat, all mages had more in common than not.

"The werewolf energy is more...eh, more focused. Grigori can be very single-minded. He reminds me of Scylla sometimes, or the Kraken."

"Those reference points don't mean much to me," I told her. "I know the stories, but I bet you've actually met them."

"Of course. All sea creatures are interconnected."

Before she could add information, the distinct sound of paws reached me. Grigori was almost here. His energy pulsed as he approached.

"I'm still uncertain," Ciara said.

"He'll understand," I replied. "And he'll respect you for having the guts to speak up."

The black-and-silver wolf loped into the grove, shifting into his human body as soon as he cleared the perimeter of tree trunks. "I'll understand what?" he asked.

Ciara took a couple of steps from where she'd been leaning against a tree and rolled her shoulders back. Standing tall, she said, "Do you honestly believe the scourge killing the virus in your body resulted from a demon attack two years ago?"

"Why would you ask?"

A carefully worded response. So carefully worded, I zoned in on Grigori. It was looking like Ciara had been right about him playing with a concealed hand. "Because a delayed reaction to demon taint seems unlikely," I replied.

"I, uh, took the liberty of doing some research," Ciara said.

"Into werewolves. Quinn figured it out since I knew where to shelve all the books and scrolls he'd selected without consulting the central registry."

A corner of Grigori's mouth twisted downward. "You have to get up pretty early to slide anything past Quinn."

"Apparently." Ciara didn't alter her stance. "Once he busted me, we talked a little, behind a sound shield."

"What'd you come up with?" Grigori prodded.

"We believe the Circle's been infiltrated," she said flatly. "I'm nowhere near certain of that, but it would make sense to have a two-pronged effort with mages both outside and within the Circle intent on bringing it down."

"To what end?" Grigori was still in Q&A mode.

"Maybe it's been a thorn in someone's hide for a long while," Ciara suggested. "Most of the targets you've selected would have it in for you."

"Perhaps they want to co-opt the Circle's machinery and turn it to their own ends," I cut in.

"Why not both?" Grigori's mild tone told me those ideas weren't new to him.

"You already knew, didn't you?" I said.

"Know is too strong a word, but I've had my suspicions for a while." He crafted a canopy and gestured us closer. "The grove is sealed, but I'm making doubly certain no one listens in. I'm who created and endorsed the demon taint theory. The White Fae who work as healers are complicit, but I trust them. We haven't added any new White Fae to the Circle for over four hundred years."

"If you believe you have traitors within the Circle, why haven't you kicked them out?" I asked, and added, "You've never hesitated to cull the ranks before."

"If you think about it, you already have the answer," Grigori replied.

"So I'm correct. They are part of the big picture threat," Ciara muttered.

"Aye. I believe so." Grigori looked pleased by Ciara's deductive logic.

"Are you going to tell us whom you suspect?" I asked pointblank.

Grigori shook his head. "It's critical you come up with the same mages I did. If not, we need to dig deeper."

"You have to be more forthcoming than that," I groused. "I'd never accept a job with so little information attached to it."

The weave of his power tightened around us, proof he was almost back to his full capacity. "When I was fading," he began, "few paths were available. Merely appearing outside my quarters took what little strength I possessed. Because I was so diminished, I had Aidyrth introduce me to the dream guardian. I'd known of his existence but had never met him."

"I'm surprised the dragon had any use for him," I said.

"It's how she found her new bondmate," Grigori explained. "Don't interrupt until I'm finished. "None of the sidebar topics are relevant."

I held up a hand indicating I'd do my best, but biting my tongue isn't one of my long suits.

"Walking the dreamers' paths did not tax me," Grigori went on. "I tapped into enough nocturnal musings to convince me..." He stopped, maybe collecting his thoughts. "To convince me someone views the Circle as a threat to their plans."

I opened my mouth but shut it. Nothing I said—or didn't say—would drag the information out of Grigori any faster than he chose to share it.

"Which brings me," he went on, "to a loosely associated set of data points. You will be the first to hear them, so listen with critical ears." He held up an index finger. "The veil holding

Earth separate from other worlds has grown thin, a casualty of carbon emissions."

He added another finger. "Earth has always been a highly desired location were it not for all the pesky mortals."

"Who's planning an end run?" I blurted.

He skewered me with eyes that had darkened as his virus count improved. "Quinn. For once in your life, shut up."

I mimed a salute. "Copy that."

He smirked. "It happens you're correct. Demons are sick of being consigned to the underworld. The few lucky enough to be sent topside don't wish to return. Satan and his princes have grown weary of riding herd on their restive minions. The obvious occurred to them. If they moved their base of operations, everyone would be happier."

"They knew they couldn't do it alone," Ciara mumbled, "so they conscripted shills to do some of their dirty work."

"For the love of Fenrir, do I have to muzzle both of you?" Grigori demanded.

"We'll be good," I promised, knowing full well it wasn't necessarily true.

"The Circle is the only organized group of magic wielders who've polished their power specifically for the assassin trade," Grigori went on. "We could chop a hole in Hell's plans, but at least so far they believe they're flying beneath my radar.

"They assumed if they planted mages within the Circle—and cut the knees out from under me—we'd fall apart." He drew his red brows into a thick, bushy line. "They're not far off the mark. I've never shared power. The Circle was my idea, and I've held the reins tightly. Twenty-twenty hindsight is always crystal clear, but I'm rethinking how we're organized. It occurred to me when I was so depleted that if I faded, the Circle would wither along with me. No one would be prepared to assume leadership."

"How many, um, problems managed to pass muster here?" Ciara asked.

Grigori didn't chide her for speaking, so maybe the moratorium on questions had passed. "Four that I know of," he said.

"How did you determine that?" I chimed in.

"Patterns of unexplained absences to undisclosed locations and restive bondmates. They've all complained to me privately that their bonded ones have held them at arm's length. While that's not uncommon for newly bonded mage pairs, it passes quickly. It's bad enough, a coyote requested to be relieved of the bond.

"I instructed him to try harder. Any alteration in the status quo could tip them off we're onto them."

"Were you candid with the coyote?" Ciara asked.

Grigori shook his head. "How could I have been? He'd have told another bond animal, in absolute confidence, and my hunches would have ignited into an inferno."

"How did you find out anything about Hell's upper management?" It was a weak place in his theory, and he'd asked us to listen closely.

"I didn't. Not directly."

"You mentioned a coyote." I slid into the hole he'd created, hoping to widen it. "Are all the traitors shifters?"

"Possibly. You may come up with a different working theory," Grigori replied. "The shifters in question talk. And they dream. I could be off base, but I don't believe I am. Particularly since all four bond animals are unhappy. I could see one, or even two, but all of them?"

"Since you've said this much, what are they beyond the coyote?" Ciara asked.

"A hawk, a wolf, and a hyena. He's particularly annoyed, but they have a short fuse going into the game. For all I know, he's severed the bond himself and moved on. I always ask my people how their animals are, and the hyena's mage has been quite closemouthed of late."

"So you told us the bond animals, not which animals the shifters change into?" I clarified. Grigori nodded tersely.

I'd always wondered how things worked with shifters and a bond animal. It seemed like there'd be one extra entity in the mix. Grigori's bond animal was his wolf. Yet he'd set a different standard for other Circle shifters. He must have had his reasons. This wasn't the time to delve into them.

"But you can see the bond," I pointed out. "The one to their bondmates."

"Aye, and if I examine him that closely, he'll feel the prick of my power."

"There must be some way we can rid ourselves of them," Ciara said. "Something accidental where it might look fishy, but no one could figure it out for certain."

"I expect you to exercise due diligence, do your research, and come to your own conclusions. They may differ from mine, so keep your minds open," Grigori said flatly. " Besides, they can't all meet their end in the same event."

"Picking them off one by one isn't much better," I mumbled. "If they'd even stick around after the first one or two were killed."

"You can see why I've been stuck gathering information," Grigori added. "We can't very well have an all-Circle meeting to plan."

"Sure we could," I argued. "Except we plant false data. Break us up into teams, and then draw each one aside in the grove for updated instructions. Except the targets, of course."

Grigori cracked a wicked smile. "You're pure evil, Quinn."

I grinned back. "Thank you, oh fearless leader."

"Won't assigning the four shifters to the same group look suspicious?" Ciara asked.

"Not at all," Grigori replied. "They stick together like limpets without any instructions from me. Assuming they'd prefer to work as a unit shouldn't raise any flags. The pretend mission could be to Fire Mountain. Once they're there, dragons can dump them into a fumarole."

"Did you already talk with Aidyrth?" I inquired.

"Aye, but in general terms," he replied. "As in if we had a problem within the Circle, would the dragons be willing to corral them. Her answer wasn't immediate. She had to confer with her council before saying yes."

"I bet you've already thought up a cover story," I murmured.

"More or less. It's right out of science fiction. Tell me if it sounds too hokey."

"Before you go there," Ciara broke in, "let me make certain I have this straight. We'll need to deal with a bunch of demons seeking to overrun Earth, but first we have to get rid of the spies in our midst. And we have to do it in a way that doesn't raise anyone's hackles."

"Not sure of that last part," I said. I'd been thinking about timing and staging and come up with a somewhat different conclusion. Grigori crooked two fingers my way, so I obliged him and added, "Frankly, I don't see any problem with hauling the conspirators out of the Circle and immolating them. We don't need the dragons for that. So what if Hell Central knows we're onto something?"

"They could move up their timetable before we're fully ready," Grigori replied.

"You're underestimating your subordinates," I told him. "When I was in residence, we were always ready for damn near everything."

"I vote for rousting them out and dealing with them," Ciara

said. "The whole gig. Separation from the bond—because the bond animals are innocent—and then mage fire."

"Do it publicly." My enthusiasm was growing. "To discourage anyone else who might fall prey to Satan's inducements in a weak moment."

"Let me think about it," Grigori said.

"What's to think about?" I clapped him across the shoulders. "Blood, baby, blood. It's where we live."

Grigori started to laugh. Between gouts of mirth, he said, "I love it. A new motto in the making. BBB for short. Before we do anything, I expect both of you to move quietly among the resident mages gathering impressions. Give it a couple of days, and—"

The eagles flew through gaps in oak branches. "You have to come," Gwaihir croaked.

"Yes, now," Tory squawked agreement. "The courtyard."

I knew Gwaihir far too well to hesitate. He'd never have interrupted if it wasn't critical. Grigori shifted and loped from the grove with the four of us behind him.

CHAPTER 12

Howls, yowls, baying, and outraged voices buffeted me as we closed the distance to the guild house. Dragon fire painted the sky. Aidyrth was the only dragon in the Circle unless Grigori had added another since I'd left. Usually, she was fairly even-tempered—for a dragon. What had moved her to trumpet outrage?

Grigori leapt atop the flight of steps leading into the guild house and spun to face the crowd of mages. I couldn't see through the tightly packed bodies, but Gwaihir had an aerial vantage point.

"It's a hyena," he said, right before a piercing shriek blasted my eardrums.

Ciara scrambled to the top of the stone fence around the courtyard. I joined her and wound a few bands of magic around our ankles to make our position less precarious.

A man stood facing a pissed off hyena with its hackles elevated and every tooth on display. "I thought the hyena was part of his shifter power, not his bondmate," Ciara said.

"Uh-uh. Grigori disclosed their bond animals, not their shifter alter egos, but it would have been easy to miss."

The man, a mage named Mort who I knew vaguely, was saying, "You can't do this. Not unilaterally."

Because he'd never notice, not with everything else going on, I probed him with magic. Ciara intuited what I was about and sent power along the same channel I'd opened. It was like peeling the layers of an onion. The top ones looked pretty normal, but the deeper we went, the more rotten he became.

"This isn't right," Ciara said softly.

It wasn't. No matter how deeply we probed, something even worse lay beneath. The hyena was screeching at Grigori. "Dissolve the bond. This isn't a shifter. He lied to us all."

"You're the crazy one," Mort shouted at his bondmate. "Batshit nuts."

Grigori was back in human form. Jets of blue-white magic shot from his hands, encompassing Mort. I withdrew my power quickly. No need to muck up the works.

"Has anyone seen him in his shifted form?" Aidyrth demanded of the assembled mages. A gout of fire shot from her mouth and wrapped around Mort's feet, burning merrily and effectively hemming him in.

"Of course, we have." Another man stepped away from the crowd.

"How much do you want to bet he's one of the four?" Ciara hissed.

"Why guess?" I said smoothly and redirected my exploration his way.

Ciara jumped in behind me, and we found the same pattern as before. Layers and layers covering putrefaction. "Christ," I muttered. "He's a demon. Bet they all are."

"Where do you see that?" she demanded.

I guided our shared power. "Look there," I told her. "And over here. The striations are a product of living in Hell."

"How do you know?"

"I was trapped there once. Had to fight my way out, but I took a passel of those fuckers down along the way. I had to understand how they were put together to determine how to end them."

"Separate us!" the hyena screeched again. "Or I will do it myself, and you won't like the result."

"Give me another chance," Mort pleaded. "You're wrong about me. Sorry for calling you crazy, but your accusations got me going."

The mage who'd defended him had faded into the crowd. Or maybe he'd gotten the hell out of there while he had the cover of a noisy fight to cover his exit. Regardless, I was done standing on the sidelines. "You're a demon," I bellowed and netted Mort in a visible truth weave. "I dare you to deny it. You'll activate my spell, and everyone will know."

"Someone believes me!" The hyena charged toward me. I was afraid he'd unbalance us in his enthusiasm, so I grabbed Ciara's hand and jumped the six feet to the ground before he arrived.

My assertion must have been good enough for Aidyrth because the courtyard lit with dragon fire as she extended her circle upward to encompass the faux mage's body. Mort's pleas turned to screams and squeals. I didn't think any kind of fire would end one of Hell's denizens, but anything that caused him to yelp like that had to be a strong start.

The hyena jumped on me, licking my face. Ciara ran her hands down his rough spotted coat. "This is almost over," she said, earning a bevy of mewling barks.

The air around the hyena turned golden as the bond animal, pushed beyond his ability to tolerate the mage shackled to him, severed the connection. I'd only seen such a thing once before. Quick and powerful, it served as a potent reminder how sacred the linkage was—and how fragile if the beast half of the partnership was finished.

We pushed through the outer edge of the circle of mages in time to see Grigori add something magical to make Aidyrth's fire bite deeper. A mage I'd never seen before with pink-and-purple tresses leapt atop the gunmetal-colored dragon. Between the mage's hair and the dragon's reddish wings, they were quite the colorful pair. Power shaped like javelins flew from the mage's outstretched hands.

"The more the merrier," I cried and added my own magic to the mix. The hyena was licking my pants, my knees, anything it could reach. If there'd been time, I'd have felt sorry for him. When evil gets too close, it bites deep. The net result is feeling dirty, used, smarmy. After my sojourn among Hell's minions, I'd taken one of my very few breaks from work to put myself back together.

Demons are devious. They plant insidious suggestions, tell you you're worthless, damaged until you begin to question your sanity. I couldn't imagine what the last few years had been like for the hyena, but I bet it would be a good long time—if ever—before he volunteered to bond with a mage again.

Between dragon fire and Grigori's dual casting, one part to finish severing the bond with the hyena and the other to hold Aidyrth's fire up close and personal, Mort's human illusion melted leaving horns, a red scaly hide, a tail, and cloven hoofs.

"Fuck me," Ciara muttered. "Never seen one before."

The hyena was so delighted, he was rolling around on his back snorting like a puppy as he squealed, "Told you. Told you." In one lightning-quick movement, he bounced up, twisted in the air, and landed on all fours. "The other bond animals," he howled. "We have to save them."

Grigori's spell had a long way to go. The fire that had flayed Mort amused the demon. I felt him cycling through magic as he attempted to escape, but the dragon was on top of every bid for freedom. The woman sitting between her shoulders had to be her bondmate. Mostly Dark Fae mixed with something I couldn't quite determine, she was strong and fearless. A perfect addition to the Circle.

How had Grigori missed the mark so comprehensively and allowed four demons to slip through?

"Do you know where the other three are?" Ciara asked the hyena.

He tilted his head, nostrils flaring as he scented the air while his rounded ears swiveled from front to side and back again. "Gone," he pronounced, "and their bondmates with them."

What had Grigori said they were? A coyote, a hawk, and a wolf. "Surely they can break free," I said.

"I couldn't until now when Mort was besieged." The hyena reared up on his haunches. "And I tried."

A roar grew in volume along with the stench of roasting meat. Rather than clean and inviting, this smelled of decayed corpses. I've run into plenty of those on deserted battlefields, places where so many have fallen their companions walked off and left them.

Or ran away to save themselves. A line from a Bob Dylan song about not counting the dead when you had God on your side made me wince. Mortals were saps. Convinced they were making the world a better place, they swung blades and hoisted automatic rifles. Except nothing ever changed. One crappy leader was followed by another and another. Each more willing than the last to send men and women to their deaths.

"Quinn." Ciara nudged me.

"Yeah?"

"What do you want to do about the bond animals?"

"It's Grigori's call," I said.

She tilted her head, nailed me with her blue eyes, and said, "Really?"

I nodded slowly as the roar turned to cheers. The demon must have breathed his last. Damn they were a lot of work to kill. More than they were worth. After my brush with them, I'd avoided missions that had them anywhere in the equation.

Crap. Was that the problem? I didn't want to deal with them because they were so creepy. *Strap on a set* I told myself, totally ashamed.

"We should hustle and track them down," she insisted. "Before they go to ground."

"You mean return to Hell," I growled.

"We can retrieve them from there. Look, we don't have to kill them, but we owe it to the bond animals to make certain they have a path to freedom. The hyena says he'll help. His name is Kai."

"We need to leave now," he barked, "or the track will grow cold."

"I have to tell Grigori what we're doing," I said and threaded my way around mages to reach him. His arms were still extended, but the flow of magic had slowed. Not much left of the demon but a puddle of fetid goo.

"We're off to rescue the other bond animals," I said.

He didn't take his attention away from the decomposing demon. "Good. One thing I can check off my list."

"If it's possible, we'll end the demons, but our principal focus is the animals."

Grigori glanced my way. "Take Aidyrth and Shira. The dragon will come in useful, and Shira's solid."

"More of us means we can split forces, cover more ground," I agreed. I was the only one who had no idea what the other three looked like, or two of them anyway. The mage who'd spoken up for Mort had to be one of his buddies. Except they'd probably revert to their true forms, which would make their animals' lives even more miserable.

Grigori dropped his arms to his sides. "One down. Inconvenient the others took off."

"But not unexpected. If I'd been in their position, I'd be gone too. How in the hell did you let them into the Circle in the first place?"

He cast a pained glance my way. "I deserved that. I can't even claim a weak moment since they showed up before my tryst in Hell. They were smart about it. One approached me, and then another months later. It won't happen again."

I was certain it wouldn't. Nothing like being burned to make a man cautious. I started to ask if he'd changed his methods. When I'd been active in the Circle, it found you, not the other way round, but the clock was ticking.

"I'll report in if I can," I said.

"Good to have you back, Quinn."

I nodded brusquely. It felt good to be back, but I'd be damned if I'd admit it. Ciara was waiting impatiently, the hyena nowhere in sight. I motioned her toward Aidyrth and her passenger. "Well met," I called to the dragon. Smoke eddied around her long neck, but she'd stopped spitting fire.

"Good to see you too, Quinn," she bugled back. "May I present my bondmate, Shira."

Raising a hand in greeting, I said, "We're going after the other three."

"I already know something about them," Aidyrth bugled. "I've had my suspicions for a while now, but Grigori was so ill I was waiting to approach him with my concerns."

"Kai and I mapped out a plan while Quinn was with Grigori," Ciara told all of us. "He's already left to track the wolf.

If it works for you, Quinn and I will go after the hawk with our eagles."

"We'll find that coyote," Aidyrth said.

"Goody. More demons to slay. I hate those fuckers," Shira spoke up.

"Dead demons are a bonus. Our mission is freeing the bond animals," I clarified.

"Got it. We'll probably run into you in Hell." Shira mimed a salute just before she and Aidyrth faded from sight.

Gwaihir and Tory dropped out of the sky and flew around our heads, clearly anxious to get moving. I signaled the eagles to land. "Do either of you know the hawk?"

"I do," Tory said.

"Any idea where we might start our search?" Ciara asked her.

"No gateways to Hell from this world," the eagle replied.

"We'll teleport to Earth and find the nearest entry point," I said as a strategy shaped up. "I agree about the three returning to Hell. Soldiers always retreat to their home base when things turn to shit."

"We should be able to find him," Gwaihir said.

"How?" I asked. Hell was a big place.

"We have our ways," he informed me. "Bond animals are interconnected."

It was news to me. "Kind of like angel radio," I muttered.

"What's that?" Ciara asked.

"It's not important." I set a teleport spell encompassing the four of us in motion and kindled it.

"I really want to know," she pressed as the darkness of a travel channel eddied about us.

"It's from a television series," I clarified. "*Supernatural* ran for a whole lot of seasons. It offered a snapshot into how mortals view those like us. They got a few things right, but most details were laughable. Anyway, angel radio was how angels communicated across distances. From what Gwaihir said, the bond animals have a similar network, one I didn't know existed, by the way."

"Nor did I," she said and leaned into me.

Because it was familiar and would give us a base of operations, I brought us out at my house in the Highlands. I could have picked a different one in the US, but the Old Country offers more portals into Hell. We could always switch things up if our first forays proved futile.

Ciara said she'd never seen a demon before. Presumably, it meant she'd never crossed Hell's borders. Protectiveness surged to the fore. "Not very pleasant down there," I said as the walls of my living room formed around us. "You and Tory can sit this one out if you'd like."

She narrowed her eyes, said, "Bite me," and followed it with, "Where's the nearest entry point? I can scope it out on my own, but if you already know, it will save time."

Ciara had glided to a spot in front of me, keeping a few feet of distance between us. I cleared my throat and gave it one more shot. "I've seen a lot of shit, and Hell is by far and away the worst. It's extremely dangerous, and—"

"Now you look here," she spoke over me and moved close enough to thump my chest with an extended index finger. "I've battled Krakens, Leviathans, and Jengu. I've snuck into witch's domains to steal from under their pointed noses. Do not patronize me."

Narrowing her eyes, she shook her head. "Shit. I figured you'd be the last person I'd have to justify myself to. Grigori trusts me. Why don't you?"

"This has nothing to do with trust," I said stiffly. "I want you to be safe."

"Yeah, well, you picked the wrong woman to play that card

with." Turning away, she whistled for Tory. "We're leaving. Guess we'll do this separately."

I made a grab for her arm. She eluded me. "I'm sorry," I gritted fully aware that having her dredging through Hell on her own was a hundred times worse than the two of us together. If she was with me, I could watch her back.

"Are you?" She didn't turn around.

I softened my tone. "I hurt your feelings. I didn't mean to. I was trying to do a good thing, but sometimes they don't turn out like I hope. Let's get moving. We can sort everything else out later."

To forestall digging myself in deeper or stuffing my other foot into my mouth, I snatched up keys from a hook near the door and shooed everyone outside and into my aging Land Rover. We could have teleported to the spot I had in mind, but I didn't want to alert the sentry—if they'd posted one.

If one of my men retreated to base, tail between his legs, I'd sure as fuck post sentries at every entry point. No reason to assume Satan was stupid.

The birds rode in the back. Ciara sat in the passenger seat, spine ramrod straight. We'd been en route for a quarter hour before she asked, "Where are we going?"

"The nearest portal is close to Hadrian's wall. Try and get some rest. It will be a few hours until we get there."

"I'll spell you," she said. "You take the first shift driving. Wake me in ninety minutes, and I'll take over."

Grateful she hadn't written me off—or maybe she had and was waiting until this mission was over—I said, "You got it."

"Tell me what you have planned once we cross beneath the lintel." I directed my words at Gwaihir.

"We will try to establish contact," Tory answered.

"What happens if you can't?" I asked her.

"Means we're not close enough," Gwaihir squawked.

"We can't skip from portal to portal," I protested. "It could take days to home in on where the hawk is."

"We can triangulate," Gwaihir informed me.

I understood the word, but not in this context. "If you can't find the hawk in the first spot, what do you have to triangulate off of?"

"Trust us," Tory said.

Clearly, the birds weren't about to divulge any more of their secret comm system than they had to.

Ciara had fallen asleep. Her head lolled onto my shoulder. It felt good there, but I warned myself not to presume too much. Or anything at all. I had almost zero practice with the welter of emotions buffeting me.

This was why I'd maintained my solo status. So I could put the mission first. As I drove, afternoon shaded to night, and I came up with what I hoped would be a workable compromise. It was simple and straightforward. We'd operate as co-team leaders. I weeded out the tender places, the spots I was attracted to her, cared about her, and buried them.

A shade over ninety minutes had passed, but I'd wanted to make certain I wouldn't slip up, that the heat and need and attraction I felt wouldn't get in the way. It wasn't all that difficult. I was a master at subverting the personal.

The next pull out, I stopped the car and said, "Your turn. Do you need me to dial in GPS guidance?"

CHAPTER 13

Another two hours brought us to a deserted shepherd's track. "We'll walk from here," I announced.

"You've been quiet," Ciara said as she cut the engine and handed me the keys. "You weren't asleep."

Pleased she'd noticed what I was doing—or not doing—I drew myself up short. This was exactly the kind of trap I didn't want to fall into. The hawk required my undivided attention.

"Mostly, I've been paying out options and testing them for pitfalls," I replied.

"I've been doing the same," she said in a neutral tone. "We should compare notes."

"We will once we're done here."

"But what if our bondmates locate the hawk? It's remote but possible."

They'd flown ahead. Gwaihir knew the way. We'd spied on Hell from this spot before, but never gone much farther than the area just beyond the gate.

"Possible but unlikely," I told her. "Hell is huge. It exists in its own dimension, and I've never mapped its boundaries."

"What did the eagles mean by triangulating? And if Hell is as large as you say, why'd Shira mention they'd likely meet us there?"

"She was assuming the three not-shifters would be together. It's a logical hypothesis. I'm guessing the eagles will sense something, maybe traces too faint to tell them much, but the more bits they piece together, the closer we'll come to a location."

"Makes sense," she replied. "Probably, it's something only they're tuned into, and if they notice whatever it is from a couple of locations, it will help them determine where the hawk is.

"While we're kicking ideas around, what makes you think the demon will even want to hang onto his bondmate?" she went on. "I kept coming back to that when I was driving. Seems to me any type of positive magic would be a real clod in Hell's churn."

My thoughts hadn't strayed in that direction, and I didn't care for the possibilities. "Satan or his princes can probably break the bond, but they'll kill the hawk."

"You can't know that. I assumed they'd imprison it. Bond animals are tough to do away with."

"Either way, it's not good." I'd been constructing a ward and draped it around us. "Hard right," I said, "and then silence. No mind speech, either." I cringed. After all my big talk about co-leading this mission, I'd slid right back into issuing orders—and assuming she'd obey them.

"Turn right? Are you certain of that?" she muttered just before an opening formed in what appeared to be an impenetrable hillside.

The characteristic buzz of a medium-strength electric shock blitzed us. It had to be an early-warning system, but Hell didn't possess enough minions to keep an eye on every entry point.

Satan and his crew weren't especially tech savvy. They'd imported mortals to set things up for them, but then they did away with them, which didn't leave anyone to ride herd on complicated networks. From time to time, they attempted to conscript souls who'd been black to their bones and knew computers upside down. The dead don't have much interest in cooperating, though. Nothing in it for them.

I called up my psychic vision to cut through the gloom. Soon the darkness would be absolute. Hooking a hand under Ciara's arm, I made certain she remained within my ward. I expected pushback but didn't get any, maybe because I'd effectively silenced communication. We started along a downward-sloping corridor. It was tempting to pay out bits of a seeking spell, but we were better off cloaked. The eagles had come this way. I sensed Gwaihir, but only because of our bond.

The state of the tunnel reinforced my belief no one was monitoring the doorbell. Mini cave-ins required navigation around rocks of varying sizes. A stone circle loomed ahead. As with most entrances to the nether realm, hardworking demons had piled rocks to form a circular opening, except this particular one was in far worse shape than the last time I'd been here a few years back.

"We don't need the ward," Ciara said softly. "No one is anywhere near."

"Tory told you?"

She nodded, and I quietly dismantled my spell, pulling the power back within me. Normally, I'd have sent elements outward. Before I did that, I tested the stone circle, expecting to find it loaded with more of the same dark enchantment that had zapped us before.

It was dead. Motioning to Ciara, I stepped through.

"Sloppy, aren't they," she whispered.

"More than they used to be," I agreed. We pressed forward

slowly, picking our way around rubble piles. It appeared no one had used this tunnel in a long while. Demon taint with its scent of decay was present but quite faded. The gradual incline steepened, but I'd expected that. Some portals plunged straight down. Guess it depended how industrious Satan's minions of the hour had been during the construction phase.

A squawk deep in my mind drew me up short. I sent a reflexive arc of seeking magic in front of our position.

"What is it?" Ciara moved off to one side into a solid defensive position.

"Gwaihir warned me. Just a cry, nothing else." Anticipating her, I said, "Do not reach for Tory. If the two of them ran into trouble, that will make it worse."

"Goes against the grain," she muttered. "We've almost never separated."

I remembered how the Circle operated. One of Grigori's tactics was to urge newly bonded pairs to do everything together. In that way, each learned the pattern and cadence of their bondmate's magic.

Three choices presented themselves. Retreat, stay put, or teleport to Gwaihir's location. Each had plusses and drawbacks, but I've never been conservative when it comes to a fight. The rich smells of damp earth rose as I crafted a spell.

"Talk with me, goddammit," Ciara growled.

I started to make excuses for myself, tell her I usually worked with mortals who followed my lead without question. Instead, I settled on, "We can retreat, stay where we are and wait for further clues, or join our bondmates. My vote falls with the last of those options Yours?"

"Same," she said tersely. "What if your eagle isn't in the same spot he was when he alerted you?"

"We'll be closer to him, and—"

A muted grinding was followed by a whooshing sound. Air

currents surrounded us, and my perspective shifted once and then again. The sensation was familiar, yet not, and I grappled with locating the proper "magic running amok" classification to interpret our situation. Ciara barreled into me, driven by the disturbance.

Thanks be to Danu she ended up next to me. Shit like this could have gone the other way just as easily. "What in the hell is happening?" Ciara gritted as we were tossed about like flotsam in a riptide.

"We're shooting through barriers between Earth and Hell, but at breakneck speed. I've had this happen before, but never with the underworld. Usually, it's a way to short-circuit long journeys between worlds."

Yeah, and usually I was in control of the transition points, rather than being abused by them. I didn't mention that part. The rounded tunnel we'd been in was no more, replaced by a whirling cylinder. Light flickered and flared, replaced by blackness, and then light once again.

Could we teleport out of this? Did we want to? It wasn't just my decision. "We might be able to teleport," I said.

"What? And leave the eagles?"

I'd looped an arm around her shoulders; I tightened it. "Gwaihir is resourceful. Tory too. They're together, and they're more than a match for whatever they run up against. Wherever this construct spits us out could be a long way from them."

"How do you know they didn't get caught up in it?"

"I don't. This is a major magical disturbance. We'd have felt it even from outside the entry point in that hill."

Ciara pressed her mouth into a thin line. "Every time I think I'm ahead of the game, I get a major wakeup call."

"You lived in a different environment for most of your life. Our best bet is trying to break free. Wherever this spits us out, I guarantee we won't like it."

"Tell me what you need from me," she said tightlipped, obviously not totally on board because of her bondmate.

I visualized our starting point and poured power into my spell, borrowing liberally from Ciara. The vortex should have vanished; it didn't so much as flicker. Fuck. Double fuck. Not good news at all. Rather than giving voice to my rising concerns, I said, "Different approach. You lead this time, heavy on water. I'll manage the air. No earth or fire at all."

"But that should have worked," she said, stating the obvious. "We should have shot out of there as if we'd been launched from a catapult."

"We have to try again. Now." I didn't modulate the urgency in my voice. We should have tried everything in our repertoire to break free the moment we were snared. Had Gwaihir known what was headed our way? Made sense. If I'd heeded his heads up...

I wrenched my full attention back to Ciara and loomed power in with hers. A tidal wave of magic bounced between her hands. This had to work.

If it didn't, we were stuck riding this pony to the bitter end.

All her attention was caught up in her spell. I goosed it with air and a whopping dose of concepting for success. Believing in results is more than half the battle. Magic is a fickle bitch; she knows when a mage is lukewarm about potential results.

The roar of a hundred waterfalls battered my ears. "More!" I shouted.

"There isn't any more," she yelled back.

"There has to be. Dig deep." I cinched up the linkage between us and gave it everything I had. Not the best move—but only if we failed. "Come on, come on, work goddammit," I growled. Ciara probably didn't hear me over the pounding water.

Power drained from me far faster than I could replenish it. Fine. I'd deal with the fallout later. Next to me, Ciara was panting, but she didn't complain. She knew better than to waste energy on anything other than our objective. Finally, when I was hanging on by a thread, the fucking vortex shimmered. Either our efforts were paying off—or we were reaching a natural end to our journey.

When did I turn into such a cynic? "We've got this," I wheezed and did my own digging. The transition from whirling, spinning, and falling to the spot we'd entered the hillside was almost instantaneous. With this much magic in play, it didn't surprise me.

I hit the ground hard, doing my damnedest to shield Ciara. My lungs burned, and I felt like I'd been licking the bottom of a birdcage, my mouth bitter and dry.

"That was too close," she rasped.

"Nothing is too close when you make good on an escape." I lay on the ground, arms around her, not even trying to get up. For one thing, I wasn't certain my legs would hold me. For another, she felt amazing.

"All the bond animals are here," Gwaihir croaked. The comforting sweep of wings surrounded us as he landed next to me.

"Ciara." Tory settled on the other side of us and ran her beak up and down her bondmate's cheek.

"Yes, love, we're all right, although we very nearly weren't." Ciara dragged herself out of my arms, her movements weak and sluggish as she rolled to a sit on the cold, damp ground. Somehow, it was still night. Judging from the position of the partial moon and stars we hadn't been gone all that long.

It only felt like hours had passed.

"I warned you," Gwaihir chided.

If Ciara could sit up, well then I could too. Every muscle in my body ached; my head pounded, but I managed a cross-legged sit. "Thank you," I told my bondmate.

"I'd have been more specific," he continued, "but I would have been overheard. This way, I could easily have been mistaken for the fallen ravens in Satan's court."

"You infiltrated that far?" My eyebrows would have shot up if I'd had the energy.

Gwaihir clacked his beak. "We did."

"We found all the phony shifters," Tory crowed.

"That's marvelous." Ciara wrapped her arms around the eagle.

"Finding them was," Gwaihir agreed."

"A couple of Satan's underlings were kicking them out of Hell for failing," Tory clarified. "They'd been beaten and were quite torn up."

"I've never heard such a pack of sniveling cowards." Gwaihir sounded disgusted. "Nothing was their fault. Mort was the dumb one, the reason they were discovered."

"Blame the dead one," I sneered. "Works every time."

"Not this time, it didn't," Tory said.

My head was clearing. I unclipped a water bottle from my belt and offered it to Ciara before dealing with my parched throat. "The vortex wasn't accidental, was it?"

Gwaihir shook his head. "It took a while, but someone ran into the cave shouting they'd been invaded."

Ciara shook a fisted hand at the air. "Next time we'll do more than sightsee."

"We'll be quicker on the uptake, but there might not be a next time if our targets are getting the boot," I replied. It wasn't wise to let myself think about how close we'd come to being captured. I'd end up so angry, I'd be tempted to teleport smack dab into the center of Satan's realm and challenge him to a duel. It stank of machismo and was a stupid idea.

"Did you run into Cai down there?" Ciara asked after the hyena.

"No. Or the dragon, either," Tory replied.

Sitting had gone all right, so I took a chance and got my feet under me. Once I was stable, only swaying a little, I offered Ciara a hand up. We started toward my car. I keep provisions in the boot, and the prospect of replenishing my depleted magic with food was attractive.

"We need to catch up with Cai and Aidyrth and her bondmate," I said. "If Satan is really kicking those demons out, we'll require help running them down."

"It should be somewhere on Earth, right?" Ciara asked as she stumbled along next to me.

"Not necessarily. Depends how pissed off he is."

"It wasn't Satan," Gwaihir reminded me.

I had no idea if the not-Satan part would alter anything. We'd reached the car, and I passed Ciara a couple of energy bars. After inhaling three of them, I had enough magic back online to raise my mind voice hunting for Cai and Aidyrth.

The place I'd parked the Land Rover was private. For how populated the northern UK is, there are quite a few spots like this where a man could lose himself for weeks. Tory perched on Ciara's shoulders. Gwaihir had taken up a post on a nearby stone fence. Kilometers of them dotted the countryside because stones were plentiful; wood wasn't.

I handed Ciara a bottle of water and cracked another for myself since the one hanging from my belt was dry. Next, I rustled through my field pack to take stock of what I had with me. Ciara bent over my shoulder, watching as I reorganized the pack's jumbled contents.

"Not a bad idea," she said.

"You carry a bag. Why are you interested in mine?" I asked as I clipped the pack together.

"Not the sack so much as what you choose to put in it. I rely mostly on magic. A lot of what you have in there"—she flicked a finger at my duffel—"would be dead weight in the ocean."

The shadow of a generous wingspan crossed the moon. My bet was on Aidyrth, an impression that solidified as she grew closer. The dragon, Shira on her back, circled to land. Jealousy pricked. I'd always wanted to ride a dragon, or a unicorn, but neither were inclined to schlepp passengers.

"I already told her everything," Gwaihir informed me.

I nodded my thanks. We needed to hit the ground running. So far our efforts had netted a big fat dead end. "Can you find Cai through your bond-animal network?" I asked him.

"Already put out a call," the eagle replied.

Good because the hyena hadn't responded when I'd tried to raise him.

Shira jumped from her spiny perch. "We accessed Hell from a couple of spots we've been to before. Nothing cooking in either of them. We were on our way back here when Aidyrth intercepted your call."

"Shira and I talked about it," the dragon said. "You were wise to stick closer to Satan's seat of power. It never migrated beyond the Old Country."

I've never matched up a set of data points linking specific spots in Hell with places on Earth. Until Aidyrth mentioned it, I'd assumed Hell was its own entity and didn't relate to anything. Maybe I should spend more time at a guild house. Either I was forgetting things, or I hadn't known them in the first place.

"I'm worried about the hyena," Ciara murmured.

"He can take care of himself," Tory said.

"If he was taken, we'd know," Aidyrth agreed.

I considered her words. "If he hasn't been imprisoned, and he's not here, he must be in the middle of something."

"Something too critical to abandon." Aidyrth pounced on my line of reasoning.

"Can you locate him?" I posed a general question to the bond animals. "If he has the wolf in his gunsights, I bet the hawk and coyote are nearby."

Power surged, pricking me as the air filled with various smells. Fire, ash, greenery, and wet stones. I waited impatiently, but kept my mouth shut. Neither the eagles nor the dragon would appreciate me snapping my fingers and telling them to hurry.

"Not sure," Aidyrth said.

"Comes and goes," Gwaihir agreed.

I was done being quiet. "Can we get close?"

"Maybe." Tory sounded more hopeful than the other two.

No one seemed willing to pick up the reins, so I said, "Worst that can happen is we're wrong."

"No," Ciara corrected me. "We could be walking into a trap."

"Cai is smarter than that." Aidyrth punctuated her words with a stream of fiery ash.

I shuffled through possibilities out loud. "Let's look at what we know. Cai isn't a prisoner. He's not responding to our summons, which means either he doesn't want to or he can't."

"Or he was more of a willing participant with Mort than he's letting on," Ciara said. "It pains me to even suggest this because I like him, but did he seem too exuberant after the bond was broken?"

"Going after the others was his idea." I narrowed my eyes as I reconstructed the sequence of events.

"Cai would never betray the Circle or the other bond animals," Aidyrth said firmly.

"Never is a big word," I told her. "I'd love to be proven wrong, but we can't ignore any possibility."

"We have enough to go on to take a stab at locating him." Gwaihir joined the conversation.

"Where is he?" Shira asked.

"Baffin Island in the Arctic, near as I can tell," the eagle replied.

"Odd spot for any of Hell's minions," Ciara said.

"Could be smoke and mirrors to make us chase our tails," Shira spoke up.

"We're going to take a look," I said, trusting Gwaihir to steer our journey spell.

"Let's be smart about this," Aidyrth trumpeted and rattled off coordinates. "Prudent if we arrive separately."

"Fifteen minutes apart," I agreed. Before anyone else volunteered, I said, "Gwaihir and I will go first." To avoid further discussion, I whipped my still somewhat depleted magic into a teleport spell, tapped into the dragon's destination, and left.

It accomplished two things. The show was up and running, and Ciara wouldn't be the one to show up alone. Damn it. I was still protecting her. Even though she'd made her needs in that regard painfully clear, I couldn't help myself. Dragging my full attention to the task ahead, I did what planning I could. The Arctic is a desolate place. No trees and virtually no cover. Once we popped out, we'd be visible for miles as long as it wasn't storming.

I could fix the visibility problem and settled a ward into place. A partial one. Still sucking fumes, I couldn't afford to be wasteful with how I deployed magic. This transport spell would take a while as it was...

Crap. What if Ciara arrived before me? Before I got too spun out, I reminded myself it was much more likely Aidyrth would be the first to arrive. Even on her worst days, her magic trumped mine.

"Awk." Gwaihir croaked. "Cai is hooting and laughing, but for his kind, it's a strong warning."

"Is he cautioning us?"

"I don't know," my bird replied.

"Tell me what you do know," I said. "Every minute detail."

CHAPTER 14

"We need to hurry this up," Gwaihir hooted, not answering my question.

Probably, he didn't want to split his attention, so I tapped into the flow of his perceptive mind. Birds don't think the same way I do. They rely on imagery, not words. Over the long years of our partnership, I've grown proficient at piecing pictures together.

Imagery flowed, scenes butting up against others in a confusing array.

Cai had nabbed one of the false shifters, presumably the one bonded with the wolf. He'd taken him to the remotest spot possible in hopes of eluding any who'd been assigned to follow them. So far, his reasoning was sound. I started to relax about him batting for the other team. Not completely, but a little.

The demon had shucked any pretense of humanity and was in full bloom with horns, tail, and hoofs. The ones I'd come across loved to break things, but they weren't overly industrious. It was the only reason Satan and his princes had managed to avoid a full-out insurrection all these years. Leaving Hell required planning and patience, two qualities in short supply in demon-dom.

If the flow of images had stopped there, this would be a slam dunk, but demons were popping up from crevasses. Maybe they'd drilled up from below, but they'd probably hunted for the simplest way through. A quick scan didn't reveal any others who'd been battered, so the hawk and coyote had to be elsewhere.

My bondmate had counseled haste, but stealth shot to the top of the heap. I hadn't thought we'd require much warding. Wrong. Despite being worried about not blowing through the power at my disposal, I shored up the invisibility casting around Gwaihir and me. In the nick of time as it turned out. The transition between travel and a vast expanse of ice and snow was sudden. Illuminated by moonlight, ice crystals glittered in a perpetual winter wonderland. The far north holds a strange beauty. Nothing grew except a few species of lichen and moss clinging to ice-choked rocks.

Maybe my power wasn't as depleted as all that because no one had beaten us here. Aidyrth might be hiding behind her own concealment spell, but it wasn't her style. She was formidable enough to intimidate almost anything.

Clearly visible from my vantage point, demons formed a ring around Cai. I couldn't see him or the beat-to-shit demon through the wall of scales, but his snarling and hissing and weird shrill laugher escalated. Hyenas are remarkably tough.

"I don't need warding," Gwaihir announced. "By the time any of them shift into something capable of flight—if they even bother—I'll be long gone." Spreading his wings, he shot into the clear, frigid night sky cawing fiercely.

Excellent. I took advantage of the diversion to burrow jets

of power into the frozen tundra. Earth is my native element, my strong suit. The permafrost parted, sensing my need. If this worked, it would be quicker than struggling to fry those fuckers with magic. My earth-based enchantment wouldn't get them all, but Aidyrth could finish them off when she showed up. Or Ciara could drown them in ice water.

My first victim scrambled as the surface beneath him caved in. Working fast, I widened the crack drawing him downward. It wasn't as simple as I'd hoped, but then very little is.

I spend so much time jousting with shitty windmills, I opt for the glass-half-full perspective. Many of my half-baked stunts would never draw breath otherwise. A couple of other demons had crouched next to the one doing his damnedest to crawl out of my pit. They were trying to pull him out, but not especially hard. No friends in Hell's army.

Perfect. The more the merrier. I enlarged the hole, forming a crater. Three had far more bulk than one, doing part of my work for me.

I didn't need them all the way under. Once arms and legs were below ground level, I cinched the frozen earth tight forming an impenetrable layer. By the time I was done, their prison had all the endearing traits of concrete. Magic wouldn't make a dent. The two would-be rescuers cursed roundly, blaming my original target for their plight.

The other demons had drawn away from my victims. Most cast uncertain glances at their ugly cloven hoofs clearly wondering if maybe leaving wasn't the smarter course of action.

That's right, you lazy sacks of crap. Vamoose.

Except they couldn't leave. They had bosses to report back to. Demons who'd make them sorry they'd ever drawn breath if their mission crashed and burned. Gwaihir cawed again, the cry that meant he was contemplating whom to kill. High and piercing, it was an attention-getter. When he swooped down and landed between Cai and the battered demon, no one made a move in his direction.

Why weren't they looking for me? Surely, they'd determined the eagle was part of a bonded pair. Or not. Cai was on his own. Gwaihir could be an independent agent too. How much did Satan's minions know about bond animals? Hopefully very little. Underestimating demons could be quite a miscalculation, but I didn't believe I was.

The next part happened fast. Aidyrth and Shira burst through. Cai and Gwaihir caught the demon scissors-fashion in power that cleaved through scales along his breastbone. The wolf clawed his way out, his gray fur coated in black gore.

Fury sheeted from him. No sooner free, he twisted midair and closed his jaws around the demon's neck severing every vessel. Black blood spewed everywhere, polluting the clear air with the stench of rotten meat. Gwaihir jumped into the carnage, ripping the shit out of the demon's trashed neck. If he did enough damage, no amount of dark power could repair it. Cai faced outward, tail lashing, daring any of the others to come closer while the wolf and eagle destroyed the demon.

I dropped my ward. Didn't need it any longer. Without it as a perpetual drain, the rest of my enchantment would last longer.

Where was Ciara? She and Tory should be here by now.

Aidyrth had landed; fire streamed from the dragon's mouth and lethal magic from Shira's hands as they felled one target after the next. Any loyalty the remaining demons might have for their masters melted away. They tried to use the same crevasse system they'd engineered as exit points, but I was ready for them. As soon as one jumped into the icy ground, I focused power to seal the opening. From both ends.

There's something clean and honorable about ending scum. I fell into a rhythm, a cadence that energized me. Done with their first target, the wolf and Cai chivied the few remaining Hellspawn this way and that. They were playing with them, a deadly game of cat and mouse.

Aidyrth shuffled toward me, shouting, "Look left."

Her warning saved me from a world of hurt. A new demon had emerged out of nowhere. Twin long blades whirled where my head had been moments before. The dragon doused the newcomer with fire until he turned into a pyre. He'd looked different from the others, acted different too. More confident.

Maybe Satan had deployed one of his inner circle. The question was why a few trapped bond animals merited anything beyond a shoulder shrug.

"Thanks," I yelled Aidyrth's way and surveyed the cracked, icy landscape. Nothing moved. We'd either ended them all, or a few lucky ones had seen the writing on the wall and scurried back to Hell.

Ciara still wasn't here. "Where are Ciara and Tory?" I sucked in a breath. My question presumed the dragon knew.

"Tory got a line on the other two," Shira explained. "She was afraid if she didn't follow the trail, it would vanish."

Relief surged, strong and intoxicating. Other possibilities would have been far worse. Like being apprehended out of a travel spell. It was rare, but not unheard of. Or being set upon after everyone else had left. I had to get over my Papa Bear impersonation. Ciara had been a mage for a long time, one who'd managed the notorious intrigue of Poseidon's court. I should trust her ability—and her instincts.

Cai and the wolf trotted over, looking pleased with themselves. "Revenge was long overdue," the wolf snarled.

Cai batted him with a paw. "You got that right, brother."

Gwaihir dropped out of the sky and onto my shoulders. "Two down," he crowed.

"We have to go after Ciara." A sense of urgency swept through me. "If we return to where we started, we can track her and Tory."

"Maybe," Aidyrth corrected me.

She was right. Depending on where Ciara and her bird had gone, and if they'd taken care to cover their footsteps, we might have a hard go of things, but I'd cross that barrier if it materialized.

The return trip went quicker, but then they always do. Something about having blazed a path through psychic space makes it part faster the second time around. A hasty scan was disappointing. Ciara had obliterated her tracks.

Cai and the wolf ran this way and that, noses twitching. Gwaihir overflew the area. "Won't find them this way," the wolf rumbled. The air around him came alive with lupine-saturated power. Judging from him and the hyena, their stint locked within demons hadn't diluted their magic.

Where in the hell were Aidyrth and Shira? I reined in annoyance. So far, I'd expended a ridiculous amount of energy trying to keep the team together. It reminded me why I preferred to work alone—or with humans who were far more malleable than my fellow mages.

Gwaihir settled heavily onto my shoulders. "Tell me you know where they are," I muttered.

"Possibly."

A stout bugle announced the dragon. Dawn was finally breaking; I hoped no one had heard her. Dragon vocalizations aren't the kind of thing mortals have a point of reference for. The last thing I wanted was for a party of do-gooders to pop over a ridge carting rifles.

Aidyrth settled to the ground quickly, cutting her usual aerial circling short. I bit back words instructing her to be quiet. It wasn't my place to order her about.

"I sent power along the standard travel paths," she explained. A minimal amount of smoke and ash trailed after her words, but nothing a campfire wouldn't produce.

"We know which way she went," Shira spoke up.

"Us too." Cai and the wolf padded close.

"I found them," the wolf made a point of clarifying.

"Them being the other bond animals?" I asked.

"All of them," Cai said.

Twisting my neck I glanced at my oversized eagle. "Presumably, you know too."

"I do."

Before he'd said possibly, but he was probably buying time for Aidyrth to materialize. The bond animals stuck together, their loyalty to each other almost as strong as their allegiance to us.

"Coordinates?" I resisted snapping my fingers. Working as a mercenary all these years hasn't improved my patience, or my temper. A set of numbers rolled through my mind. I didn't bother to interpret them, just grabbed onto a hunk of magic and powered Gwaihir and me forward.

"On the hasty side," my bondmate observed. "We could have done with a plan."

"We'll improvise," I growled driven by desperation to rescue Ciara, which was not only stupid but ill-conceived. She did not need me. No matter how much I wanted to slot her into a damsel-in-distress-who'd-be-grateful-as-fuck-I-saved her-bacon role, it wasn't her.

She was capable, with power rivaling my own. Why was her ability so tough for me to accept? I've worked with women before. It's not my first choice. Not because they aren't strong, they are. But they're unpredictable, and they don't take orders especially well. Before I sank too deep dredging uncomfortable truths from my soul, the characteristic reek of Hell burned my lungs and nostrils.

I did a quick check of the destination I'd wired into my spell. Yup. Right place. My power would stick out like a rock-and-roll number in an opera. I slapped up a ward and hoped I hadn't been too late.

"Is that what improvising looks like?" Gwaihir hooted quiet laughter. Still perched on my shoulders, he dug his talons in deep to remind me looking before leaping was a time-tested strategy.

Fascinating. Had the last two banished demons returned home of their own accord? Or had they been forced back? A perversion of an old saying taunted me. Be it ever so shitty, there's no place like home. Given what had happened to Mort —probably not his real name—and Cai sweeping in like a whirling dervish to scoop up the wolf's temporary captor, the remaining two had probably beaten a track to Satan's domain.

Safety lay in numbers and familiarity. Except Gwaihir said they'd been banished.

"You can run, but you can't hide," I mumbled as a low squared-off tunnel flickered into view. Smoking torches had been stuck into spaces between stones at haphazard angles. Not enough to provide much beyond a flickering glimmer that cut through absolute blackness. God only knew what the combustible material was. It stank even worse than the rest of the place. My money was on excrement. Rich in methane gas, it provided an inexhaustible fuel source.

A light brush against my mind told me Aidyrth was nearby. Cai and the wolf must be as well, but everyone was well-shielded. Even the dragon wasn't willing to display her presence here.

So far, we were alone. Us and the torches. They suggested we were deep in the netherworld. So far, none of the other places I'd been in the underworld featured illumination of any sort.

"Tory knows we're here," Gwaihir breathed into my mind.

I took his use of telepathy as a message that perhaps we weren't as alone as I'd thought. His senses are far more acute than mine, and I've learned to trust them. I took stock of our surroundings. Unlike my other forays into Hell, we stood on a level stretch that had been so well-trodden a path was visible. It suggested we were at the bottom. If such a thing existed.

"Which way?" I asked my bondmate about the time I felt a mild disturbance as the dragon pushed past. Left to my own devices, I'd have taken off running, but Aidyrth was moving slowly. Her senses were sharper than mine too, reminding me of my deficiencies. Removed from the Circle and working on my own, I'd been so much more competent than mortals, I'd forgotten what it's like to defer to anyone. Chafing at my virtual lack of useful intel, I fell in behind,

If I used seeking magic, I'd drag attention our way. A surprise attack that came out of nowhere was our most promising tactic. A couple of right angle bends in the still flat tunnel brought us to the opening of an enormous chamber. The same stinking torches provided light. At the far end several demons lounged atop serpents on a raised dais. I'd known they kept them for pets but viewing them held a big ick factor. Slime from the snakes left a visible film on the demon's scaly hides. Bones, some of them huge, littered the floor. Streaks of black and crimson decorated the walls, no doubt blood from unbridled slaughter.

I couldn't see Ciara. Big sigh of relief on that one. Meant

she hadn't been captured and was hanging back on the sidelines much as we were. The two demons we sought groveled on the floor a few feet in front of the dais. Their version of the tale was interesting.

Nothing new on the Mort front, but to hear them tell it, a sabertoothed tiger and a wooly mammoth had teamed up, dragged the demon bonded with the wolf to the Arctic, and massacred the rescue party. No mention of the dragon at all. I hadn't expected demons would have principles; hearing lies roll from their lips in fits and starts reinforced my already rock-bottom opinion of them.

They'd been there when Cai kidnapped their buddy, but they'd never gotten close to the Arctic.

Once they finished embellishing their dilemma, they got around to begging for asylum.

The demons on the dais trundled around in more snake slime and laughed.

Without moving from his prone position, one of the demons said, "Eh, I suppose you can stay, but remove the bond animals."

"Aye, that way the Circle will quit pursuing us," one of the two seeking clemency mumbled around a mouthful of broken teeth. The injury appeared recent, probably courtesy of a hoof to the jaw.

"Could be interesting," one of the dais demons chortled.

"Bond animals for dinner," another chimed in.

Gwaihir's claws tightened in a death grip. Blood flowed down my back and chest. I hustled to obliterate it, but every demon's head snapped up, nostrils flaring. Yeah. It figured blood would be one of their go-to scents.

Knowing he'd made a mistake, the eagle relaxed his talons, but the damage was done. All the demons on the dais shot to their feet. "Show yourselves," one shouted and shook a fist.

"Only cowards hide behind wards," another said smugly.

If he was aiming to bait us, it worked. The odds weren't especially epic. Two dozen demons versus three mages and five bond animals, not counting the hawk and the coyote who had yet to break free. Eh, I've had worse.

Battle lust took over, and I jettisoned my ward. The demons nearest me jumped back. I laughed, letting it roll from me. "Who's the coward now?"

"You brought food," one of the dais demons purred. "How thoughtful of you."

Gwaihir launched from my shoulders and scribed circles in the smoky air, cawing a challenge. Aidyrth burst forth next in a showy blaze of dragon fireworks. Shira was still hidden. Wise of them to break things up like that.

"Dinner, is it?" the dragon cooed. "We'll see who eats whom."

"Long way from Fire Mountain, aren't you?" a demon challenged.

"Depends on who's traveling there," she retorted and flexed a taloned foreleg. "I could scoop you up and drop you into a caldera in no time at all." Fire shot from her mouth, but demon scales needed a whopping dose before they'd disintegrate.

Tory joined Gwaihir, and the eagles feinted and swooped. A shrill cry was followed by, "Give it back." Predictably, Gwaihir held an eyeball in his hooked beak. I've never figured out what it is with hawks and eagles and eyes, but they're quite the delicacy.

A muted roar grew in volume. Water rushed through the cavern, gallons of it, the brine a welcome change from burning shit. Ciara was at work behind the scenes. I called on the dirt under our feet. It was sluggish, slow to respond, probably because it had played host to demonkind for far too long.

"Your chance to get back at them," I suggested in silken tones.

Demons charged me, but running through thigh-deep water takes time. Once I turned it to a viscous mud, they had no chance at all. Standing at the edge of the mess their chamber had turned into, I slopped through mud as if it weren't there. It parted for me, recognizing its maker. The two false shifters were on their feet. If they were smart, they'd have used all the ruckus to make a run for it.

If they'd been smart, Hell would have been the last place to go.

The demons on the dais hadn't moved, but the serpents were winding their way up the walls, using any protuberance to aid their movements. They could swim, but breathing underwater wasn't one of their talents. The rounded entry point we'd used was the only way in or out that I could see. If those fuckers had tunnels, they'd be flooded by now.

"You've got this," Aidyrth told me.

I didn't necessarily see it that way, but the battle seemed at least a draw for now. Why the vote of confidence? And then I understood. She sucked the demons still housing bond animals close and vanished in an explosion so brilliant it left after-images stamped on my corneas.

Yeehaw. Our job was done. All we needed to do was teleport out of this shithole. A bloodcurdling yowl added my ears to the list of senses under attack. Ciara plonked herself down behind one of the demons on the dais and swung a wicked serrated blade hard enough to separate head from spine.

Impressed by her courage, I was also infuriated. She might want every demon who'd ever walked dead, but our mission was over. The idea was to get in, do the deed, and get out. We had the demons—and the bond animals. The dragon would break the bond and toss the demons onto a slagheap.

Cai and the wolf joined the party, leaping and snarling and meting out maximum damage. Common sense took a hike.

Everybody was having such a good time, I leapt into the fray with Shira—a finally visible Shira—right behind me.

"Start with the dais," I shouted since three of us were already there and making staunch progress.

"By the time they're dead," Shira yelled back, "wanna bet no one else is left in here?"

CHAPTER 15

I got in a few good licks, but Shira's words were prophetic. Once we were done with the fuckers on the dais, the chamber was empty of demons. I'd been avoiding Ciara. Simple enough since we were knee-deep in meting out death blows. I may have mentioned how stunningly hard demons are to kill. They remind me of kewpie dolls in a shooting gallery. Knock 'em down, and they bounce right back.

Beautiful, graceful, light on her feet, Ciara danced past, blades twirling. They must be a new addition since she'd said she relied on magic. Or maybe they were linked to her power. If she'd been in my direct line of command, I'd have read her the riot act for engaging the enemy after our work was done.

She wasn't. I had no jurisdiction over her actions, nor did I want to. My hopes for us had nothing to do with warfare. Gwaihir swooped past with an empty beak. Guess he'd eaten all the eyeballs, or he'd been sharing them with Tory.

Ciara barked a few words; the water withdrew leaving scattered puddles and uncovering fallen demons. Maybe not as many had left as I assumed. Cai and the wolf and the eagles had been kicking some serious ass while we'd been occupied on the dais.

"Nice work," I called out.

"We did good," Shira agreed enthusiastically. "Shit. I'd never seen a demon before Grigori signed me up. Now they're all over the fucking place. Every time I turn around. Here a demon. There a demon. Everywhere a demon." She chuckled, pleased by her own narrative.

A few more spell words from Ciara, and the blades disappeared. So they were an extension of her power. "Thanks for the help," she said, "but I pretty much had this. Me and Cai and the wolf."

"What's his name?" Shira asked.

"No idea." Ciara shrugged. Tory landed on her shoulders and spread her wings, fanning them.

Shira extended a hand. We shook all around, and I readied a spell to move us out of here. The longer we remained, the greater the chance more of Satan's ilk would show up. Or not. We'd trounced them soundly. Loyalty isn't part of their rulebook. Satan or his princes could be screaming their heads off at their minions—if they could find any—to no avail.

"I'll travel independently," Shira said. "Think I'll take advantage of Aidyrth being busy to go home for a few days. Maybe Jake and Arrow will join me."

Once she'd left, I asked Ciara, "Who are Jake and Arrow?"

Ciara grinned. It lightened something uncomfortable eddying between us. "Jake's a mobster she met on her first mission with the Circle. Turned out he sprang from gypsy and witch stock, had nascent power, and became a Circle recruit. Arrow is his wolf."

"Are Shira and Jake an item?"

"They hang around together, yes." Ciara motioned the wolf and hyena close. "Where will you go next?"

"Where did the dragon take the others?" Cai asked.

"Probably to Fire Mountain," I replied.

"We will return to the guild house and wait to make certain they're all right," the wolf said in solemn tones. His devotion to the other trapped bond animals touched me, reminded me how lucky I was to have Gwaihir in my corner.

"You damn betcha," my bird cawed before landing on my shoulders.

"Stop stealing my thoughts," I chided him and got a peck in the side of the head for my efforts. Meanwhile, the wolf and Cai had left. We needed to also, and I seized the spell I'd begun a few minutes before.

Once we were solidly settled in a travel channel, I hunted for a neutral way to talk about choices and how her end run against the demons might not have been the smartest move. In the end, I couldn't craft anything that didn't sound like a lecture, so I let it go. A circle of standing stones not far from my car morphed into view. I'd been sloppy and neglected a ward. It didn't cost anything. No one saw us. Both birds took flight.

Ciara glanced around. "I figured we'd go back to the guild house."

"We will. We have to report in, and I want to see if there's news about Aidyrth and the two bond animals."

"Then why are we here?" Ciara trudged next to me as we covered the half mile to the Land Rover.

"I have to take the car home."

"You don't need me for that. Tory and I can leave from here."

The prudent course would have been to say nothing. But I've never been the cautious sort. "You could," I agreed, "but I'd like it if you hung around."

"Why?"

"I like your company, and I'm curious as hell about those blades." The last was a cheap shot. Assassins love to crow about the tools of our trade, and I wasn't above cheating to get what I wanted, which was more of her time. My rebuke could wait. If I launched into it now, she'd be gone in a heartbeat.

Her brows unknitted, and she smiled softly. "Quite a tale behind them."

"I'd enjoy hearing it."

We reached the car, and I opened the boot for the eagles who'd been pacing us from fifty feet in the air. They swooped in while I opened the passenger door for Ciara. She shook her head. "I'd like to drive for a bit. It's one of the ways I unwind."

"Of course." I dropped the keys into her hand and walked around the car, shutting the hatch as I passed it.

We'd been on the road for a few minutes when she said, "A sea witch gifted me those blades, but it wasn't out of the goodness of her heart. She managed poisons for Poseidon and wasting spells. Everyone feared Brocca, so she spent centuries mostly alone.

"I first met her when I was quite young. My mother was one of the few who befriended her, but it was very one-sided. Brocca never had anything good to say. She wore a perpetual scowl and swam around her cavern in a fury. Before I learned to watch my tongue I told her she was scary because she never smiled or had a kind word to say about anyone.

"Not even about Mother who left delicacies like crab cakes and seaweed gruel."

"What was in it for your mother?" I asked, curious why anyone would put up with abuse over an extended period.

"I asked her the same thing," Ciara said. "More than once. Turned out they went way back. They'd been children together, played together, although the concept of Brocca engaging in anything fun was tough to fathom."

"I see. Go on. And let me know when you want me to drive."

"Will do." She nodded. "Brocca and I both killed for Poseidon. We had that in common even though we employed different methods. Once after I'd walked into a trap, she took me aside and fashioned the blades, matching them to my magic. Her instructions were to chop Poseidon's balls off."

I chuckled. "I like the crusty old bitch, and I don't even know her. Was the trap Poseidon's fault?"

Ciara nodded tersely. "You'd think I'd have been smarter after all that time. He rarely researched anything, just parceled out targets. Half the time, he told the unfortunate mark I'd be coming for them."

A long, low whistle erupted from me. Nothing like being hung out to dry by your boss. "That's just rude," I growled.

"He'll never change." She paused and took a measured breath. "I'd already decided to leave the sea. Poseidon didn't value any of us. He was a narcissistic pig. His first question was always what was in it for him. If he couldn't find anything, whatever project was up for discussion died on the chopping block."

"I've had commanders like that."

She spared a glance my way. "How'd you handle it?"

"Killed the last one."

She snorted. "So you get it."

"Yeah. I do."

"I told Brocca I was leaving," Ciara went on. "It was a risk, but since she'd given me the blades, she deserved to know I wouldn't be around to turn them on Poseidon. She fussed and fumed, called me ungrateful, but in the end, she provided the diversion I needed for my escape."

"Good for her. Was it hard to leave? You mentioned a mother. Do you have other blood kin?"

"I did. Hell, I still do, but none of them can know where I am. It would lead Poseidon right to me."

I frowned, confused. "They could find you easily enough. Blood calls to its own."

She shook her head and nosed the car into the parking lot for a market. "Grigori had the White Fae make a few alterations. No one can track the old me because she no longer exists." She shut off the ignition. "You hungry?"

"It's a perpetual condition. We'll pick up some grain for the birds too."

"Meat." Gwaihir pulled his head from beneath a wing long enough to correct me.

I'd have ruffled his feathers, but I couldn't reach him. "Meat it is," I agreed.

I took over driving, and we scarfed down sandwiches and beer as we drove. Ciara had found raw frozen steaks in the cold case and bought one for each bird. By the time we reached my house, light was fading from the day and Scotland's perpetual drizzle was back.

I killed the ignition and said, "I'd like it very much if you'd come in, but I understand if you'd rather not."

Her full lips curved into a smile. "How much time did you waste coming up with such a stilted invitation?"

I grinned back. "Too much. I'll be the first to admit I'm out of practice, but we both need to shower. I can whip something up for dinner, and you can tell me more about yourself over steaks and brandy."

"But we just ate," she protested.

"So? I'm still hungry. We blew through a lot of power." I waited, trying to tamp down hope burning a path through me. I hadn't been especially eloquent. Quite the opposite, since she'd made fun of me, but I couldn't be other than who I was.

A rush of power flickered between Ciara and Tory. They

must be talking. I could have listened in, but it would have been rude, so I opened my door. Once I was on my feet, every muscle lodged a complaint. Eh, I've felt worse. Far worse. A button on my key fob opened the boot. I reached around for my field pack, and Gwaihir hopped to the edge before taking flight.

"Good hunting," I called after him and shouldered my sack. I hadn't needed any of its contents this trip. Ciara and Tory were still talking. Turning away from the Land Rover, I looked upward, losing myself in the flow of clouds as they scudded across the night sky. Every once in a while, I'd catch a glimpse of the quarter moon or the odd star.

Ciara's door opened and closed. Tory followed Gwaihir's path out the hatch I'd left open for her. She was smaller than Gwaihir, elegant as she extended her wings, letting the wind carry her aloft. I sent a bit of magic to close the hatch.

"That steak sounds good," Ciara said, walking until she stood next to me.

I turned to her wanting to ask a million things like had staying been Tory's idea or hers. Instead, I smiled and said, "Excellent. Come on inside. We'll get a fire going, and I'll start supper. You can have the first shower."

"Do you have an outside burn barrel for trash?" She held up the bag with the remains of our foraging through the market.

"Nah. We'll toss it in the fireplace inside. This cottage was originally built in the 1700s. It's been modernized, added onto, but I kept some elements like the original stone hearth and firepit."

"When did you buy it?"

"Long ago," I admitted. "I've changed the name on the registry a few times, but it's getting harder."

"Why would that be?" she asked as I slipped the deadbolt

with a smidgeon of magic while checking if the front door had been disturbed.

"A hundred years back, all I had to do was waltz into the local land office with a sheaf of paperwork. Everything's computerized now."

"It requires a different skillset," she admitted while she looked around the great room before heading for the far end where a fireplace took up the entire wall from floor to ceiling.

"Are you a hacker as well as an assassin?" I teased.

"I get by." She tossed the garbage into the fireplace and ran a hand along the rockwork. "This is gorgeous. Stonemasons are a dying breed."

"Thank you, and yes they are. The fancy bathroom is up the main staircase and to the right. I'll be in the kitchen."

"And the unfancy one?"

"Off the kitchen, but go upstairs, please. I did all the work on that one, and I'd love to hear your opinions."

She nodded pleasantly, chucked a few lengths of wood into the fireplace, and lit it with magic. Once a blaze crackled merrily, she moved toward the hallway. I loped into the kitchen, both relieved and disappointed. Having her naked only a few feet away would have been tough, but part of me wished she'd opted for cleaning up with only a wall separating us.

She hadn't asked how I came to have firewood. Probably, she hadn't spent enough time in the Highlands to know how scarce a commodity it was. The few trees were owned by the government; cutting them earned a stiff sentence. What little wood I had was transported from the dense forests covering eastern Europe courtesy of various enchantments.

The sound of water rushing through pipes told me the upstairs tub was filling, or maybe she'd opted for a shower.

I hustled through dinner preparations, gathering spinach and leaf lettuce from a greenhouse beyond the kitchen door.

I'm far from chef quality, but I can turn out luscious, rare steaks and crisp salads. Once the meat was done and in a warming oven and the salad tossed and ready, I ducked into the downstairs bathroom intent on washing off the stench of Hell. The nose accommodates to almost anything given time, but I still caught whiffs of sulfur and decay.

Hot water pelted me—and my hard-on. My clothes were loose enough, maybe it hadn't been noticeable. Making dinner hadn't deflated its enthusiasm in the least. The bathroom filled with steam and the sandalwood scent of a soap I import from London. I lathered up, but my hand kept straying to my cock. Should I? It felt perverse to bring myself off with Ciara so near.

My engorged member strained against my hand. Lust gained momentum; my balls tightened. Everywhere I touched my soapy body sent a thrill through me. Aw hell, I was stronger than this. It wasn't as if I was fifteen. My breathing had escalated. Christ. I was a fucking mess.

"Get hold of yourself," I mumbled.

"Or I could get hold of you." A smoky, sultry voice hit me with all the force of a tornado. Ciara stepped over the rim of the tub. She'd slid the glass door open without me even noticing. What kind of assassin was I? With such a stellar lack of attention to my surroundings, it was amazing I hadn't been seriously damaged.

Too embarrassed to turn around, I stood there like a dolt while water bounced off my chest. Ciara wrapped her arms around me from behind, smushing her breasts against my back and her sex against my butt.

"I, uh, I thought you were upstairs," I sputtered.

"I was. Lovely marble work, by the way." She laughed; mirth made her breasts bounce. Their already distended nipples hardened still more. "I had you pegged for a lot of things, Quinn, but a prude wasn't one of them."

She ran her fingertips lightly down my soaked chest. When they grazed my nipples, I groaned and made a grab for her hands. They were moving lower. If she touched me, I'd be lost. My member beat like a second heart, perilously close to a look-Ma-no-hands climax.

Disconcerting as fuck.

I turned to face her, determined to regain control of the situation. Yeah. Right. I could add delusional to perilously inattentive. Her long fair hair hung in saturated strands surrounding her breasts. Up close like this, I noticed golden flecks around the pupils in her oh-so-blue eyes. Breath caught in my throat. She was lovely, but her beauty was far more than the perfection of her face and body. It was like adding two and two and coming up with a hundred.

"You're incredible," I said taking in gracefully muscled shoulders, high firm breasts tipped with strawberry nipples, and a flat stomach stretched between pronounced hipbones. The vee between her legs sported spiky blonde curls, and her acres of legs were icing on the cake.

"So are you." Her gaze raked me, leaving heat in its wake. The only thing she wore was the silver trident necklace. I had a feeling it was linked to her magic somehow, maybe to the blades.

Ah fuck, my mind was all over the place.

She moved her gaze to my face, adding frank appraisal to the mix. "Did I read you wrong?"

I shook my head. "Not at all." Flicking fingers downward in the direction of my cock, I added, "Being around you is exhilarating. So is fantasizing about your body."

Her mouth curved into a soft smile. "Is the reality as pleasing?"

"More, but why are you fishing for compliments? You must know how striking you are."

"Something's in the way," she murmured. "What is it. We're both here. You want me. I felt your desire all the way upstairs, but you're hesitating."

I swallowed once and then again. Talking about feelings is so not on my agenda. Ever. I'm the original tough dude. The one who eats nails for breakfast, spits them out, and rushes into battle.

"Do you want me to get dressed?" she asked softly.

"No."

"You don't want me here. And you don't want me dressed. What do you want?"

I wouldn't get a better invitation, so I wrapped my arms around her. "You're not fuck-'em-and-leave-'em material. I've picked partners for their transient qualities. Women I could walk away from without a second thought. Even the occasional man, but they're not my thing."

She molded her body to mine. The water was turning cold, but neither of us minded—or even noticed. "We could be transient," she said. "Friends with privileges."

I threaded fingers through her silky hair, feeling the wet strands snag on my fingers. "I can't be that way with you," I replied. "Once we come together, I'll want you again and again and again. I don't know how to be someone's lover beyond casual sex, never wanted the responsibility."

"Do you now?" Her question was soft, probing.

I felt like an idiot. We barely knew one another, and I was nailing down our future. Cupping the side of her face and meeting her gaze, I said, "I don't know what I want, and it scares the crap out of me."

Once I'd said that much, words followed with little or no censorship. Mr. Always in Control had taken a hike. "I'm probably shitty partner material. I'm self-absorbed. Comes from only having me to consider forever. I'm not good at checking in. Even Gwaihir chides me for being a dick, but we understand one another."

She wound her arms around me, fingers splayed across my shoulders. "How about if we worry about all the rest of that later?"

I was almost lost. Before I fell off the cliff into sexual oblivion, I managed, "I got the impression you didn't even like me very well."

"Sometimes I don't, but there's something about you that draws me. You're a pretty man, Quinn." Her eyes trained on my face turned liquid with need. "I've spent my years out of the ocean figuring things out. My magic is the same, but everything else is different."

"Am I one more experiment?"

"Maybe we both are." Reaching between us, she wrapped her fingers around my cock. A wild, savage cry burst from me. Every pent-up fantasy I'd had about her spilled through my entire body. I'd pick up the pieces later. Now was for us.

CHAPTER 16

Heat from her fingers seared me as she squeezed my errant appendage. I strung kisses down her neck before bending to take a nipple into my mouth. A low breathy moan told me I'd done a good thing. I teased her breast with my tongue, suckling and biting. The hold she had on my cock tightened, and she stroked from base to tip and back again.

After swirling my tongue around her nipple, I kissed my way up her breastbone to her collarbone and her cheek before claiming her lips. Firm beneath my mine, they felt even better than they had the first time we'd kissed. The scents of the sea rose around us as her magic sang to mine. Ciara opened her mouth, welcoming the thrust of my tongue, sparring with it and exploring the inside of my mouth in return.

Reaching around us, I shut off the water—no longer tepid, it was stone cold—without abandoning her mouth. Kissing, sucking, biting, playing. She felt amazing in my arms, like she'd been born to be there. Her body fit perfectly against mine. The nipples I'd played with rubbed my chest, hard as polished stones. I ran my fingers down her back and cupped her ass, snugging her belly against my hard-on and capturing her hand between our bodies.

She had one arm between us. The other curved around my back as she kneaded my butt. The same savage growl wasn't far from the surface. Desire clawed at me like a live thing, urging me forward. Earthy scents of evergreen and damp granite mingled with her musk and brine, the combination intoxicating. Between her crushed against me and getting higher with each strained breath, sex turned into a whole new phenomenon. Far beyond delighting my body, Ciara captured my soul, my mind, my magic.

It was like I'd never bedded a woman before.

Her heart thudded against my chest. Breath rasped from her as she worked me and rubbed her body against mine. I wanted to scoop her up, carry her to bed, but I was too aroused to take the time. I had to be inside her. Waiting wasn't an option.

With a downward swooping motion, I positioned my forearms beneath her thighs and lifted her. After an awkward moment when she relinquished her hold on my cock, she wrapped her legs around my waist and her arms around my shoulders. The head of my penis was poised at the entrance to her body. I eased my way in.

Searing heat and slick walls met me as I did my damnedest to press forward slowly. A cry reminding me of the eagles rushed from her. She held onto me with her legs while jamming the length of me all the way inside. A torrent in a language I'd never heard before followed, and she raised herself a few inches before thrusting downward again.

A rambunctious bite marked my mouth, and then another seared the junction of neck and shoulder. I might not understand what she'd said, but I knew what she wanted. No holding back. Maybe next time, but not now. She was as desperate for release as me. Holding her steady, I bent my knees enough to withdraw and drive the length of me into her. She bit me again. This time in the neck. I gripped her upper thighs, digging my nails in. A high, wild cry told me she liked rough play.

We'd moved beyond the subtleties of lovemaking, the touches and kisses reserved for lazy lust-saturated nights. I took her, fucked her fast and hard, willing her to come as I hovered on the edge of release, my cock as hard as it had ever been. Our mouths came together again; we devoured each other, breathing each other's air as we pushed ever higher.

I cheated, used magic to wind our heat into a single pulsing strand of unslaked need. It was like we dared ourselves to push for one more notch of desire. Another glistening step on the lust ladder. How high could we go before we fell back to Earth?

She broke first. A low moan turned to a shriek. Nails scudded down my back; teeth tore at my lower lip. Her vault turned to liquid heat as it shuddered around me. I thrust faster, so quickly my movements were a blur. Her climax fed my soul, my heart. Sweet and fiery and passionate, she writhed in my arms, her sex clamped tight around my cock.

The line I'd been holding, mostly with a magical assist, crashed. The floodgates opened, and semen juddered from me. I've never come so hard. Or so much. I've always been jealous of women's orgasmic capability. Tonight, I joined their ranks. Our bodies ground together as we crested once and then again. The muscles in my arms had long since turned to rocks, but my attention was elsewhere. On the miraculous place our bodies were joined.

We stood with me holding her for a long time. Long enough when we finally untangled ourselves and I flipped the taps back on, the hot water had recovered.

"What language was that?" I asked after we'd rinsed off and I was enjoying drying her in the steamy bathroom.

"The sea people's. I'm not surprised you've never heard it." She snagged another towel and blotted water from my chest and legs.

"Did you learn spells in Gaelic too?"

She shook her head. "I have since I left the ocean out of necessity."

"Why's that?" I'd moved to wrapping her tresses in another towel to soak up excess liquid.

"Expediency. My native tongue kindles spells here, but not quickly. Sometimes they don't work especially well, either. Grigori was kind enough to find me a scroll with equivalent commands in Gaelic."

I'd had no idea any mages on Earth used other than our common magical language, but I was sidetracking. Doing my usual two-step to run away from anything that touched me deeply, anything that might get in the way of my carefully constructed life.

"Do you have clothes I might borrow?" she asked. "Mine are having their own bath in your washer."

I plucked two robes off the back of the bathroom door and handed her one. She slipped it on and tied the sash. I did the same, but then I stood in front of the door blocking our exit. If we left the small, intimate room where we'd shared such passion, I'd do what I always did and cover up feelings with diversions and small talk.

In truth, we had plenty of complex topics facing us, issues that should command all our attention. Rightfully so. Dealing with Satan and the demon problem had to take priority, but before we returned to our commitments within the Circle, I motioned her close and folded my arms around her.

"What we did, making love, was special for me. You're quite extraordinary."

"Bet you say that to all the girls." Her voice was muffled by the shoulder of my robe.

"I do not. I may be a cad, but I've never taken a woman to bed under false pretenses."

She straightened and angled her head to look at me. "I didn't mean to strike a nerve."

"I want, um, I hope we can find a path forward. Together."

"But we scarcely know one another."

I nodded. "How do things work in the ocean? Do mages pair up?"

Ciara shook her head. "Rarely. My longstanding affair with the Selkie was an anomaly. The naiads sometimes mate, but more in trios and quartets than pairs."

"They're all female, right?" When she nodded, I went on. "We can take things slowly, but this is important to me. You're important to me."

"What makes me different?" Her eyes had shaded to a deeper blue. "Lovemaking was pretty damned spectacular. Is that it?"

"Nope. I felt that way before you crawled into my shower buck naked."

She crinkled her nose my way. "Like you weren't practically begging me. The pheromones were so thick I smelled them all the way upstairs."

"Do you make a point of shedding your clothes for every man who thinks you're hot?" I countered.

Her full mouth stretched into a grin. "Touché. I ignore most of them. Some are so obnoxious, I make certain their equipment won't work for a month."

I grinned back. "Wicked."

"Nope. Practical. Means they won't bother me."

I kissed her forehead and both cheeks. "So, where are we?"

"Standing barefoot in your bathroom."

"Not what I meant." I wasn't about to let her off the hook so easily.

She nodded. Her hair was starting to fluff as it dried, softening the planes of her face and lending her an angelic look. "I know. This kind of thing isn't easy for me, either."

I remained silent, offering encouragement in my own way. I could live without her. Of course, I could, but I didn't want to.

"I'm interested in seeing where this leads," she said softly. "You and me. That first night I showed up here, after Grigori sent me to run you down, I wasn't expecting to do anything except deliver his message." Her smile developed a crooked aspect. "I wasn't counting on a one-two punch to the guts the moment I laid eyes on you."

Relief cascaded through me, rich and exhilarating. She was going to give us a chance. "Makes two of us," I murmured. "After you weren't trying to kill me any longer."

She shrugged. "I had to do something with all that free-floating yearning."

Promises rose to my lips, but I kept them inside. The hard truth was I didn't know what I was capable of, how well I could hold up my end of anything that smacked of the personal. I was hell on wheels as a comrade-in-arms, but what I hoped to build with Ciara was terra incognita.

"Feel like dinner?" I asked. "The meat's cold, but the salad will be okay."

"Dinner would be perfect. I already found the washer and dryer. It was why I was downstairs when you were in the shower. My clothes should be done with one and ready for the next by now."

"The only reason you were downstairs?" I teased.

"It was the one I let myself believe, but the flesh turned out to be far weaker than I'd figured."

Laughing, I said, "Let's hear it for lust."

I hooked a hand with hers, and we walked into the kitchen. Ciara detoured to the alcove where my laundry machines sat. The eagles were perched on the table, obviously waiting for us. Tory cooed, sounding like a mourning dove. Gwaihir extended his wings before settling them back into place.

"Was the hunt good?" I asked them as I rescued the steaks, plated them, and put the salad bowl on the counter. The brandy had had plenty of time to breathe, and I poured two generous goblets.

"Very," Gwaihir cawed.

Ciara made shooing motions. "Move you two. We need to eat, and then we'll head back to the guild house."

Gwaihir never would have moved for me, but he hopped down obligingly for Ciara. Tory did too. My bondmate waited until we were seated to say, "About the guild house, we heard from Aidyrth."

I glanced up from my meal. Between blowing through magic and opening the door I usually barricade my emotions behind, I was starving. "Are the coyote and hawk all right?"

"Yes and no. The hawk is fine," Gwaihir replied.

"Our healers are not sure about the coyote," Tory added. "The separation process wasn't as clean. Dragons killed the demon before the coyote was well and truly clear of it."

I frowned and took a generous slug of brandy, savoring the twenty-year-old Armagnac. "Their healers are skilled. It's not like them to make a rookie error like that."

"Aidyrth was confident they could repair the damage," Tory said.

I thought back to her earlier statement. "You mentioned your healers. Did some of the White Fae come along to help?"

"We have our own healers," Gwaihir clarified. "Owls and foxes, for the most part."

First I'd heard about it, but I kept my own counsel. The food in front of me was fast disappearing, the brandy too. Despite her assertion she wasn't hungry on the drive back here, Ciara had almost finished her meal.

"Was everyone at Fire Mountain?" she asked.

Tory clacked her beak in assent. "Aidyrth says our healers were at fault. I am certain when we talk with them, they'll tell a different tale."

"Maybe no one did anything wrong," I said. "Fire Mountain is a difficult place to employ magic for everyone except dragons." My statement earned another beak clack, this time from Gwaihir.

I got up and brought the brandy decanter to the table, pouring myself a little more and leaving it next to Ciara's place in case she wished to do the same. As I plotted where we should aim for, I asked, "Where is everyone now?"

"They won't welcome us in the dragons' world," Ciara warned.

"Have you been there?" I raised a brow.

She shook her head. "Only heard about it."

"Their bark is worse than their fire," I said. "They fuss and grumble, but they don't eat you for breakfast or chuck you into a fumarole."

"We'll be outside," Gwaihir said and hopped toward the back door. He was more than capable of opening it, but I sent a thread of magic to prop it open for him and Tory.

Ciara poured a couple more fingers of brandy into her goblet. "This is quite good," she said.

"Thanks. I'm fond of brandy, and Armagnac is one of my favorites. It's only produced by a few boutique wineries, and it gains a lot after ten years or so in an oak cask."

She smiled. "You're full of surprises." She held up a finger. "One, you can cook." Another finger, "Two, you know spirits."

"If I couldn't wend my way around a kitchen I'd have starved to death before takeout became popular. Keep the sugar coming." I reached across the table and placed a hand over hers.

"You're even hotter in bed than I'd imagined."

This was getting better and better. "Have you spent much time thinking about how sex with me would be?"

Her pale complexion turned rosy. "Maybe a little bit."

"I fantasized about you too. A lot," I tossed out, so she'd know she was in good company.

"Did I meet muster?"

"In spades, darling." I got up, walked to her side of the table, and gave her a quick hug before moving my plate to the sink.

She followed me, plate in hand. "That was wonderful. Thanks for catering dinner. Next time, it's my turn."

I rinsed plates and left them in the sink. "What will we have?"

"Lobster. Scallops. Sea bass. Depends on what I come up with."

"I can't wait." Turning, I held out my arms. She walked into them and turned her mouth up for a kiss. My body should have been drained, but it responded so quickly it took me by surprise. I crushed her against me, hungry for more of the same.

We'd run out the clock. I could justify a meal and our earlier tryst, but a second time was pure paganism. Her mouth moved beneath mine. Her hands grasped my butt. Our breath quickened with our tangling tongues. The alluring scent of the sea wafted through my kitchen; I breathed it in, greedy for more of everything. Her scent. Her body. Her breathy moans.

I tore my mouth from hers. Our eyes locked; what I saw in

the depths of hers tantalized me. My same push-pull—desire and hope versus apprehension—reflected back at me.

"We should go," I said softly.

"We should." Ciara looked away. "I mean, I should want to go, but I don't, and I don't understand it. We have work to do."

Work. It's been my rallying cry all the years of my life. Killing has molded me, shaped me, made me what I am. No time for a philosophical discussion about how we could maintain who we'd been and still make space for us. It seemed possible on paper, but translating theory to reality would take a quantum leap of faith.

On both our parts.

"Meet you back here in a few," I told her. "Your clothes are probably dry, and I'll grab something clean from upstairs."

A good soldier like me, she was ready to go when I returned. "Come on." Grabbing her hand, I walked us out of the kitchen, through the great room, and out the front door before swathing my house in the same protections I always provided.

"We were about to roust you out of there," Gwaihir squawked.

"Sorry," Ciara said.

"Fuck," I muttered and turned back for the house. "Forgot my duffel. Get the transport spell cooking."

Clucking over being sloppy and squandering power setting a ward only to dismantle it minutes later, I lectured myself about getting a grip. About doing better. About not letting my newly ignited lust for Ciara erode my razor-sharp instincts.

What was it about her? She was like a drug, potent and addictive. I'd broken away from our latest embrace by the thinnest of margins. My cock still throbbed, reminding me it had been cheated out of another taste of ecstasy. This was why I'd remained alone. To ensure my focus was absolute. No distractions meant fewer mistakes.

Beyond forgetting the field bag slung over my shoulder, I hadn't made any fatal errors yet. As I joined the others and jumped into Ciara's simmering transport spell, I vowed to keep it that way no matter what it took.

I've always had solid instincts. They've kept me out of trouble and my companions alive—most of the time. Maybe it wasn't possible to do what I did and have enough left over to share my life with another. Over the years, the Circle has had a few mated mages. Not many, though. The pairings occasionally ended in a blaze of acrimony, but more frequently the people involved had walked away from one another.

I'd never dug too deep, but I've always suspected the pressure of keeping too many balls in the air wore on them until they decided it wasn't worth it. A couple of hundred years had passed since my Circle days, though. Eh, more than that. Shira was part of a dyad. Maybe more matings had cropped up in the time since I'd left.

"We're almost there," Ciara said. "You're quiet. Is everything all right?"

Everything was far from "all right," but I nodded anyway in what I hoped looked like reassurance. "Just running scenarios for after we arrive."

Daylight flared around us as the courtyard came into view. I'd expected it to be deserted since it almost always was, but mages had gathered. Grigori, in human form and appearing his old self, stood on the steps. He broke off whatever he'd been saying to turn to us.

"It's about time. Didn't Aidyrth tell you to hurry back?"

Gwaihir squawked. "No. She didn't."

"Her only message was about the bond animals," Tory seconded.

A staunch trumpet from the dragon was followed by fire and smoke belching upward, staining the clear air. "They're correct," Aidyrth said. "I missed that part because I was making certain Shira hurried back."

I shook off the dregs of the travel spell and Ciara's lush scent. "We're here now," I announced. "No harm. No foul. And we're ready for whatever lies ahead."

A woman slipped out the front door of the guild house and made her way to Grigori's side. Surprise thrummed through me. I'd been certain Rhea Lockhart and her wolf were long gone, yet here she was dressed in the same robes the White Fae favored.

Ciara nudged me. I glanced at her and shrugged. We'd untangle the mystery soon enough, but a sudden jolt of worry pummeled me; I angled a subtle bit of power toward Rhea. Grigori was vulnerable, and Rhea had said something about creating stores of virus to keep him going.

What if she'd perverted them somehow? Maybe her wolf was furious with him and pulling strings behind the scenes.

I was quick with my seeking spell; her attention didn't flicker from Grigori. Damn. Double damn. Solid instincts all right, but this was one place I'd have preferred to be wrong. Reining myself in, I listened to Grigori. He'd begun laying out our next steps to deal with Satan and his minions—before they regrouped after our last go-round.

Ciara elbowed me again, harder this time, before rising on tiptoe and placing her mouth right next to my ear. "Rhea's werewolf is too close to the surface," she whispered so low I'd have thought I misunderstood.

If I hadn't sensed the exact same thing.

If we knew, why didn't everyone else?

I mirrored her actions and spoke into her ear. "We do nothing, say nothing. Not until we know more."

"What if Grigori's in danger?" she hissed back.

I shook my head and returned my attention to Grigori. He'd

been taking care of himself for an exceedingly long while. I had faith in him honed by years of proximity.

Ciara hadn't liked my edict. Her mulish expression and the tight line of her jaw reminded me I wasn't in charge of her. Maybe not in her mind, but I outranked her in the Circle.

"Six teams," Grigori was saying. It snapped my attention back where it belonged. I'd made a commitment, given my word. Once we were done with Hell's spawn, I had decisions to make. Or maybe Ciara would make them for me. We'd never had it out about her impromptu "stick around and kick some demon butt" move.

It had been fun, satisfying, but not part of our game plan. We should have left in Aidyrth's wake. I wrenched my focus back to Grigori. Apparently, one of the teams would be mine. If I didn't listen up, I'd be clueless.

CHAPTER 17

Despite admonitions to myself, I listened to Grigori with one ear and pieced together where events had been when I'd left. Rhea and the werewolf had committed to finding common ground, and it had sounded as if they'd be headed for a werewolf pack to reprogram the terms of their partnership. Yet, they were still here.

Why? What had transpired? She looked damned cozy with Grigori. Gwaihir swooped close and landed on my shoulders. Eagerness streamed from my bondmate. The specter of battle excited him as much as it did me. It was why we made such good partners.

"Quinn. Select six mages to fight with you," Grigori said as he parceled out assignments and locations.

"Why him?" Loren the other earth mage shouted. "Hell, he hasn't been here in 300 years."

Where Grigori had stood in man form, a snarling wolf sprang forward planting himself in front of Loren. Loren's wolf shrank away, deferring to the were. "If you question me again"—

Grigori growled to punctuate his words—"you will leave the Circle."

"Why wait?" Loren sneered.

I felt him summon magic. If I hesitated for even a second, he'd be gone for good. While part of me thought that was a grand idea, we earth mages are few and far between. I'd never understood what happened that made Loren so bitter, but he'd been that way from the day I met him.

"Loren." I shouted his name and bolted between him and Grigori.

"You." His sneer deepened. "Stay out of this."

"Where will you go?" I asked.

"What's it to you?" he shot back. "You never cared one way or the other when you were here."

Ciara had closed on us. "Let him go," she blurted. "No big loss."

"But it is," I corrected her. "The Circle used to be a family of mages. It's what made our partnership work. We trusted one another not only because we had to with the work we did, but also because we wanted to."

"You've been gone a long time," Loren said. "Things change."

"You haven't," I pointed out. "What made you so resentful?"

He glared at me. I held his gaze and a neutral expression. I didn't like Loren, and neither did anyone else. The other mages had barely tolerated him when I was in residence. Clearly, that part hadn't changed. But he hadn't made any effort to develop a likeable side. He wore his rancor like a hair shirt.

Grigori shifted back. His keen eyes moved from Loren to me and back again before he said, "Loren. You're assigned to Quinn's group."

Before my fellow earth mage said something that ensured

his removal from the Circle, I clapped him across the back and said, "We'll make it work."

"Like hell we will," Ciara muttered.

Ignoring her comment, I glanced around to see who I had to choose from. The other team leaders were already working their way through the assemblage. Because of her antipathy toward Loren, Ciara was an unknown at this point, so I chose Shira, Jake—who I had yet to formally meet—Mae, and Rolf, a mix of Dark Fae and witch.

Our assignment was the Ninth Circle, the deepest level of Hell, far beneath Satan's court. One of Grigori's concerns was Satan would recall the gatekeeper. Once he was out of the picture, an untold number of ills would be visited on Earth as the bleakest of dark souls ran free.

Since we had no way to force the gatekeeper to perform his duties, our task was to seal him within the Ninth Circle and bar the entrance so no one could leave. It meant Satan would have to make new arrangements for unruly dead, but we'd deal with one problem at a time.

Grigori had mentioned asking Hel to take over the worst of souls, holding them in Niflheim, but that task was above my paygrade.

Ciara had moved a few feet away. She stood, arms crossed under her breasts, with a thousand-yard stare. I walked to her and said, "I'm holding a place for you."

She flapped a hand. "Pick someone else."

I'd anticipated her response, but it angered and disappointed me. I'd worked with plenty of people—magical and otherwise—who weren't exactly my favorites. Loren was a dick, but he was professional. He'd get the job done with his usual efficiency.

"What will you be doing?" I asked.

She shrugged. "My own thing."

The same visceral reaction to her doing just that in the cavern where we'd located the trapped bond animals pounded through me. I switched to telepathy to spare her embarrassment, never mind anyone could listen in.

"No. You will not," I told her. *"You work within a group, a structure. When you make snap unilateral decisions, they put others in harm's way."*

"I do not," she bristled, not bothering with mind speech.

Fine. If she wanted our conversation out in the open, so be it. "Yeah, you do. When you chose to engage demons in battle once our last objective was complete, you kicked open a precarious door."

She faced me squarely, shoulders back. "We won."

I nodded. "We did, but we might not have if demons weren't so self-serving, and more had joined the fight."

Grigori glided close. "What's this about?"

Ciara opened her mouth, but I jumped in first. "Nothing. Ciara declined my invitation. She's free to join another group, but not to freelance."

"Of course." Grigori sounded confused. "Was there ever any question?"

Ciara sidled away before turning and loping out of the courtyard.

"Explain," Grigori said bluntly.

So I did. When I was done, he drew his thick brows together and blew out a tired breath. "She's used to working alone."

"Not an excuse," I snapped. "So am I." As long as he was next to me, I addressed my nagging concern about Rhea. "Why's Rhea still here? Her wolf is really close to the surface."

Grigori nodded. "I ran into some problems. The werewolf council wasn't enthusiastic about assigning them to another pack. They were furious the Morak had left Delta world. Even though their alpha lied to his people, and Rhea wasn't even around when the whole mess rolled out, they still didn't want her werewolf potentially tainting anyone else."

What a stick-up-their-butts crew they must be, but I didn't say a word. It wasn't my place to criticize any more than it was Grigori's to weigh in on earth mage matters.

"You had a reason for asking." Grigori sought more information.

"Only because I expected her to be gone. Her wolf treading so close didn't seem right, either."

"They're getting to know one another, so the wolf is nearer than another might be. Thanks for your work extricating the bond animals."

"It turned out okay," I replied.

"I'll keep an eye on Ciara," he said softly.

"No need. She was fine before. Maybe I bring out the worst in her. Kind of a one-upmanship thing."

He frowned. Before the conversation got any thornier, I raised a hand in farewell and joined my team. We were short a mage, so I asked for suggestions.

"What happened to Ciara?" Aidyrth asked.

"Me," Loren replied bluntly. "She's never cared for me."

"You are a dick most of the time." Mae pursed her mouth into a sour expression.

I chopped a hand downward. "Enough. We need a sixth mage, and then we're gone."

Mae whistled loudly; her hawk flew toward her, landing a few feet away. As I considered the remaining mages, discarding one after another because their magic wasn't a great fit, an idea took shape. Since Hel might be taking over the Ninth Circle, perhaps she'd want to lead the charge. No love lost between her and Satan. They hated each other.

"Grigori," I shouted. When he turned, I asked, "Can we add

Hel to our group?"

A corner of his mouth twisted downward before he nodded slowly. "Interesting idea. Give me a few minutes."

"Have you met her?" Aidyrth demanded.

I nodded. "If she agrees, we're lucky," I told the others. "She's as fierce as warriors come. Half her skeleton is visible. It's why Odin banished her from Valhalla. He found her appearance unsettling."

"She's Loki's daughter," Aidyrth said. "And sister to Fenrir, which is probably why Grigori knows her."

"She's also Jormungand's sister," Loren spoke up. "Two serpents accompany her everywhere. I've run into them a time or two."

"I thought the Norse dead went to Valhalla," Shira said.

"Only the good ones," Jake replied. "The ones who didn't die valiantly end up in Niflheim, the dark place."

I felt an alteration in the warp and weft of the border world's underpinnings. It wavered and shuddered before Hel strode toward us. Swathed in a black robe that covered most of her half-skeletal body, she was imposing. Taller than me and with part of her face exposed bones, she was the stuff night terrors were made of.

Two large black snakes slithered next to her. Maybe ten feet long with enormous bodies and tongues perpetually flicking out to scent the air, they formed an effective barrier. I bet no one got too close.

Rings adorned most of her fingers clanking against the bones of her right hand. Black hair sprinkled with silver fell past her waist. She halted and held each of us in her dark gaze for a long moment. I winced under her appraisal. Apparently, my leadership role had come to an end. Normally, it would bother me, but not this time.

"We shall solidify my new realm," she said in a hoarse,

throaty voice.

I bowed, not too low, but enough to establish deference to the goddess and said, "My team will do your bidding."

"This is how we shall proceed," she went on. "I will forge a path through all of Hell's gates. It will remain open for the rest of you to travel through one at a time. When we are gathered at the Ninth Circle, the gatekeeper is mine."

No one argued. None of us had been looking forward to subduing him.

"What happens then?" Loren asked.

Hel narrowed her eyes his way. "Earth mage, eh? I suspect you'll call down boulders to seal the opening. We will require a physical barrier we can glue with magic to ensure the gates never open again."

"But then how will you come and go?" Shira asked.

"By a different path, of course." Hel didn't offer details, and Shira didn't delve any deeper. The less we knew about the inner workings of the netherworld, the better.

The snakes had glided over to Aidyrth and were working their way up her sides as she bathed them with steam. Hel's forbidding face split into something that might have been a smile. "Not much tempts my babies from my side."

"Blood calls to its own," Aidyrth said, "and Odin barred all dragons save his from Valhalla."

Grigori moved from group to group with last-minute instructions. I'd assumed he'd join one, but apparently he'd oversee this operation from the guild house. When he reached us, Hel inclined her head. "Thank you for the invitation. Fenrir sends his regards."

"Please convey mine in return," Grigori said.

A low sibilant hiss from Hel must have touched a nerve because the snakes beat a track to her side. "Pay attention," she barked at us, "or you won't be able to follow my trail."

I rather doubted that. Her magic was so unique, such a powerhouse, I could have tracked her blindfolded. My thoughts strayed to Ciara. I redirected them fast. She'd placed me in an impossible bind. Grigori had saddled me with Loren. When she'd made it seem I'd chosen the earth mage over her, she'd mingled personal with professional.

I'd worried about my ability to keep the two separate, but she'd crossed what for me has always been an unwritten line. Work was work, not to be confused with anything else, and certainly not to be muddied by crap like she'd pulled.

Tough to lose what I'd never had, but I couldn't think about any of it now.

Aidyrth and Shira left, followed by Jake and his wolf, then Mae and her hawk. I waited until everyone had gone before bringing up the rear. It's an important position since if anyone got into trouble, I was their best hope of recovery. Rear guards have always been underappreciated. The guys in front get all the glory.

Hel had forged an extraordinarily direct path. The moment I left the courtyard, I passed the first gate of Satan's domain. I have no idea how she managed it, but I wasn't complaining. The less time we spent in transit, the more time we had to devote to the task at hand.

Ozone and sulfur were becoming familiar enough, my nose barely twitched. The chemicals still burned, though. The deeper I went into Hell, the worse it looked. Whoever was in charge of maintenance had fallen asleep at the switch. The only gate that appeared to be in decent repair was the first. All the others had fallen inward, hanging on rusted hinges and creaking in the strange wind that always blew down here.

Maybe Grigori's hunch the king of Hell was facing a full-on insurrection wasn't so far off the mark. Yellow muck floated in the air. Random clouds of something toxic. I'd been counting gates. The seventh had been a gaping maw, as had the eighth. If the ninth looked that way, we were wasting our efforts. Everyone slimy had already escaped.

Would Hel bother hunting them down? Somehow I doubted it. She'd blame Satan. He'd shrug his scaly shoulders, and the problem would get punted down the road. Mortals would pay when depraved spirits wreaked havoc, driving men to their doom via any number of inventive methods.

Accidents. Nightmares. Petty jealousies that developed a life of their own. Lies that promised untold riches in exchange for unspeakable acts. The dead aren't corporeal, but they're masters at planting suggestions.

The earlier gates had been spaced at fairly even intervals, but the wreckage of the eighth gate had flashed past quite a while ago. I'm attuned to the Earth. The deeper we went, the more she implored me to save her from the indignity of demons tunneling into her substrate. Knowing it was far too little, I sent calming magic all around me.

The Earth groaned before pelting me with bitter laughter.

The channel I'd been falling through widened. I somersaulted to break my fall and landed next to Loren. Gwaihir had already arrived. Perched on a six-foot-tall boulder he cawed raucously.

This gate was intact. Guess Satan must have determined it would cost him less over the long haul to keep it in decent repair than to deal with twisted, perverse dead running amok through his domain.

Hel stood before gates made of stout timbers banded with iron. Staunch bolts connected them to boulders at the top, middle, and bottom. Deep moans shook me to my core. Loren flinched, so he must hear the source of our magic lamenting her fate.

"Gatekeeper. I command your presence," Hel bellowed.

The air around her turned a deep, dusky violet, and her snakes commenced crawling up the gates. They went from ground to the cavern's top and had been carved so they fit perfectly with no gaps. I hadn't expected that level of craftsmanship from anything under Satan's oversight.

The left gate swung open just far enough for a burly demon to shoulder through. It thudded shut behind him. Coal black with eyes like curdled milk, he was bigger than most demons. I'd never seen one that wasn't red before.

He hissed, showing a mouthful of rotten teeth. The snakes had been clinging to the gates. With acrobatic ease, they wound their tails around hinges and dropped their heads onto the demon's shoulders. Once they had a secure perch, the rest of their bodies followed, winding around the demon from both sides.

The Earth's moans died away, followed by a silence I interpreted as hopeful. In her own way, the Earth was cheering Hel on. The serpents were impressive, but why wasn't the demon fighting back? He'd stood passively and let them imprison him.

"Your rights here are forfeit," Hel pronounced. "Niflheim will be your new home. The snakes are preparing you for the journey."

Another hiss. The demon tilted his head at a defiant angle. I kept careful watch on everyone, from mages to bondmates. Our orders had been to seal the guardian inside the Ninth Gate, but moving him to the Norse darklands achieved much the same end. I wasn't about to quibble, or to challenge Hel's edict.

Something wasn't right, though. I've taken on a lot of demons, and none put their heads willingly on the chopping block. I reached deep into the earth, seeking information—and ran into Loren who was doing the same thing.

He might be a son of a bitch, but there was nothing wrong

with his mind. No one could hear us if we spoke through our land-link. Before I could suggest we split up to cover more ground, a shudder percolated through rock and dirt. It was followed by another. And one more. No longer hopeful, the panicked earth heaved and buckled.

Demon stench, already overpowering in this subterranean hellhole thickened. Realization kicked me in the guts. Talk about rookie mistakes. "Ready yourselves," I shouted. "The gatekeeper was bait. Others are almost upon us."

"Nooooo," Hel roared. Black lightning forked from an upraised hand and augured into the hapless guardian, splitting him from stem to stern. I didn't feel sorry for him. No matter whose orders I'd been following, I'd never have agreed to stand by and let anyone truss me up like a festival pig.

Aidyrth's fire lit the cavern. Piles of bones littered the floor. In addition to being a stooge, the gatekeeper had been a slob. A new vibration joined the outraged earth. Feet, hundreds of them from the sound of things, all headed straight for us.

How had anyone intercepted our plans? They were so new we hadn't known about them until a couple of hours before. A grunt escaped. Ask a simple question, get a simple answer. Only one way. Grigori had a traitor in his midst. At least one, maybe more. Or it might have been the four who'd infiltrated passing information. They wouldn't have known about today's attack, but they'd picked up the rough bones of it before Grigori caught and expelled them.

Demons flowed into the cave around the Ninth Gate. It wasn't all that big a space, and they had numbers on their side. When I looked at Hel, I saw Odin's fierceness and Loki's treachery. Her mouth spread in a vicious grin, and she beckoned with the fingers of one hand and the bones of another.

"Come on little demons," she purred. "Come out and play with Momma Hel."

CHAPTER 18

I longed to fill my lungs with something fresh. Stuffy and stinking to start with, the air in the deeply submerged cave only grew worse. An endless supply of demons converged on us, oozing through walls, the ceiling, the ground. The only ones who seemed to be getting a kick out of the ceaseless carnage were Hel and Aidyrth. Jake was holding his own too.

I liked killing as well as the next assassin, but when I'm fifty bodies into it, I'm ready for a break. Demons are a bitch to kill, and now I'm just whining. No recess on the horizon. Far from it, they kept right on coming. For every abomination we killed, two rose to take his place. Demons smell rancid when they're alive. Dead, they're worse by a factor of ten. Spilled guts, geysering blood, shit, and piss all blended into a nauseating brew.

Loren had edged close, slipping and sliding on a trail of demon innards. Our magic slotted perfectly. It had been a long while since I'd worked with one of my own kind. Easy, almost enjoyable, it took the edge off my weariness. We lobbed power until our target died, and then we moved to the next. At least we weren't losing ground, but eventually we'd run our magic down to bedrock.

"The earth wants to help," he said.

"Yeah," I grunted agreement.

"We can end this." He spoke into my mind.

"How?"

"Find the spaces those fuckers are sliding through, and use earth magic to close them. No entry points, no more problem."

Like all simple solutions, the execution would be far sketchier than his description. We'd need the bond animals, but even with four of us, the project was a crapshoot. If the demons were inclined, they could simply open new channels.

Gwaihir was having the time of his life, munching on a boundless supply of eyeballs. Loren's wolf stuck by his side, snapping and snarling if any demon dared get too near. We also had to let Hel know what we were about.

I hooted softly. The eagle understood and perched on my shoulders while I outlined what he should tell Hel. He'd just taken to the dense, putrid air when something plowed into me from behind, knocking me to the ground. More weight suggested demons were turning me into a pig pile—until I heard barks and growls.

Loren's wolf must have attacked the demon who held me down. I head-butted upward and heard the satisfying crunch of facial bones breaking. One of my hands was free. I floundered around with it until I latched onto something scaled and sent power scudding into the fucker who had me pinned.

He yelped. Score one for the team.

All of a sudden the weight was gone. I leapt to my feet. Loren and his wolf were ripping the demon into bite-sized pieces. I have to hand it to Satan's minions. They don't whine, neither do they beg for mercy. Once they're caught, they fight back until there's no point. Then they fold.

Gwaihir was back. Bending gracefully, he relieved our latest victim of an eyeball. "Hel agreed," he crowed around a beak full of crunchy retina.

Loren didn't waste any time. His spell snared the four of us, moving our group through rock and earth. Every place we found an opening, we marked and sealed it. Christ. There were hundreds of them from every direction imaginable. Some of the portals had demons inside. Their mistake. They'd be locked within earth's clutches until she absorbed their magic and spit out their husks.

Dragons served fire. I served earth. If Ciara had been here, she could have married her sea-linked power with ours. Elements were created to work together. We'd have been quicker with her.

"Yeah, and Santa Claus is real," I muttered.

"What was that?" Loren was panting from effort. We had less breathable air here than we'd had in the cavern, but at least it was cleaner.

"Nothing."

"Why'd we have to get Hel's permission?" he asked.

"Not permission. It's a courtesy to let your team leader know what you have in mind."

"But she could have nixed the idea," Loren protested.

"If she had, there'd be reasons." I took a small break and turned toward him. He was weaving a jagged opening shut and borrowing liberally from an obliging earth. "Christ, Loren. It's not as if you haven't worked as part of a group."

"Not for a long time. Mostly, Grigori assigns me solo tasks."

"You prefer it that way."

Loren didn't answer, but his wolf growled protectively. Gwaihir had been fading in and out as he used his brand of magic to locate breaks allowing demons access to the Ninth Circle. Time passed. Tough to judge how much. The telltale spidery markings around each breach thinned out. Finally, when I looked for another rift, I couldn't locate any.

"Are we done?"

"Done enough," Loren replied. "The earth is delighted. You feel the change in her, don't you?"

"Yeah, I do. Too bad we can't make Satan close up shop and move somewhere else."

"No world would welcome him or his minions."

"True enough. We're not going to solve that problem today. Let's return to the others."

Loren shepherded us through a series of cascading psychic spaces. His technique was flawless, elegant. I'd known he was a talented mage, but he possessed a subtlety I'd never have guessed existed. The Ninth Gate shimmered into view.

"Nicely done," I told the other earth mage. The compliment seemed to please him, but he was tough to read.

"Did you shut all the gateways?" Hel asked.

"Enough to discourage them," I told her and did a quick nose count. All mages and bond animals were present and accounted for. Excellent. We hadn't sustained any casualties.

"We sealed some passages with demons inside." Loren offered a cocky grin. "Our treat for the earth. She'll feast on their power and cast them aside."

"Do you have enough juice left to bar the Ninth Gate permanently?" Hel looked from Loren to me.

"Probably," I said.

"Depends how we do it," Loren added.

"My land-links are to the Nine Worlds," Hel explained. "I'm not as effective here, but I'll assist as I can."

Beneath my feet, the dirt fairly hummed with anticipation. Something it had considered a blight was about to be hobbled.

Forever. I didn't worry about titrating my ability. The source of my magic was prepared to open the floodgates.

"Ready?" I looked Loren's way.

He nodded and extended his arms. I did the same, and we faced the gates. Enchantment rushed through me, used me as a conduit. Rocks crashed before the gates, piling high and ensuring they'd never open again. Once we had an impenetrable wall of dirt and granite, everything melted together courtesy of dragonfire.

Hel surveyed our work and dusted her hands together. "A good day's effort all in all," she pronounced, snakes gliding and hissing around her lower legs. "I shall see you back through the gauntlet." The same evil smile turned her odd face into something predatory. "I transitioned the guardian to Niflheim, and I imagine Satan's out for my blood."

I'd assumed he was dead, but then so was everything else in her realm.

Dusky violet power sheeted from her hands; a vortex formed, pulsing and swirling. This time, Hel waited, shooing all of us through. The return trip was even quicker than the outbound leg had been. The guild house courtyard shaped around us. Night had fallen, and we were alone.

What did it mean? Were we the first group back—or the last?

Grigori pelted down the steps, reaching us the same time Hel did. She sealed the portal behind her, and said, "Our task is done."

"Is anyone else back?" I asked.

Hel scribed another glowing rectangle, clearly intent on returning to the Nine Worlds with her pet snakes.

"Hold a moment," Grigori said. "Please."

The skeleton half of her face might have smiled. "I appreciate your faith in me, but one favor is all I'm inclined to grant." She stepped into her spell amid hissing and crackling. Moments later, no evidence remained of her passing.

"What's wrong?" Aidyrth bellowed.

"Someone set us up." I met her whirling gaze.

"You think I don't know that?" the dragon shot back. Fire came within an inch of my boots.

Rhea ran across the courtyard. "Thank God you're back. Two of the teams are in trouble."

"Silence!" Grigori thundered.

It had the desired effect. Not a growl, squawk, trumpet, or whisper broke the clear, chilly afternoon. Muscles rippled along the line of his jaw. "Three of the teams are on their way back. Two require extraction. I was inside grilling mages since I trust no one."

"We'll go," I said, my response automatic. One of the first rules of combat is never leave companions in the field.

"I want to help," Rhea said.

It surprised me. Had she finally come to appreciate her magical side?

"My answer hasn't changed. It's still no," Grigori growled.

"Why not, and because I said so doesn't cut it."

I smothered a grin, glad Rhea was reclaiming her strength, but we needed to get moving. "Which teams and where exactly are they?" I asked. Before Grigori could answer, I told my group, "We're all in, right?"

A quick array of yesses and ayes was reassuring. They had to be as sick of demons as I was, but we'd do whatever it took. No one fared well in demon hands. Grigori provided coordinates and rattled off names of the mages.

"How do you know they're in trouble?" Shira asked. It was a logical question.

"I can't reach them. Any of them," he replied. "I sent scouts to both locations. They said they couldn't move past the liminal space betwixt Hell and Earth. Neither were they able to connect with anyone despite being close."

"Are the scouts up for coming with us?" I asked Grigori. "Them and three or four mages inside who passed inspection." In full command mode, I was plotting my moves. We'd split forces. It would save time over stopping two places.

"I'll take one location," Aidyrth said, anticipating my strategy. "Jake and Mae will come with us. Loren and Rolf will remain with you."

"Will you take me?" Rhea asked in a clear, ringing voice.

Grigori's no and Shira's yes collided with one another. A handful of mages and bond animals swarmed across the courtyard. My attention had been on Shira and Aidyrth, but Gwaihir's joyful squawk told me Tory had to be nearby. If she was there, so was Ciara.

My gut tightened. I did not need complications, and I didn't trust the sea mage to follow a line of command, particularly not if the orders came from me.

"You can't protect me forever," Rhea was saying. "My wolf agrees we're ready to do something other than sitting around."

"We will not have this discussion here." Grigori used his strictest tone, the one that sent acolytes scurrying to do his bidding.

Rhea wasn't impressed. "No need to have it at all," she said brightly and sprinted to stand next to the dragon.

Dragons aren't especially swift on the uptake where social cues are concerned, but Aidyrth gathered her team and headed out quickly to avoid an argument with Grigori. In the space between two breaths, the lot of them were gone.

Damn it. I'd been hoping Ciara would go with them. "We're good," I said before anyone could piggyback onto our team. "I asked for reinforcements, but we'll figure things out."

Gwaihir and Tory were flying rings around the courtyard, cooing delightedly. "Get down here now," I told my bondmate.

His cooing changed to a derisive hoot. From mourning dove to owl, eh? *"Not how it works,"* he told me.

"Time to leave."

"I'll find you when I'm ready."

I grimaced. Tough to argue with precedent, and it was how our partnership had always been.

Ciara strode forward until she stood in front of me. I tried to look over her or through her to avoid the smackdown effect her beauty had on me. Blerg. Wasn't working. Even if I avoided gazing at her, her scent was everywhere, piquant and enticing.

"I was one of the scouts, and I'd like to be included." Her musical voice shot holes in my resolve. Turning to Loren, she said, "I owe you an apology."

He made a slight shrugging motion. "It's okay. Nobody likes me except my wolf."

"My opinions aren't important. They shouldn't matter, and they won't ever again," she replied. "Not when we have a job to do."

Against my better judgment, I asked, "Can you commit to following orders? Even if they come from me."

She nodded. "Aye. Grigori and I had a...chat."

Mmph. I'd have liked to have been a fly on that wall, but we were out of time. Did I bring her or not? The old saw about fuck me once shame on you, fuck me twice, shame on me rattled around in my head.

"Quinn?" Grigori's pointed tone lit a fire under me.

"You're in," I told Ciara and selected two more mages out of the group milling about. Both were female Sidhe I'd known long ago. One was bonded with a fox and the other with a civet. With the team complete, I built the bones of a spell to take us to Grigori's indicated coordinates. Part of me was pathetically thrilled to have Ciara close, but a much larger part was worried I'd just made the biggest mistake of my career.

Some mages managed to blend their personal lives with their work persona, but not many. I'd never been inclined to try. Phooey. The die was cast, and I couldn't think about any of it. Not now. Lives were on the line. Ciara would either come through, or she wouldn't. What she did, how she behaved, wasn't under my control.

Nothing mattered beyond kicking demon ass and freeing our companions—and their bond animals. We'd come full circle. Freeing bond animals from demons masquerading as mages had been the leading edge of this mess.

I vowed not to let another bond animal suffer beneath demon hands. If there was a way to wipe out Hell entirely, I'd sign on. We'd figure out some other way to establish a needed balance between light and dark, good and evil.

Watch what you wish for, I admonished myself. Better the evil I knew than an unknown quantity. My spell was well in hand, and we shot toward a spot close to our target. I wanted a window to regroup before we engaged the enemy, a relatively safe spot to parcel out assignments.

Ciara stood next to me. "I owe you an apology too," she said softly.

"Later," I snapped, my tone sharper than I'd meant it to be.

"You're right," she murmured. "I scouted this location; let me describe what I found."

Disappointment vied with relief. She'd backed off and was being appropriate. Why in the hell did I feel let down?

CHAPTER 19

Whatever passed between Ciara and Grigori had made a difference, a big one. She walked our group through her attempt to reach the other team so she could determine what happened. Her narrative was concise, highlighting the important parts and glossing over the rest.

"I found evidence the team had been there," she went on. "They'd entered one of Hell's many portals. I buried myself in wards—turned out to be a waste of magic—and tracked them. Just past the stone circle, Hell's early warning system, I ran up against a barrier. I couldn't see it or sense it until it blocked further forward movement."

"Did you try to find a way under, over, or around it?" Rolf asked.

Ciara nodded. "Of course. Dark power stung no matter what I did. I might have been able to punch through, but there was only one of me. At the point I left, demons were closing fast. They're boors but they're not stupid. Someone was expecting the cavalry to show up. Returning to report to

Grigori was more important than ending up trapped just like the team I'd tried to locate."

"Good call," I said, followed by, "We're nearly there. Conceal yourselves in case we have unexpected company."

I'd known we'd come out in eastern Siberia with perpetual howling winds scouring the tundra. The vista that took shape around us was every bit as desolate as I'd expected. I redirected a few shards of power to keep my hands and feet from freezing solid. Christ, but it was cold. It would have been frosty minus the windchill, which was icing on the cake. I was grateful this expedition didn't include anything airborne. Choppers wouldn't have been able to fly.

I herded us to the opening. It was simple to find. Follow the faint miasma of Hell's soldiers, no tracking magic required. Any footprints the mage team or Ciara had left in the snow had been obliterated. We'd determine who'd do what once we got out of the wind. I didn't know what the lost team's original assignment had been, so I asked. Luckily, Loren had been paying closer attention than me when Grigori parceled out tasks.

"All the groups were the same except ours," he clarified. "Stealth attack to take out as many demons as possible and destroy anything critical to maintaining Satan's systems."

"Like what?" a Sidhe asked.

"Blocking channels into the earth that sapped her power, sealing off caves, dismantling electronics. Shit like that," Loren replied.

Interesting. I'd assumed each team had a specific objective, not a slash-and-burn approach. Didn't matter. We were here now. "We're moving beyond the barrier," I announced. "Once we regroup, speed is our friend."

"Over stealth?" Rolf, the Dark Fae-witch combo asked. Tall

and spare, he projected quiet competence. A badger stretched across his shoulders, showing lots of sharp teeth.

"Yup. They'll know we're here," I replied. "When we show up on the far side of the stone circle, they'll figure it out. We may as well take full advantage of every second.

"Loren and I will blend with the earth and aim for maybe 500 yards down the tunnel."

"Hopefully," Loren muttered. "If we're not intercepted before that."

I'd have chided him for questioning my lead, but it wouldn't do any good. Loren was who he was, and I'd rather hear his opinions than muzzle him. The Sidhe and Rolf opted to teleport past the barrier. "What will you do?" I asked Ciara.

"Join you and Loren if you'll have me. Our powers are complementary."

I offered a curt nod.

A squawk told me Gwaihir and Tory were close by. I'd been annoyed they hadn't traveled with us. All the other bond animals had. My eagle was teaching Ciara's bad habits, but she'd have plenty of time to reprogram her once we were done here.

Guess I'd made my decision. My life might be on the arid side, but I didn't have anything left over for domestic squabbles, for smoothing rough spots and misunderstandings.

We all needed to leave at the same time. I took charge of the magic that would propel the three of us and our animals through layers of earth. Rolf gathered the Sidhe close. He gave me a thumbs-up when they were ready, and we all left on my count of three. I hadn't said anything to Gwaihir, but he was next to me and ready. We had enough miles under our belts, he knew he'd pissed me off.

He had ulterior motives, but if he wanted to continue to coo at Tory, it would have to be on his own time. I wasn't at all sure how that would work, but so long as he was available when I needed him for work, we'd figure things out.

Sinking into earth, inhaling its rich loamy smells, was second nature. The break from demon stench was welcome. Ciara's magic was similar enough, the earth allowed her to pass without incident. I hadn't run across a fire mage or an air mage for hundreds of years. I'd figured they abandoned Earth for more commodious worlds. There are some habitable border worlds, but they're few and far between. Usually, the inhabitants guard their turf, and strangers aren't welcome.

"You're going to overshoot it," Loren noted.

He was right. I blanked out every stray thought—and there were bunches of them. A few adjustments, and the tunnel was back, the reek of Hell's spawn thicker than ever. Where were our companions? We needed to get moving, but not without everybody.

I couldn't risk calling out names, so I sent pulses of seeking magic. "They're ahead of us," I said and took off at a run. Silence and speed are at odds with one other, but I'd already made that choice. Rocks clattered against each other as we pelted along a narrow channel. In contrast to the minus forty temperatures aboveground, it was too warm down here.

We reached Rolf and the Fae just in time for demons to surround us. Much as they had at the Ninth Gate, they oozed out of nooks and crannies. Anger bled through me, filling me with determination.

"Where are the mages?" I thundered, layering compulsion into my question.

"Like we'd tell you," a demon snarled.

I hadn't expected any of them to roll over. Prepared to address pushback and take a stand, I loosed a bolt of death at the soft place beneath his chin. My aim was true. I dragged power in the form of a glowing javelin downward until he split in two, innards spilling on the ground and making little splatting noises. He pawed at his gaping gut before pitching headfirst into his own organs.

Excellent. Grabbing the upper hand and hanging onto it has always been my preferred approach. If this bunch of rotters caught the slightest whiff of weakness, we were done for.

Rolf danced from foot to foot. His badger was loose, running this way and that as if he were playing the children's game, eeny meeny miney moe. Badgers are right up there with hyenas in the nasty department, and I felt sorry for whichever demon he sank his fangs into.

"Who's next?" I asked in my best bring-it-on tone, so they'd know we meant business.

"Or you can tell us where our friends are," Ciara purred.

"You invaded us," another demon yelled. Others took up his chant, repeating "invaded us" over and over again. Yeah, as if us showing up were some kind of outrage.

"Eh-eh," I snarled. "You started it. Satan sent minions posing as mages to infiltrate the Circle of Assassins. You even took on bond animals."

"It will require time, a lot of it, for my kin to recover from the nightmare," Gwaihir squawked.

"More like an honor than a nightmare," the same demon replied.

"Aye," another said. "Bet those beasts will never be satisfied with you puny mages again."

"They're lying," another demon said. "Never happened, or we'd have heard about it."

"Where are our companions?" I snapped my fingers, not in the mood to deal with proving my point. If the demons thought my tale was fake news, so be it.

"Or?" a demon leered at me.

I shrugged. "Absent information, you're of no use, so we

may as well kill you. Same treatment that one received." I hooked a thumb at the one I'd eviscerated.

"Why are you chatting over high tea?" a new voice shrieked. "You're supposed to be fighting, not talking. Fighting. Where you knock heads together, drain magic, end lives, that type of thing. Get moving, mates. Now!"

Interesting. Fresh meat, and higher up the food chain from the sound of it. I couldn't locate whoever the voice belonged to, but I should be able to work around it. Focusing the same type of power in the direction the voice had come from, I ran up against empty air.

"Show yourself," I gritted.

Ciara and Loren joined forces. The opposite of a ward shot from them, and my unseen opponent took shape. I didn't hesitate. So long as I had a target, I was good. This one wasn't as easy to overpower. It took mixed magic from us all before he lay twitching in the dirt.

The other demons were nowhere to be found when we were done. Guess they didn't want to be next, but it left us emptyhanded. "Come on." I motioned everyone to fall in and follow me. We'd stick with this track, clearly a main thoroughfare judging from all the hoofprints, until something more promising showed up.

"I sense them," one of the Sidhe said.

"Aye, me as well," her companion confirmed. "They're to our right."

"Look for side channels," I said. "Weak places where the walls aren't solid."

We needed to move quickly before another phalanx of demons closed on our position. This time, we'd face more of them, and someone was bound to be furious we'd done away with one of their platoon leaders.

"Something's wrong," Loren muttered. "I'm triangulating, but every time I get a different reading."

"Because they aren't there," I said and ran forward. Someone had found a way to trick us, maybe draining mage essence and planting it in several locations.

"We shouldn't have fallen for that," Ciara said as she loped next to me.

"Yeah, well, we did. Didn't cost us much, luckily." I tried not to pay attention to her nearness, but it was tough. I was still smitten, but I had to pick up the pieces and move on.

The track ended abruptly. A ladder bolted into rock led downward. "Let's be smart about this," I said once everyone was close. "I'm going to become one with the earth and locate the mages that way. Once I have a target, I'll let you know."

"We'll teleport to you," Rolf said.

"Want company?" Loren asked.

I shook my head. "I move faster alone. The odds of another batch of demons showing up is high. Ready defensive power. If there are too many of them, get the fuck out of here."

"What about you?" Ciara asked.

"Assuming I find the others, I'll stage a mass exodus. We can regroup back at the guild house."

"You shouldn't go alone," she insisted.

I did look at her then and the caring I saw in her eyes almost broke me. "What is this?" I barked to cover my discomfiture. "Kindergarten where we need partners? I'll be fine." Before anyone else raised an argument, I sank into the earth and borrowed liberally from her protective cover as I sent a seeking spell in a 360-degree arc.

Something about the perverted acoustics of Hell stymied my efforts, so I changed up my parameters until I found a combination that worked. The mages were still alive, but one, a faery, was in rough shape. Her bond animal, a lynx, crouched over her, licking her face and wings.

The earth led me downward. Goddess only knew how deep we were, but the dungeon where I ended up had seen heavy use. It reeked of blood and hopelessness. I fought my way through a final barrier someone had erected around rocks surrounding the prison.

I was breathing hard and sweating before I punched through. Guess they didn't need to post many guards if it was this tough to get inside. Magic had to be the only way in. I didn't see a door as I glided across a foyer littered with bones and grisly bits of flesh.

A flash of familiar magic brought me spinning around. "Yell at me later." Ciara offered a crooked smile. "Magic goes better with two."

"The others needed you. Furthermore, I ordered you to remain."

She rolled her shoulders back. "The others are on their way out of here. At least a hundred demons showed up within seconds of your egress."

It explained why no one was guarding the prisoners, but we couldn't count on that to last. A tiny little bit of me was delighted to see her. I put the kibosh on it immediately. I was her ranking officer. She'd disobeyed me. Made her own decisions and thumbed her nose at the chain of command. I would have ordered her to leave, but she'd have defied me again.

We'd deal with it later.

"Come on." I edged forward, intent on the cell with the mages. We rounded a corner, and it came into view. Fuck. They'd posted a sentry, but he hadn't noticed us. Not yet.

Using hand signals, I motioned Ciara to my right. We pummeled him with the one-two punch of earth and sea while

Ciara sliced a blade through his throat, jumping out of the way of his stinking black blood. If we got very lucky, he hadn't dispatched a frantic telepathic message to Hell Central on his way out.

She finished off the guard while I rattled through a few combinations before I got the cell door to open.

"Quinn, you old son of a bitch," a Fae shouted.

"Sight for sore eyes," a shifter agreed.

"Everyone out of here," I ordered, certain we wouldn't be able to teleport from inside the cell. Demons wouldn't be that stupid.

The lynx made a low mewling sound. I scooped the faery into my arms and ran for the edge of the dungeons with Ciara next to me and the others and their animals spread out behind her.

Gwaihir morphed into view. I'd felt his magic but not seen him since we'd left the main group back in the tunnel. He opened a channel to his power, sensing I'd need it. We'd come to the crux of my plan, the place I had the least assurance I could pull things off. My bondmate was privy to my thoughts. Interesting how that worked since I didn't have access to his.

"We need to blend with the earth so I can leverage her power and move us out of here," I told everyone. "The sensation will be claustrophobic, but don't fight it. Whatever you do, do not raise magic. It will get in the way of mine and make this harder."

"Got it," the Fae said.

"Ready?" I asked. Seeing nods all around, I opened a channel and dragged everyone through. I hadn't exactly forgotten the extra barrier around the dungeon, but it dragged at me, tripped me up. My lungs burned from effort, and power flowed out of me far faster than was wise.

A hand on my arm was followed by a river of sea mage

enchantment mixing with mine. The barrier parted handily, but then Ciara had found a way through on her own when she'd snuck after me.

I never argue with success. Ever. As soon as we were in the clear and dark power wasn't hot on our heels, I snapped up an assist from Gwaihir and Ciara and visualized the guild house. The faery clutched in my arms was barely breathing, but she'd be with White Fae soon. If anyone could pull her through, they could.

The transport spell seemed to take a long time, longer than I thought it should, but even with help I was running on fumes. Our escape had been far narrower than I'd have liked. And it would have been tougher still if Satan's army had chosen the moment of our escape to ooze through rock and dirt en masse.

"But they did show up," Ciara said, having helped herself to my inner dialogue. Disconcerting as fuck since it meant she'd probably intercepted my ambivalence about her.

"They weren't there when we left the dungeon," I pointed out.

"No, but they arrived within minutes of us leaving. I felt them but didn't say anything because I didn't want to distract you." She hesitated. "What you did was difficult."

"Dicey shit is my specialty." I deflected her compliment, not wanting to open a door to anything not strictly professional.

She nodded soberly. "It's why Grigori sent me to fetch you. Some of our newer members lack experience."

The lynx wound around my legs making the same sad little mewling noise. Ciara held out her arms. "I can take her. I have some healing skills."

News to me. Elemental mages could do many things, but large-scale healing wasn't one of them. "What do you think?" I asked the lynx.

Ciara knelt next to the faery's bond animal and remained

still while the animal examined her. When she crawled into Ciara's lap, I handed the faery to her.

"We should be back soon," I told everyone.

"Thank you so much for locating us," the shifter said.

"We'd given up on anyone launching a rescue," the Fae I'd known long ago chimed in. "We did everything we could combining our various magics, but it bounced back in our faces and slapped us."

"Every time," the shifter said.

"Did you have a plan?" Ciara asked. Tory balanced on her shoulders, wings spread for balance as we rocked and rolled through my teleport channel.

The Fae gave a curt nod. "We did. We'd already killed one guard. The one you axed was new. Big gap between the dead one and the next recruit. Guess they drew straws or something."

"Nah, Satan forced someone to pick up the slack," the shifter muttered. "Our plan was waiting for the next time the cell door opened and mobbing whoever was on the other side."

The lynx growled. I'd have ruffled its fur, but it wouldn't have taken the gesture in the spirit I intended it. "I'm with you," I told the bond animal. "I loathe those fuckers."

"The only good demon is a dead demon," the Fae said and chortled.

The edges of my spell finally took on a pearlescent shading. Our journey was almost over. I was trashed, but I had enough magic left to teleport to my country house in Scotland before I fell on my face and slept for a week.

Not so fast.

First, I needed to make certain Aidyrth and her group were safely back. Not that we were in any shape to launch a rescue right this minute, but we could be in a few hours.

We plopped into the courtyard. From the looks of the sky, it was the middle of the night. Grigori must have sensed when we drew near because he was waiting. Relief streamed from him as we all piled out of the channel. Healers were standing by; Ciara walked with them, the injured mage cradled tenderly in her arms. The lynx kept pace as did Tory. Apparently, they knew each other.

"Aidyrth's team?" I asked, my voice rough and scratchy.

"Everyone is back," Grigori said. "Get some rest. Eat something. This war is far from over."

I blinked stupidly at him. "You're not done with me?"

"Only if you want me to be." He slugged my upper arm. "I could use you, Quinn. You're dependable, seasoned."

"Let me think about it," I mumbled, so weary finding even simple words was a chore.

I wrapped myself in a transport spell and aimed for the Highlands. Somehow, my field pack was still latched to my body, and Gwaihir hadn't pulled another disappearing act.

"Thanks for your help today," I told my bondmate.

"You needed it," he said with his usual bluntness. It didn't bother me. We had no secrets.

"That I did," I agreed. "But thanks anyway. I appreciate you knowing when to be there and when to back off."

Dawn was breaking when the flagstones outside my front door shimmered into view. I tried opening the door with magic. When that failed, I dredged out a key.

"How prosaic," a rich, musical voice said from a few feet away.

What little adrenaline I had left shot to the fore, and I spun to face Ciara and Tory. The eagle lifted off her shoulders; Gwaihir flew after her.

"Are you going to tell me to leave?" Ciara arched a fair brow.

Bluntness seemed to run in my immediate circle. "I should,"

I told her, "but I'm too tired to think about anything right now."

"Good call," she said. "Discussion tabled until we've had a few hours' sleep and a meal or two."

Feeling weak and dumb and vulnerable, I pushed the door open and held it for her to walk through. Just because I was conflicted as hell was no reason for me to be rude.

Keep telling yourself that, one of my snarky inner voices piped up. *Keep telling yourself that.*

"Take your pick of rooms," I slurred. "Most of them are made up."

With a jaunty gesture that looked vaguely like a salute, she melted into the downstairs hallway. I trudged to the next floor up and my suite of rooms. I didn't remember stripping off my clothes until hot water pelting me told me I was in the shower. Ciara had used this bathroom last.

When I grabbed a towel, her scent was all over it. South of my hips, my body stirred to life. I told my cock to take a hike and fell into bed. Ciara was close, but I had zero idea what we'd have to say to one another once we woke.

This wasn't a field operation. I didn't have to plan anything. Good thing because I was two steps from sleep when my body crashed onto the bed. Groggy, disoriented, I tugged the duvet around me and called it even.

The strains of a haunting, lyrical instrument woke me. Or maybe it was the smell of food from the kitchen one floor down. My resolve to keep everything between Ciara and me work-related was definitely on the fritz because I hustled into clean clothes—jeans and a sweater—and was brushing my hair before I reminded myself of all the reasons she and I were a bad idea.

It punched a big fat hole in my enthusiasm to hurry downstairs, and I took my time pulling my hair into a queue and stuffing my feet into a pair of well-worn sheepskin slippers. Why had she followed me? Not much in the way of unfinished business between us.

One of the generous French-paned windows rattled under Gwaihir's determined beak. I crossed the room, opened the drapes, and unlatched the window. Dingy, gray daylight streamed through. I figured it was maybe two in the afternoon, but which afternoon? It had been dawn when we arrived. Had we slept the clock round and then some?

A quick check of my magical reservoir suggested we'd been

asleep for more than a handful of hours. I was pretty much back up to snuff. My bondmate flapped around the room a few times before perching on the edge of an antique mahogany desk.

I crossed my arms and looked at him. "What is it?"

"Hear her out."

No need to ask who "her" referred to. "Look," I began, "you and Tory found something special. I won't stand in the way, so long as you're front and center when we're heading into trouble."

"This is more about you," he said. On that enigmatic note, he flew back through the still-open window. I directed a thread of magic to close it behind him.

Picking up the filthy garments sprinkled across my floor, I slung them over an arm. I'd drop them in the washer on my way to the kitchen. Ciara was putting plates on the table when I walked in. I started to ask if she had clothes to toss in the wash but didn't. She wouldn't be here long enough for them to cycle through wash and dry mode.

An old-fashioned lyre was propped against one wall, no doubt the source of the music I'd heard on awakening.

Fruit, eggs, and toast had been artfully arranged on a dinner-sized plate. The coffee pot was full. "Thank you for making us something to eat," I said, keeping my tone formal.

She shrugged. "I'm not much of a cook, but I can manage simple fare. Everything in the sea is raw."

I waited for her to sit before doing so myself. For a time, we ate in silence. I was hungry, and enjoying food I hadn't cooked was a luxury.

Ciara set down her fork. "Up for a spot of conversation?"

"The price of my breakfast?" I tried for a joking tone, but it fell flat.

"Nope. I considered ambushing you once you woke, but we

need to get back to the guild house. Teleport spells go better when you're not half-starved, at least that's how it works for me."

"You've been up for a while." I nodded toward the lyre. "The music was nice."

"Thank you, but I can't take all the credit. Magical instruments are accommodating as hell." With a flick of her fingers, the lyre disappeared.

"You mentioned the guild house. I'm not sure I'm going back," I said flatly.

Her fair brows shot up in surprise. "Our work is far from done."

"My part could be. I need to think about it."

"The Circle needs you," she said and sipped some coffee. "If I'm the sticky wicket, the reason you're hesitating, I can make certain we're not assigned to the same team." She shook hair back over her shoulders. It hung loose and shiny, framing her face in small curls. "Do you treat men under your command the same way?"

I frowned. Talk about a shift in topics. "What do you mean?"

"You take it as a personal affront when I don't follow each and every order. Is that how you are with everyone?"

"It depends."

"On?" She spun one hand.

"Circumstances. I really don't want to pick this apart. I've chosen to be alone for many reasons."

"Because you're a dick?" she shot back.

"I can be, but that's not why."

"What is?"

I'd been holding my coffee mug; I set it down harder than I meant. Luckily, it didn't shatter. "I'm not going to answer that. I care about you, but we're a bad idea. I've been tied up in knots inside ever since you walked into my life. Part of me wants to protect you. Another part is furious when you don't follow directions meant to keep you safe. When I'm worried about you, the absolute focus I need for the task at hand is impacted."

I stopped to take a measured breath. "I don't want to live like that. I'm good at what I do. My skills are sought after, especially in the human world. I can't be the assassin I've been, can't stay at the top of my game when you're in the picture. So far, nothing significant has slipped off my plate, but it's bound to happen."

Her pale eyes latched onto mine. "Coward."

I winced. "Ouch."

"Do you think you're the only one struggling with the unknown?" she went on. "When you bark orders, viewing them as absolutes, I want to slap you. Grigori says you're how you are because you've worked with mortals for so long. You're superior to them, so it never occurs to you to ask what any of your mercenary pals think about your edicts. They trust you to bail them out—and you do."

This was getting interesting. "You and Grigori must have had quite the chat."

"We did. He rebuked me for carrying on the fight once we had the bond animals in hand, and—"

"See?" I broke in. "It's not just me."

"In that instance, no it isn't." She picked up her fork but put it back down. "Not much of a chain of command in the sea. Poseidon gave orders, but he never bothered to follow through to see how well—or if—I'd carried them out. Sometimes years passed between times when I saw him."

She spread honey on a bit of toast and ate it before adding, "The Circle took a lot of getting used to. I almost left many times."

"What drew you back?" I asked, curious about her reply.

"The fellowship aspect. Many working toward a common goal. It's clumsy and awkward sometimes, but in the sea it was every mage for themselves."

"Except the ones who were traitors," I said sourly.

"Between Poseidon and the Nereids, turncoats didn't last long in the sea. Everyone was loyal when Grigori convinced me to give the Circle a try."

"You're wrong," I said flatly. "Whoever infiltrated the Circle of Assassins started the process more than seventy-five years ago."

"How do you know?"

"Grigori is picky about whom he selects. Sometimes, he'll spend twenty years—or fifty—deciding on a recruit. The new mage always believes their selection occurred yesterday, but that's never true."

Ciara cocked her head to one side. "Explains why he's so worried."

"He should be," I told her. "Someone hatched a plan to devour the Circle long ago. It's been years in the making, and it's finally coming into its own. Grigori allowed tainted mages, and some who weren't mages at all, into our midst. He did so with the best of intentions, but he has to be kicking himself and questioning his judgment."

"This runs deeper than the four faux mages, huh?"

I nodded. "Much deeper. I've had an opportunity to think about it, and it's not good. If I do return to the Circle—not permanently, but long enough to sort this out—that will be why."

"What will be?"

"I believe in what Grigori built. I was around before the Circle, and he added pride and professionalism to the assassin trade. He set standards. We upheld them. The addition of bond animals was a stroke of brilliance. They're intuitive and bring out the best in us."

Deep in my mind, Gwaihir hooted doing his owl imitation. It also meant he was listening to every word that passed between Ciara and me. I hadn't made him any promises, but I was listening with as open a mind as I could manage.

She blew out a tight breath. "Good to know you haven't ditched the possibility of returning. I was worried you being angry with me would cut Grigori off from your talent. He needs mages he can trust right now."

"And a permanent solution to his werewolf virus problem, although he may have found it in Rhea. She seems devoted."

"She should be." Ciara sounded fiercely protective. "He saved her, resurrected the bond between her and her wolf."

Something about talking, sharing thoughts and ideas with a mage whose talents were similar to my own, loosened my resolve. I reached across the table and laid a hand over hers. "I can come off harsh, but I'm not angry with you. Disappointed, maybe, but that's on me. The one I'm angry with is myself. I know better than to get sidetracked, but the combination of your magic and beauty and intelligence is nearly impossible to withstand."

A crooked smile formed on her full lips. "You're doing okay resisting."

"It's costing me. Every time I turn around, I want to cave, to say we should find a way. Except it wouldn't work."

"Interesting you seem so certain about that. Why does this have to be all or none?" She flexed her hand beneath mine.

I'd tried to explain it before. "You bring out the best in me —and the worst. I can't have a casual fling. Not with you."

"Why? We could craft one of those friends-with-privileges arrangements I've seen on television. See where things lead."

"Where they'd lead," I growled, "is me killing anyone who looked at you in a way I didn't like."

"It's the elemental mage tie," she said with a knowing little nod.

"Huh? Not something I've heard about."

She drew her brows together. "With all the books and scrolls in the various guild houses, I figured everyone knew about it. Plus, you were raised on elemental mage lore."

"Studying for its own sake has never been my thing. Even when I was very young, I preferred being out in the field experimenting rather than stuck inside with a dusty scroll. Loren's the only other earth mage I've come across in over 600 years. From what I can tell, he doesn't study, either. How about if you tell me, so I don't have to dig up the information."

"I can do that," she replied. "Back when there were a lot of us, elemental mages frequently mated across the various element lines. Each aspect complements the other three, so mated mages were stronger as a dyad—or trio or quartet—than they were alone. We were sought after by our own kind for that very reason."

"But most of us have been gone for centuries."

Ciara nodded. "True, but it doesn't dilute the yearning for another elemental mage when we come across someone special." She gave a little shrug. "Who knows why these things happen, but I got this major zing the night I stopped by to deliver Grigori's message. It's done nothing but grow stronger, even though I've felt like an idiot pushing myself on you when you clearly didn't feel the same way. I wormed my way into your bed, and it wasn't all that hard, but men are weak when a naked woman jumps them."

"So are women," I pointed out. "Or you wouldn't have violated the sanctity of my shower."

"Sanctity? That's rich."

She tried to joke. Instead, she sounded resigned and sad, but she was being honest. I opened my mouth to thank her for her candor and tell her it was for the best if we cut our losses before they dug a hole in our hearts.

I couldn't get the words out.

The salt scent of her power had been muted; it swelled around us. The lyre was back in her hands, and she coaxed a mystical tune from its strings. It transported me, reminded me of tenderness, of warmth, of love. All the things I never let myself think about as I flitted from one hellhole to another leaving a trail of dead in my wake.

"You're cheating," I said when her fingers stilled and the instrument fell silent.

"Music is its own language," she murmured, offering back the hand I'd been holding. "Often a more potent one than any other because it relies on emotions."

The ball was in my court. What had happened to my sharper-than-glass split-second decision making? I've never been one to look back or to perseverate over choices. I'd put this particular one behind me, thinking it was over and done, but Ciara hadn't given up on me. On us.

"Why me?" I asked, my voice thick with rarely expressed feelings.

She set the instrument on the floor next to her chair and turned the hand I wasn't holding palm up. "I've asked myself that question a hundred times. A thousand. Flogged myself for not picking one of the nice mages who have made it clear they'd waited their whole lives for me."

"Who?" I growled.

"Doesn't matter. I turned them all down. They weren't right for me. You are." She nodded forlornly. "The irony isn't lost on me. I walked away from men who were funny, magical, kind, and devoted. When I finally found one who made my heart light and my soul burst into song, he was aloof, distant, critical."

"It's simpler this way," I said aware how lame it sounded.

"I'm sure it is, but at what cost?"

I started to ask for time, but no amount would offer any guarantees. "This requires a leap of faith," I sputtered.

"Like everything we do," Ciara murmured. "How many times have you had a target in your gunsights when something unexpected showed up? You had to pivot, make adjustments, never abandoning your goal."

"Is that why you've been so relentless?"

"If I hadn't, we wouldn't be sitting here. You said the lyre was cheating. You have no idea how hard it was not to come to your bed last night. If I hadn't been three-quarters dead from exhaustion, I'd have lost the battle. I wanted a level playing field, though, not one saturated by lust."

Letting go of her hand, I got up and walked around the table, drawing her to her feet. She flowed into my arms, molding her body against mine. For long moments, we held one another.

Honesty has been both blessing and curse in my long life. I could have kissed her, swept her into my arms, and taken her to bed. Instead, I said, "I don't know if I can do this."

"Neither do I, but it's not a good reason to run away before we've even tried." Her voice was muffled against my collarbone.

I cradled the side of her head and buried my fingers in the silk of her hair. She felt beyond amazing stretched the length of me. She brushed a thumb over my mouth. "You don't have to take care of me, Quinn. Any more than I have to take care of you."

"No have tos, only want tos," I murmured before I touched her mouth with mine.

Her body came alive in my arms; sensual heat mingled with

the ancient power of the sea. My kiss had been tentative; it deepened and we wound our arms around each other as our tongues connected. A relieved squawk told me Gwaihir had severed his voyeuristic connection. He and Tory could go kill something to celebrate.

Ciara was busy with the fastenings on my jeans. I reached between us and grabbed her hand.

"What?" she said breathlessly after tearing her mouth from mine.

"We can find a bed this time."

"I love it when you talk dirty." She hooked a hand around my arm and pulled. "Mine's closest."

"Sweetheart, this place has eight bedrooms."

"Mine is still closest."

A smile found its way to the surface. Ciara had a practical side. A woman after my own heart for sure. The bedroom across the hall from the kitchen was thick with her scents. Musk and spice and the sea. I inhaled hungrily. No matter how much of that scent surrounded me, I'd always long for more.

The barriers I'd hidden my heart behind were melting. I could do this. It was long past time. She shrugged out of the robe belted around her waist. Her body was even more incredible than I remembered.

"Beautiful. Stunning. Gorgeous. No matter what word I pick, it doesn't come close to describing your charms. Men would fight wars over you."

She laughed, low and musical. "I don't know about men, but sea creatures already have."

I arched a brow. "Tell me who. I'll kill them. Every single one."

Instead of answering, she reached for my sweater and tugged it over my head. I toed off my slippers. My jeans were already undone. Her hands collided with mine as we pushed the rough fabric down my hips and legs.

"I keep telling you," she murmured, "you're the pretty one." She ran her fingertips down my torso, leaving little trails of sparks in their wake. And then she did it again before sinking to her knees.

I wove my hands into her hair as my cock strained toward her. She licked up every side, swirling her tongue around the head. Between her touch and the warmth of her breath, I was lost.

The same melody she'd coaxed from the lyre filled the room. It matched the cadence and rhythm of her mouth and hands on my engorged appendage. I merged power with hers, wanting to be as close as we could be. My legs weren't especially steady; my breathing erratic as tension built in every cell in my body.

I relinquished my hold on her head. Words weren't there; my throat was too thick to form them. I pulled away from her mouth and lay so I could return the intimate caresses. We were close to a bed, but we ended up on the floor. I opened the petals of her sex, licking and teasing as I uncovered her nub. She'd taken me back into her mouth and threaded a hand around my backside to tease my anus.

Covering her nub with my mouth, I flicked it with my tongue before suckling the precious bud. My fingers found their way inside her vault. Slick and on fire, it tightened around me. I wanted more appendages, another hand, a second mouth. Magic rose to my call, and I sent vibrating streamers to tease her nipples and wind around her upper thighs.

Music cascaded through the room, urging us on. She crested, but I urged her to go higher still. When a second peak shuddered through her, I released the hold I'd had on my passion. Semen juddered from me in long gouts that shook me to my core.

Sex has always been a surface event for me, a fun sport. This was so different it fell into a separate universe. She swallowed until nothing was left. Once our breathing had settled a bit, I turned her until we were facing one another. Covering her mouth with mine, I kissed her and tasted the bitterness of my jism. Lust skyrocketed. My cock hadn't deflated at all. It pressed into her belly, ready for more of the same.

"Not tired of me yet?" she teased.

"There aren't enough lifetimes. We could stay here for months, years, have groceries delivered, and never leave."

"It's a lovely fantasy." Her mouth curved into a smile. Swollen from kisses and lovemaking, it added a softness to her aristocratic demeanor.

It was, but we needed to get back. We'd been gone for the better part of two days as it was. Grigori wasn't unreasonable, but I'd never taken advantage of him, either.

"Maybe next time, we'll actually make it to a bed," I murmured.

"Good. Means there will be a next time." She snuggled closer.

I would have moved mountains, worlds if they got between her and me. "Yes, there will definitely be a next time," I told her.

Ciara twisted in my arms. "I don't want to leave, but I need to return to the Circle. Are you coming?"

I nodded. "I probably won't stay, but I will remain until we get to the other side of the current problem. Once I discover who's behind the attack on the Circle, their days are numbered. I won't rest until they're horsemeat."

"We can figure things out as we go," she said thoughtfully.

"We don't have to be part of the Circle to work together. Grigori has been okay with mages doing side work."

I grinned. "Guess you're never going to go away, huh?"

"Nope. You're stuck with me. If you get out of line, I'll drag you to bed and everything will come back into focus. What's important. And what's not."

"Is that a promise?"

"You bet." She nuzzled my neck.

"Wench." I fluffed her long curls.

"I'm forever asking to borrow clothes," she said and then added, "Wait a minute, didn't I leave stuff in your dryer?"

"Nope. You put them on before we left last time. And sure, I have clothes you can wear."

After a lingering kiss, we both sat up. Afternoon had come and gone; the night sky showed through the window. Time had a way of sliding by unnoticed when she and I were together. I wasn't fighting the attraction any longer. She was fast becoming an essential element in my life.

"You'll find sweats in the dresser in the corner. Meet you in the kitchen in ten minutes," I said. "Will that be enough time?" The old me wouldn't have added that question, but there was a new mage in town. Hopefully, one with a sliver of sensitivity.

"I'll be dressed and ready to leave. Want me to let the birds know?"

"How much do you want to bet they already do."

Ciara laughed. "No kidding. They sure don't miss much."

I whistled an old Irish folk tune as I trotted out of the downstairs bedroom intent on locating traveling clothes and restocking my field pack. Or at least checking it.

My reservations had taken a hike. I didn't understand why or how, but some questions don't require answers. Grigori had been Fate's messenger when he'd sent Ciara after me. The rest was a simple matter of me trusting to the process. Since it was me, and I trust no one, Fate had taken quite a chance.

The birds and Ciara were in the kitchen when I strode in, pack slung over one shoulder. They were geared up for me, a transport spell simmering and ready to launch. Joy is what you make of circumstances, where you choose to focus.

I was happy, more so than I had a right to be, and I wasn't questioning it or shutting myself off from it because it might vanish in the blink of an eye. Ciara had said I didn't have to take care of her, but I would as much as she'd let me.

"Give me a few to lock up," I told them and sprinted for the front door.

Gwaihir fluffed his feathers, squawked that he'd already taken care of the kitchen door, and focused his power to launch the transport spell. Wise bird that he was, he didn't say, "I told you so."

Feeling bold and full of hope, I took Ciara's hand as we sped toward our future. I'd kicked down the gates of my resistance, quit second guessing every stray thought. We could do this, she and I.

"You bet we can," she murmured.

"Christ, woman, you're worse than my eagle. Do you ever miss anything?"

"Not much," she purred. "Not much at all."

You've reached the end of *Quinn*, second of the Circle of Assassins books. Read on for a sample from *Rhiana*. She and her unicorn have been hiding out with a variety of traveling circuses for the past hundred years or so. She needed a break from the twenty-first century, so she jumped backward in time. Grigori doesn't know quite where she is, and Rhiana likes it that way.

BOOK DESCRIPTION, RHIANA

I'm one of the old ones. I've lived many lives, done many things. I've been called sorceress, witch, and far worse. Mortals have hung me, burned me, staked me out and left me to die. What a pack of fools. I'm immortal, and their petty attempts were laughable.

So were they when I stopped their puny, pathetic hearts. The thrill of ending someone never gets old, no matter how unbalanced the contest.

When I want a break from everything, Dorcha—my bondmate—and I bide with the Circle of Assassins. I never mean to stay long, but the years have a way of slipping by.

While I find peace within the Circle, Dorcha becomes restive. She never used to mind being the only unicorn, but she's grown silent, withdrawn. The place within me where I feel her energy is often empty.

We need a nice juicy assignment to get things back on track, a mission worthy of our skill. Excited by the prospect of free-flowing blood and the crusty stench of battle, I searched for her, but she was gone.

Worse than gone, my link with her was buried beneath layers of unicorn enchantment. Could I find her? Sure, but she didn't wish to be found.

RHIANA, CHAPTER ONE

880 London

I Calliope music swelled through the huge canvas tent. Its harsh spirited notes usually excited me, but not today. Our act would be on in a few minutes. We were popular because of how real my unicorn's horn looked. More than popular, we'd made a big enough name for ourselves we headlined every circus we were part of.

Pfft. The horn looked real because it was. My challenge was making certain we snuck off under cover of darkness so no one ever saw Dorcha for what she really was. She had a cushy stall in the stables, but she never used it. My excuse was she needed special food. Delicate stomach, and all. No one questioned me since horses are notoriously prone to colic.

Aye, 'twas a carefully balanced web of lies with me pulling the strings. I'd picked this spot, time traveling into the past to get away from everything. Dorcha was never on board with this particular plan, but I'd coddled her as days followed others assuming she'd eventually stop bitching.

I may have miscalculated. Her complaints were more strident than they'd been six week ago when we first arrived.

"I'm done." Dorcha stamped a hoof. "This is absurd. Demeaning. You're an elemental mage. Why are you wasting your time entertaining stupid mortals?"

Breath whistled through my teeth; I wound a long whip made of magic and moonlight and diamonds around one arm. Dorcha understood it was part of my costume. I'd never dream of hurting her with it. If I did, I'd feel the bite of her horn. Unicorns are more lethal than I am. That horn can cut through damn near anything, leaving destruction in its wake.

"Shall we talk about this after the show?" I added a smidgeon of compulsion to my question.

"It's what you said yesterday. And the day before that." More hoof stamping.

True enough. I'd made a point of taking us hunting after the shows in question. Usually fresh blood did the trick, mollified her, but she was canny and had my number.

The canvas flap covering our lean-to next to the big top swung open admitting a blast of cold, sooty air. London has always been a dirty town, and all the coal stoves didn't help.

"Who the hell you talking to?" John stuck his shaggy head inside the flap.

"Myself."

"Och, they say it's the first sign you're headed for Bedlam. You're on in five. Get mounted up and ready." He sidled closer and snaked out a hand to grab my ass. I pivoted out of his way.

"Someday, you'll appreciate me, darling. I'm who got you this special spot," he reminded me like he did every time he got close enough to exchange a word or two. He had booted the previous occupant of the lean-to, but only because he was intent on seducing me. I gave it another few weeks. He'd tire of my excuses and move another candidate into position. Maybe she'd be more grateful than I'd been.

"Yes, yes, now get moving." I flapped a hand in his direction. My five minutes had shrunk to three. John limped away. His story was an elephant had broken his foot, but I suspected he'd fallen when he was drunk. Or tripped over something.

I slid a long woolen cloak off my shoulders, draped it over a hook, and vaulted to Dorcha's back. "We'll get through this, and then we'll leave," I told her.

Power stabbed me as she tested my words for integrity. I hadn't been lying, but I'd be damned if I knew where we'd go next. After a quick glance to make certain my costume covered everything essential, I kneed her softly and we trotted to our place next to the entry for performers. People milled this way and that, everyone cooing over Dorcha and giving her pats.

She liked that part, but she'd rather die than admit it. Inky black with a lush mane and tail and delicate hoofs, she was beautiful. Her coat so black it shimmered with notes of blue when the light hit it at a certain angle.

The leading strains of our signature song began to play. We galloped into the arena to cheers and clapping. I wasn't under any particular illusion. Magic ebbs and flows around us. Mortals are drawn to the feel of it even though they're not certain what the attraction is.

I leapt to my feet and balanced on the unicorn's broad back as we continued to canter around the Big Top. The ringmaster did his "ladies and gentlemen" gig announcing our act. The first fifteen minutes were ours. I went through a series of gymnastics atop the unicorn. Standing, kneeling, astride, sidesaddle position, handstand. My gauzy costume billowed. The many necklaces I wore clanked together, as did long hoop earrings.

Dressed like the Romani in a colorful tunic and trousers, my feet were bare. Traditionally known as horse people, the Rom had magic too. Nothing compared with mine, but it made more sense than dressing up like a Mongol.

Thundering hoofs announced the rest of the riders were joining us. They cantered this way and that, keeping Dorcha and me in the center of an everchanging circle. I'd choreographed this particular number to maintain distance between Dorcha and the other horses.

Mortals might not know what she was, but equines have sensitive noses. They understood damn good and well Dorcha wasn't one of them. One of the other horses got too close. Dorcha bared her teeth and hissed.

"You're not a cat. Stop that," I told her.

"She will respect me."

"She probably has no idea what you are." I left it at that. Some creatures have archetypal memories. Horses aren't one of them. Nothing like Dorcha in their minds or memories to relate to. She might look like them, but they weren't fooled.

The music shifted to the final number. I jumped upright again. The crowd loved all of us standing on our mounts as they galloped wildly past churning up dust and dirt.

We swept by acrobats and a man on stilts as we exited the tent. I lowered my body until I straddled Dorcha, and we trotted across packed dirt to a river. She had a bridle and reins, which I held loosely. They were for show. I let her be as she sank her snout into the water and drank.

"Why do you hate it here?" I asked.

"Why do you like it?" she countered.

Her question wasn't rhetorical; she really wanted to know. *"It's different. A break from the Circle of Assassins and endless assignments. We don't exactly fit in there, either."*

"Better than here."

The unicorn straightened her graceful neck, nostrils flaring. I tossed a leg over her rump and landed next to her. Cold mud squished between my toes as I wound the magical whip around one arm and quashed its sparkling aspect.

"Is she real?" A street urchin of maybe six or seven with dirt-caked clothes and a grimy, snot-streaked face crept close.

Dorcha whickered and turned toward the little girl, ears pricked forward.

"Real enough," I said.

"Ooooh. May I touch her, missus?"

"Come nearer slowly. She'll let you know," I replied.

Eyes wide with wonder, the child edged forward, clearly afraid but willing to brave the horrors of hell if she could get close to Dorcha. My bondmate was in a generous mood because she stood quietly while the girl stroked her nose.

"Wisht I had a carrot for you," she murmured.

I dug an apple from my trousers and handed it to her. "Feed her this."

"All at once?"

I fished out a knife I keep strapped to my ankle, split the apple, and said, "Do it this way," as I showed her how to offer food with an open hand. As soon as the apple was gone, the child slipped away merging with lengthening shadows while afternoon ceded to evening.

I'd have asked her where her parents were, but London teemed with street urchins. This one appeared resourceful. She'd probably land on her feet if she didn't get sidetracked into a brothel.

"Feeling better?" I asked Dorcha.

"A little," she admitted.

Taking hold of her reins, I walked us to the small private enclosure where we'd waited for our turn to perform. The show was still going strong. If we were going to leave, now was as good a time as any. No one had touched my cloak, but I'd spelled it to burn any hand except mine. Grateful for its soft warmth, I tugged it around my shoulders and tied it into place.

"How about a walk on the shore?" I asked softly.

"Which shore?"

"You pick." I was so grateful her anger had run its course, I could afford to be generous.

She sent images cascading through my mind. They made me smile, and I built a quick teleport spell that incorporated time traveling elements. A short while later, we came out on a desolate section of the Washington coastline with the Pacific Ocean on one side and the Strait of Juan de Fuca to the north. Crags, wind, and beastly weather effectively sealed this spot off from casual visitors. I'd kept us well in the past to avoid modern scourges like hang gliders, helicopters, and people with fancy climbing equipment.

Dorcha cantered this way and that, tossing her head. The braids I'd put in her mane untwisted. She hated being decked out like the other show horses. For a time, I sat on a flat rock enjoying watching her kick up her heels. Salt spray scented the air with an astringent sweetness.

The tide was coming in, waves crashing and booming. I raised a hand in greeting to my old friend, Arianrhod. I couldn't see her, but she had to be in Caer Sidi, her special world, overseeing both tides and moon. I'd liked her earthy, no-nonsense approach, but some of the other Celtic gods were real pricks. Especially the men.

I inhaled deeply, willing myself not to go there. I'd been enjoying Dorcha's choice of beaches, and I didn't want to sully it with nasty recollections. Instead, I shuffled possibilities. If Dorcha truly put her hoof down about not returning to London and the circus, where would we go next? I'd figured we were good for a few more months there.

Timing was everything, but my clairvoyance skills have

never been a strong suit. Something was bound to happen. It always did. Some random event would send us scurrying away from London. The last time we'd hustled out of somewhere had been because Dorcha killed a rude stallion who'd tried to mount her. It wasn't funny—at all—but it still brought a smile to my face. I knew exactly how she felt.

I'd have stuck around to defend her honor were it not for the impossibility of explaining how her horn—supposedly a prop—had exacted so much damage. We'd been in Prague then, around 1840. Eventually, we would run out of places and eras, but it wouldn't happen for a long while. It's only been since maybe 1970 that communications have become sophisticated enough to make starting over harder.

A black unicorn and her five-foot-ten-inch mistress with matching flowing tresses exacted notice everywhere. I tone things down with a glamour to make me appear less exotic— and less threatening. It smooths the cant of my cheekbones, adds femininity to my frame, and turns my bronze eyes with their deep green centers a deep blue. In times long past, those like me controlled every element. The Celts, damn their black souls, decided we wielded too much power, so they split my kind into earth, air, fire, and water mages.

A flicker of anger licked at my innards. I ignored it. Revisiting the pyre of my fury wasn't wise. I'd thrown my power against the gods. Best I'd achieved was a draw—until another of them showed up. Eventually, I'd tired of being slapped down. Besides, I'd have to hunt for them. Most were long gone from Earth. No one believed in them anymore. Or in me. The specter of endless life weighed heavy.

I've hit sketchy patches before. Ones like this where I flounder about hunting for meaning and not finding anything but a cosmic joke. Dorcha wasn't happy, either. It ran deeper than the circus being a total waste of our talent.

The water had taken on an iridescent quality, maybe from the sun's downward trajectory. Regardless, it was alluring. Dorcha pawed at the sand with her front hoofs and walked into the water. Taking a dip in the sea held appeal. I slithered out of my cloak, trousers, and tunic, piling rocks on top of them to keep the wind from blowing everything away.

On my feet, I ran lightly across the rocky beach and into the water, following Dorcha's path. The bottom dropped away; I swam into the surf welcoming the slap of waves as I cut through them. Living in the now, welcoming the cleansing saltwater scrubbing away the smells of the circus, my world grew smaller and more manageable.

Moments were important. Good moments like when Dorcha let the street urchin pet her. All we needed was to find a spot where there were more good moments than bad ones. A tall order. Even in the Circle of Assassins, mages squabbled with one another. Grigori, head of the supernatural hit squad, kicked folks out from time to time.

A brisk whinny turned my attention to Dorcha treading water fifty feet away while Nereids crawled all over her. Faeries of the sea, they have gossamer wings, masses of hair in every shade of the rainbow, and fishtails like the mer-people.

A lissome nymph with violet hair, black wings, and rings on every finger dove off Dorcha's back and swam my way. "Greetings from Poseidon," she announced in a high, clear voice. "He welcomes you to his realm."

Oh-oh.

Selecting my response carefully, I inclined my head. "Tell him I wish him well, and we shan't remain long."

Her rosy lips parted in a slight smile. "You know our liege."

"That I do." I left it at that. If the Celts were dicks, Poseidon was a straight-up bastard. Arrogant and arbitrary, nothing was ever his fault. He slung shit at his underlings, expecting them to suck it up for the privilege of remaining his subjects.

"His favorite assassin left," the Nereid went on. "He will pay you handsomely to locate and return her."

"Be sure to thank him for his faith in me, but I'm in the middle of another job. Dorcha and I were taking a break, or we wouldn't be here at all."

I flipped over and began stroking for shore with the Nereid pacing me. She could swim rings around me, but her tail was cheating. My toes touched bottom; I switched from swimming to plodding through the water intent on dressing and getting the fuck out of here.

Poseidon's methods were legendary. He'd hunt me down if his messenger didn't return with the right answer: that I'd drop everything and do his bidding. Not that he couldn't find me no matter where I went, but I wouldn't make it easy for him. Technically, I worked for the Circle, which meant all assignments were handled by Grigori. It gave me an out—if I chose to play that card.

I wrang water out of my hair and chucked it over my shoulders. Funneling magic to dry myself, I trotted to where I'd left my clothes.

"Lovely as ever, my dear," rang from behind me.

Fuckety-fuck. Poseidon hadn't waited for the Nereid to return. He'd been listening to our conversation, and now he was here to do his damnedest to keep Dorcha and me from leaving. Eh, probably not Dorcha. I was who he was interested in. And I knew damn good and well where his escaped mage was. Hiding in plain sight and transformed by magic to ensure she'd never be captured.

Swathing my mind in strong wards—so he couldn't pluck thoughts from it—I aimed for an airy tone. "Give a lady a spot of privacy to dress."

"What for? I'd rather enjoy the view. Besides, it's not as if I haven't seen everything before."

Great. Mr. Tact-and-Diplomacy was in full bloom. We'd had a fling centuries ago. Emphasis on "a fling." I'd never been tempted into a rematch. He was as boorish and inconsiderate in bed as out. Keeping my back to him, I pulled my trousers up my still damp legs and settled my tunic over my head. The cloak came last and I savored its warmth.

Dorcha cantered close. "Ready to go?" she asked brightly.

My, "Sure," collided with Poseidon's, "Not done with her."

After wringing more water from my hair, I turned to face him. He hadn't changed a bit. Tall with a full head of silver hair that spilled to his knees, he was handsome in an imperious sort of way. The trident staff I remembered was held loosely in one hand. He's always favored robes. Today's was pale blue sashed in white with embroidered tridents.

"Sorry about your assassin, but hire someone else," I said.

"You'd be perfect," he insisted. "Being an assassin yourself and all." His voice took on a wheedling note, and I tasted compulsion, thick and cloying, clinging to the words. "I can't leave the sea for long. When I do, my powers fade, but you can operate anywhere."

I shrugged. "You're a god. I'm merely a mage. Plusses and minuses all around."

"Come on, Rhiana. For old times' sake. This wouldn't take long. I'll pay you whatever you wish."

We had no "old times" not good ones. "I really am swamped."

"I can wait. Whenever you get to this is fine."

Nice wasn't working. I shifted tactics. "I'm not interested. Period."

Nereids had slithered up the sand, forming a circle around

Dorcha and me. I had a feeling they meant to keep us here. Maybe if we'd still been in the water, it might have worked.

The next wave washed over my feet. If I tarried, the sea would come to us, and the Nereids' circle would hem us in. They only looked fluffy and harmless, but they did Poseidon's bidding because punishment for non-compliance was swift, sure, and deadly.

I vaulted atop Dorcha and married my power with hers. This should be a slam-dunk. She and I hadn't had a chance to hash out a destination, so I tried to take us back to London. She had other plans. At cross purposes, our magic crashed against itself. The craggy shoreline, which had begun to shimmer and fade, stuttered back into place.

"Dorcha. Leave off."

"I am not going back to that circus."

Water was up to her hocks. We were running out of time. "It's the easiest place," I argued having given up on telepathy. I needed all my power.

Poseidon was laughing uproariously. Yup. I bet he knew a thing or two about insurrection in his ranks. All his underlings hated him. Not that Dorcha was subservient in any way. The press of sea magic, dense with the scents of salt and seaweed, rose around us.

I switched things up and visualized one of the Circle of Assassin guild houses. It would take piles more magic to move us there since it wasn't located on Earth.

Dorcha grunted something that might have been assent and opened her magic to me again. I used every trick at my disposal, but the Nereids' circle blocked our escape. With Poseidon's laughter as a backdrop, I gave up after my third attempt boomeranged back in my face.

Whatever he had in mind—like imprisoning me until I capitulated—wouldn't fly with me.

Dorcha reared. I wasn't ready for it and slid down her haunches, landing on my butt. Screaming horsey outrage at Poseidon, her hoofs thundered against his chest driving him to the ground.

"How dare you?" Dorcha screeched. "Release us immediately."

He still had hold of his trident, and he tried to angle it to stab my unicorn in the belly. Fat fucking chance. I bolted to where he was pinned and kicked the staff out of his hand. I'd just declared a full-out war on the god of the sea. It was bound to end badly, but I didn't care.

ABOUT THE AUTHOR

Ann Gimpel is a USA Today bestselling author. A lifelong aficionado of the unusual, she began writing speculative fiction a few years ago. Since then her short fiction has appeared in many webzines and anthologies. Her longer books run the gamut from urban fantasy to paranormal romance. Once upon a time, she nurtured clients. Now she nurtures dark, gritty fantasy stories that push hard against reality. When she's not writing, she's in the backcountry getting down and dirty with her camera. She's published over 90 books to date, with several more planned for 2021 and beyond. A husband, grown children, grandchildren, and wolf hybrids round out her family.

Keep up with her at www.anngimpel.com or http://anngimpel.blogspot.com

If you enjoyed what you read, get in line for special offers and pre-release special reads. Newsletter Signup!

Blood and Magic

Blood and Sorcery

Blood and Illusion

Demon Assassins

Witch's Bounty

Witch's Bane

Witches Rule

Dragon Heir

Dragon's Call

Dragon's Blood

Dragon's Heir

Dragon Lore

Highland Secrets

To Love a Highland Dragon

Dragon Maid

Dragon's Dare

Dragon Fury

Earth Reclaimed

Earth's Requiem

Earth's Blood

Earth's Hope

Elemental Witch

Timespell

Time's Curse

Time's Hostage

Gatekeeper

Shadow Reaper

Rebel Reaper

Untamed Reaper

GenTech Rebellion

Winning Glory

Honor Bound

Claiming Charity

Loving Hope

Keeping Faith

Ice Dragon

Feral Ice

Cursed Ice

Primal Ice

Magick and Misfits

Court of Rogues

Midnight Court

Court of the Fallen

Court of Destiny

Rubicon International

Garen

Lars

Soul Dance

Tarnished Beginnings

Tarnished Legacy

Tarnished Prophecy

Tarnished Journey

Soul Storm

Dark Prophecy

Dark Pursuit

Dark Promise

Underground Heat

Roman's Gold

Wolf Born

Blood Bond

Wolf Clan Shifters

Alice's Alphas

Megan's Mates

Sophie's Shifters

Wylde Magick

Gemstone

Lion's Lair

Unbalanced

STANDALONE BOOKS

Branded, That Old Black Magic Romance (paranormal romance)

Edge of Night (short story collection, paranormal and horror)

Grit is a 4-Letter Word (nonfiction)

Heart's Flame (post-apocalyptic romance)

Icy Passage (science fiction romance)

Marked by Fortune (post-apocalyptic coming of age story)

Melis's Gambit (historical paranormal romance)

Midnight Magic (paranormal romance)

Red Dawn (post-apocalyptic paranormal romance)

Shadow Play (historical paranormal romance)

Shadows in Time (Highland time travel romance)

Since We Fell (contemporary romance)

Warin's War (paranormal romance)